"What is proper?"

~~~~~~~~

. . . he asked. "A necktie to choke me? A stiff shirt and jacket to bind my chest and arms? Trousers to smother my legs?"

"Of course not! 'Tis only proper to cover yourself appropriately."

"My African attire does not meet with your approval, then?"

"Good heavens, no."

The woman's scent caught his attention. "Do all Englishwomen cover themselves from neck to toes?"

"Of course." She fingered the sharp, white collar of her gown. "I suppose you are accustomed to much more . . ."

He watched her creamy white throat move as she swallowed, and wondered how it would feel under his fingertips. His tongue.

"On the contrary, I am accustomed to much *less*."

Other **Avon Romances**

WILD

Margo Maguire

AVON
An Imprint of HarperCollinsPublishers

AVON BOOKS
An Imprint of HarperCollins*Publishers*
10 East 53rd Street
New York, New York 10022-5299

Copyright © 2009 by Margo Wider
ISBN 978-0-06-166787-9
www.avonromance.com

First Avon Books paperback printing: January 2009

Avon Trademark Reg. U.S. Pat. Off. and in Other Countries, Marca Registrada, Hecho en U.S.A.
HarperCollins® is a registered trademark of HarperCollins Publishers.

Printed in the U.S.A.

10 9 8 7 6 5 4 3 2 1

This book is dedicated to the most hospitable group of people you can imagine, the crew at the Madison Heights Starbucks.
Many thanks to Sasha, La Kesha, Meghan, Erin, Ryan, Madison, Pete, Justin, Angie, Erica, Blair, Cheryl, Kathy, Dominique, Kenyatta, Danielle, Zachary, Angela, Natasha, Jimmie, Renell, and the two Andrews . . . for tolerating me while camped out with my laptop, swilling coffee and taking up space while I wrote this book. You guys are the best.

WILD

Chapter 1

Richmond, England
Late spring, 1829

It was not like Grace Hawthorne to waste time woolgathering when she had work to do, yet she found herself doing just that as she sat at Lady Sophia Sutton's desk in the library of Fairford Park, gazing out at the back gardens. The estate was just west of London, and vast by the standards of the city, with acres of trees and gardens, yet close enough to enjoy London's attractions.

Grace took pleasure in the peace and security she'd found at Fairford, living with Lady Sutton, easing the loneliness of the elderly countess's life. Heaven knew that Lady Sutton had done the same for Grace, not to mention having given Grace a home and employment when she had nowhere else to go.

Her Ladyship was occupied at the moment, visiting with several of her dowager friends, so Grace decided to take a walk in the bright sunshine of the late May day. Her stroll would take her past Fairford's massive, ancient trees and beds of deep purple phlox, colorful nasturtiums, sweet william, and dahlias. Being out of doors among the flowers reminded Grace of her mother, whom she'd lost a year ago.

Heavens, had it been only a year? Grace mused. It seemed she had missed her mother for ages, yet at the same time, it was almost as though Grace had just bathed that dear lady's brow and tucked her blanket round her frail shoulders for the last time.

Grace turned away from the window just as the library door squeaked open, and Faraday, the butler, entered and handed a letter to her. It was soiled and discolored, as though it had been thrown into a busy street and left for days before being delivered. "This just arrived, miss."

Grace took the missive and saw that it was addressed to the Dowager Countess Sutton, her employer.

"It's come a long distance," said Faraday. "She'll want it straight away."

The butler cleared his throat as Grace turned the letter over and saw that it had come from Africa.

Africa. Oh dear. By the look of it, the letter had taken many detours before making its way to Richmond.

Wasting no more time, Grace turned to the desk

and quickly slit open the seal with Her Ladyship's penknife. As was entirely proper, Grace did not unfold the letter, but left the library and went directly to Lady Sutton's parlor.

She placed her hand on the door latch, only to pause when she heard the sounds of quiet laughter within. Many of Lady Sutton's friends gathered there each Wednesday, to visit and to gossip. She glanced at the watch pinned to her bodice. Soon the ladies would take a short walk through the garden, for the weather was fine, and then they would leave.

Grace looked down at the letter in her hand. It could be good news, or the very worst. Lady Sutton's grandson, who'd been lost in Africa more than twenty years before, might have been found.

Or the more likely case, someone had discovered the boy's remains.

Pressing the letter to her breast, Grace decided to wait. Whatever the news, it would not be something the countess would wish to share with the ladies, at least not yet. Far better for Grace to wait and give Her Ladyship the privacy she would need to digest the contents of the missive.

Grace returned to the library and tried to concentrate on the correspondence she should be handling for Lady Sutton. But that battered letter drew her eyes more times than she cared to admit.

Poor Lady Sutton. It was well-known that she harbored a most unrealistic belief that her grandson had survived being swept away from his father's hunting party somewhere in deepest Africa. The earl had returned grief-stricken after spending many months searching for his son . . . or the boy's body. Yet Anthony had never been found. No one believed the earl's son could have survived being swept into a deep, rushing river in the midst of a torrential rainstorm, yet his grandmother had never given up hope.

Grace eyed the dreaded letter, certain it could not possibly contain good news. She considered tossing it into the fireplace and eliminating all traces of it in order to protect Lady Sutton from renewing her terrible grief. But that would be entirely irregular. It was not up to Grace to decide which correspondence the countess ought to see. Besides, it might be well for Lady Sutton to be able to close the book on Anthony here and now. To finally accept that her grandson was truly gone.

The carriages belonging to Lady Sutton's guests soon came up the drive, and when the last of the ladies had taken their leave, Grace smoothed her skirts and straightened her prim collar, picked up the tattered letter, and carried it to Her Ladyship's parlor. She could no longer delay turning over the most horrible news to the woman who had taken her in as her companion a year ago, when Grace's world had shattered.

* * *

The London sky did not seem so very different from the African heavens, but Kuabwa Mgeni could not abide the smells. Disgusting. He could not leave this place soon enough.

He'd been ill when the white men had found him, else they'd never have taken him. He had made the mistake of speaking English to them, giving them his *eupe* name. He was not sure how long he'd been gone from England, how long since his white father had abandoned him, leaving him to fare on his own in the wild jungles of the Congo. But he had become part of Africa, and it was surely part of him in a way that England could never be. He belonged in his tropical valley, with its tribal people and fresh game, with its flowing waters and open sky.

And there were no disgusting odors there.

Kuabwa still felt weak after his bout with the *gonjwa* fever. The illness that had come over the Moto Dambia village had infected him, too, leaving him vulnerable and unable to escape into the jungle. He hadn't been able to protect himself against these *eupe* voyagers who had encountered him where they'd never expected to see another white man.

On the voyage to England, he'd begun to regain some strength, but then relapsed into fever and illness again. He desperately needed his strength back, so he could defend himself against these *pumbaali marinto* captors and get himself aboard another ship that would take him home.

His few belongings were bundled into a colorful *gunia* given him by Dawa of the Tajuru village where he'd first found himself after nearly drowning in the river all those years ago. Dawa had had many children of her own, yet she'd cared for him, naming him Mgeni—Stranger. Only after he'd grown to his full height had the people added Kuabwa—Tall Man—to his name.

His captors, Lyman and Brock, led him onto the deck of their ship. The *gunia* dangled heavily from Lyman's hand. It would take but one quick move for Kuabwa to overpower the man and grab the knife inside. Even as weak as he was, he could escape these men and elude them until he could make his way onto one of the other ships that were tied to the docks.

"Lord Sutton," said one of his captors. "Can you walk down the gangway to the carriage?"

Lord Sutton. His father was Lord Sutton. A man too important to waste time searching for his son, Anthony. It had been years since Kuabwa Mgeni had thought of himself as Anthony Maddox. He was no longer an Englishman, but an African with light skin and eyes, a man with no ties but those that he chose to make.

He knew better than to trust familial ties or any other kind of loyalties. A man who relied upon his own instincts and abilities would never be betrayed.

* * *

Grace looked round at the docks of London and knew they should not be there. If anyone were to take note of Lady Sutton's carriage loitering in this part of the city . . .

"Grace." The countess placed a trembling hand over her heart as she watched intently out the window of the carriage. Grace took Lady Sutton's other hand in her own and gently squeezed.

There was a great deal of activity about the dock. Men shouted to one another as they stacked large crates near a warehouse. Grace saw row upon row of barrels lined up all along the edge of the quay, where burly-looking workers loaded them into horse-drawn carts. It was a rough and vulgar scene, but Grace understood that such coarseness was a price Britain had to pay for commerce.

"Yes, my lady," she said more calmly than she felt. They watched the seamen of a dingy old sailing vessel throw ropes to men waiting on dry land, who secured the ship to the dock. Next, a gangway was lowered and weary-looking travelers started to disembark.

"My dear heavens, it's him!" Her Ladyship whispered. "He is ill. Look at the way those two men support him as he walks."

Grace held her tongue. The man in question moved well enough, but his two escorts seemed to be keeping a firm grasp on his arms. And it remained to be seen if they could prove he was actually Lady Sutton's grandson.

It was not for Grace to caution the older woman to remain skeptical of the man purported to be Anthony Maddox, seventh Earl of Sutton. It could all be a ruse intended to wheedle a great deal of reward money from the countess. Grace knew that such a fraud had been attempted once before, soon after Anthony's disappearance. The perpetrators had been transported for their crime, and Grace had to admit that the punishment had gone far to prevent a repetition of any such fraudulent schemes.

She was also mindful that soon after that debacle, the earl had died, his grief over the loss of his only son too terrible to bear.

"He is as tall as his father—even taller. And look at all that dark hair. Straight as a stick, just like Colin's. Oh Grace, could it truly be Anthony?"

"My lady, it worries me to see you in such a state." Grace's employer was a small woman with snowy white hair, her skin as fair and fine as parchment. She looked as delicate as a sparrow, but Grace knew she could be as fierce as a hawk. Grace did not envy these men if they were attempting to swindle her. Though the countess was a venerable seventy-nine years old, she was still as sharp as anyone possessing half her years.

"I wish I could see his eyes. Then I would know."

"His eyes?" Grace asked.

"They were just like his mother's—the same pale green as the lily pads in the swimming pond near one of the guesthouses at Fairford Park. We were all so sure he . . ." Lady Sutton pressed her fingers to her lips. ". . . he would be a striking man."

The man to whom Lady Sutton referred was, indeed, striking, in spite of the ill-fitting, wrinkled linen suit he wore. He was hatless, revealing a head of thick hair that was long enough to brush his broad shoulders. It was so dark Grace believed she could see blue highlights reflecting in the sunlight.

But any number of Englishmen had dark hair and green eyes. Anyone attempting to pass off an impostor would certainly choose someone who bore a family resemblance. The loss of young Anthony Maddox in Africa had become legendary, so these adventurers would certainly have researched every detail about the family. They would have thoroughly coached the fellow they'd hired to play the part of the lost heir.

They'd chosen an exceptional-looking man, but of course any son of Colin Maddox would be stunning. Grace had never seen anyone like him.

The man stopped before he reached his carriage and stood still for a moment. Actor or not, it seemed to Grace that he was a world unto himself, completely self-contained and detached from the whirl of activities taking place on the wharf. Then he turned slowly, moving his body in a way that was reminiscent of a full-grown leopard Grace had once seen while on a private tour of the zoo at Regent's Park. The animal had possessed supreme confidence, and a cool disinterest in all that surrounded it.

And Grace had known at the time that it would be disastrous to get too close.

"He is looking this way," Lady Sutton said. "Do you think he sees me?"

Grace shivered at the thought of that predatory beast taking her measure, and reminded herself that the man before her was no giant cat. "I'm not sure, my lady. Oh . . . no, he . . . oh dear, he's falling!"

Lady Sutton reached for the door handle, but Grace stopped her. "My lady, if anyone sees . . . Oh Lord!"

The man was not falling, but *feinting*!

Grace did not know how anyone could move so fast. Like an agile predator moving in for the kill, the dark-haired man stopped abruptly and somehow tripped the bald man on his left, sending him sprawling to the ground. The second escort was a tall, blond fellow who turned quickly and attacked, but Anthony was ready for him. The man grabbed him by his jacket, but Anthony threw him off as easily as he would brush away a moth, then shrugged out of the jacket and moved. But the first man, still on the ground, grabbed his ankle before he could escape.

With the agility of a cat, Anthony sidestepped

and made a dash toward a nearby warehouse. The blond man managed to grab him from behind, taking hold of his shirt. That garment ripped with the force of Anthony's movement, but he paid it no heed, dropping down to grab the multicolored bag the bald man had been carrying.

"Get it!" he shouted as the blond fellow leaped onto Anthony.

But Anthony dodged the attempt to subdue him, and managed to escape the grasping hands of his captors, oblivious of his tattered shirt. With the dexterity of a street acrobat, he jumped two astonishing steps up the side of the nearest wall to somersault backward, landing far behind the two men. He shed the shirt and started to run, but the bald man shouted, "Get him!" and a crowd of dock men gathered and prevented him from leaving.

"They'll hurt him!" cried Lady Sutton. "I must go to him!"

"My lady—"

The man purported to be Anthony moved quickly, pulling a wicked, curved blade from the bag he'd recovered. He crouched, threatening the men closest to him. The skin of his broad back shone darkly bronze in the bright afternoon sun, his muscles rippling with strength. Grace sat in stunned silence at the sight of so much potent male flesh, and felt a frisson of awareness unlike anything she'd known before.

She hardly noticed when another group of stevedores approached, unsure whether they intended to watch the altercation or to participate. She only saw the dense muscles of Anthony's shoulders and arms as they stretched and bunched with every move. His hands were large and strong . . . utterly masculine.

Grace's mouth went dry.

"I do not understand why he fights." Lady Sutton covered her mouth with her gloved hand and watched, horrified, as the men closed ranks around her alleged grandson. "He . . . he does not wish to come home?"

With a swiftness that belied his size, Anthony jabbed the blade of his knife through his teeth like some mythical pirate and jumped up to take hold of a hook on the end of a rope dangling from a winch overhead. Chaos ensued as he raised himself over the crowd and swung across the quay toward the deck of a small sailing ship. He dropped down onto its deck, poised to fight.

A strangled sound came from the back of Her Ladyship's throat, and she went pale. Grace's senses returned at the sight of Lady Sutton's distress, and she decided she would not allow it. This was enough.

She tapped on the window of the carriage, and one of the grooms came to her. "Robert, go and see if you can help that man."

"Which, miss?" he asked, his expression one of controlled astonishment. "The one with the knife?"

"Go, right now, young man!" cried Lady Sutton, her voice wavering in an uncharacteristic manner. "That's my . . ." She swallowed, obviously remembering herself. The countess could not be too quick to accept this man, nor could she be seen with him. They still did not know if he was an impostor, although his behavior so far strongly argued against it.

For he truly did seem to be a man captured out of the wilds of Africa. And his actions showed that he was none too anxious to be taken to Fairford Park.

Grace and Lady Sutton watched in horror as the dock men came after him. To his credit, Anthony did not attack any of them with the knife, but shoved barrels and wooden boxes in their path to deter them . . . for what reason, Grace was unable to conceive. Why wouldn't he want to inherit the Sutton title and estates?

Grace's jaw dropped when he jumped like a monkey onto the ship's mast and started climbing. His antics challenged his pursuers, even though they had no reason that Grace could fathom to continue after him. It was almost like some sort of game, and Anthony was clearly winning.

She felt Lady Sutton flinch every time Anthony made another dangerous move, and soon the countess could not keep herself from stepping out of the carriage to watch him. Grace followed reluctantly, aware that it was most unseemly to be standing virtually unescorted in such rough quarters. Yet she could no more take her eyes from the spectacle unfolding before her than Lady Sutton could.

Robert and their second groom went into the fray, but neither man could get across the gangway and onto the boat because of the crowd that had gathered to watch.

Anthony swung down from his high perch and dropped onto a thick net of rope webbing that was suspended from one of the masts. Bouncing off it, he propelled himself to the side of the boat, but before he could make his dive into the water, one of the men got hold of him and pulled him back, tearing one of his trouser legs.

Anthony whirled and crashed into his pursuers, knocking several of them into the murky waters below. He jumped down and took his knife from his mouth, spreading his arms out in a half circle, challenging every man to try to take him.

"Oh!" Grace cried out as two men sneaked up from behind. Anthony turned and made for the rail again, intending to dive into the water, but the two men managed to drop a heavy net over him.

Anthony fell to the ground, and the crowd of men wrestled him into submission.

"Grace, tell Daniel to come down here."

Grace took a step and realized she was trembling as much as Lady Sutton. She went to the front of the carriage and asked the driver, who'd been in

Lady Sutton's service for many long years, to step down. Frowning, he came to the countess's side. "Aye, ma'am?"

Lady Sutton struck her cane on the wooden deck. "Go over there and see that they bring the dark-haired young man to my carriage."

"That wild man, m'lady? I don't know—"

"Just do as I say, Daniel," Lady Sutton ordered. "I will not have those ruffians in charge of the young man who might be my grandson. There's no telling what they'll do to him next."

Grace wanted to mention that it was Lady Sutton's supposed grandson who'd been the first to attack, but she held her peace when she heard high-pitched whistles frantically piercing through the chaos of the docks. Two policemen arrived as the Sutton driver approached those who were holding the wild man. Many of the brawlers hurried away.

"Where is he, Grace?" Lady Sutton asked. "Where is my . . . Wh-where is that young man?"

Grace could not see him, even as she squinted against the bright light of midday. It was hot standing there in the sun, and she could feel her nose freckling in spite of the wide brim of her straw champignon hat. She could not credit that the barbarian on the wharf was truly the Earl of Sutton. The true earl never would have fought to get away from those men and leave his heritage. Certainly he would have no desire to escape the country where he belonged.

"Look there," Grace replied when the crowd cleared enough to see. "They are lifting him."

"Oh dear heavens, is he hurt?"

Grace craned her neck to see. Something must have happened to him, for when she next caught sight of him, four men were carrying his limp body from the ship.

"What's wrong with him? Is he unconscious?" Lady Sutton asked.

Grace could not answer the countess's question. The man was not moving as the two Sutton grooms and the two original escorts hauled his unwieldy frame to the other carriage. One policeman followed, but the other came to the Sutton carriage with Daniel. His nose was bleeding, and she suspected she knew how it might have happened.

"My lady . . . There's been some difficulty," said Daniel, understating the entire episode.

Lady Sutton raised her chin. She gazed imperiously at the tall policeman in his fine suit with its brass buttons. She was unperturbed by the sight of the blood-soaked handkerchief he held just below his thick mustache, or the bruise that was already beginning to take shape about the man's nose.

She gave a quick glance to her driver. "Send him to my solicitor in Fleet Street, Daniel." Then she turned her gaze to the constable. "Mr. Lamb will see that you are compensated for your trouble, young man."

Grace was not so sure that Lady Sutton should

take responsibility for the savage actions of the captured man, but she said nothing, and the policeman was silenced by Her Ladyship's generosity. He gave a quick bow and departed, and Daniel opened the carriage door for Lady Sutton, assisting her inside.

Grace followed, but not before sneaking a quick glance toward the man who was being carried away. She took a shuddering breath and climbed into the carriage behind the countess.

"Robert will stay with the young . . . fellow . . . in the other carriage," Daniel said, "and we'll follow close behind. Do not worry, m'lady."

He closed them in, and when they were settled, Lady Sutton raised one hand in front of her. "Look at how I'm shaking, Grace."

The poor old woman was, indeed, quivering. As was Grace. She'd never seen such rough, barbaric behavior, and she wondered what kind of tempest Lady Sutton was inviting into her house. What would happen when the young man regained his senses? Grace shuddered to think.

The carriage moved, and Lady Sutton pressed one hand to her breast. "Did you see how he turned to look at me? It was almost as though he . . . No, 'tis too foolish a notion."

The countess was not given to flights of imagination, and Grace could not recall ever seeing her in such a state of agitation. It could not be good for her health, to be so markedly fretful.

But it was not Grace's place to suggest that the countess calm herself. The captured wild man might be her grandson, her only living relation. Grace tried to think of how *she* would feel, if someone told that her father's reported death had been false.

Grace's case was altogether different, of course, for she'd seen the bodies of both her parents, had seen them buried. She'd taken care of her mother during the many months of her illness, so there was no doubt that Helene Hawthorne had truly died. No hope for a miracle.

The uncertainty of what had happened to Anthony must have preyed on Lady Sutton's mind for all these years. And now she was vulnerable to any charlatan who devised a good story for her.

Daniel drove the carriage through the crowded London streets to the western road, and Lady Sutton allowed herself to ease back into the squabs. Still, she grasped the knob of her cane tightly, causing her knuckles to go white. "He is untamed. Wild, Grace."

Grace did not state the obvious, that if the contents of the fateful letter were true and correct, then Anthony had been wandering the dark, uncivilized African jungles for the last twenty-two years. She shuddered to think what kind of man he would be.

Lady Sutton released her cane for a moment and reached into her reticule for a handkerchief. When she did not find one, Grace handed her own to the countess, who dabbed the corner of her eye with it. "All that hair. And his skin so brown. I wonder how he managed to survive."

Grace had given that question a great deal of thought in the week since the battered letter had arrived. As the granddaughter of Lady Sutton's oldest friend, Grace had heard a great number of details about her son's fateful African safari. She knew that his own son, eleven-year-old Anthony, had been washed overboard during a torrential rain.

"Colin searched for months," said Lady Sutton. "But the river was swollen, flooded. It carried Anthony many miles. But he was a strong boy. A powerful swimmer—everyone said so."

"And, by all accounts, an intelligent child, too," Grace remarked, although she was not altogether sure she should contribute to Her Ladyship's fantasy. There was much to be seen about the dark-haired man who'd fought so savagely for his freedom.

"If only that fool Gerard Thornby had been closer, he might have taken hold of Anthony," said the countess. "He might have saved my grandson."

"The earl did not blame Mr. Thornby, my lady," Grace said. "Did he?"

Lady Sutton pursed her lips. "Colin was too generous to assign blame. But, by all accounts,

Thornby was closest to Anthony when their ship swamped."

Grace had heard the tale many times before, yet could not conceive of such a situation. Watching her child being washed overboard in a frothing flood would be too much to bear. She did not know how the earl had survived his loss as long as he had.

"My grandson was as sharp as a razor," the countess said. "He'd have found a way to survive."

If the ruffian in the carriage ahead was truly the Earl of Sutton, then Grace could not imagine what he'd endured, as a boy of eleven years, lost in the wilds of Africa. How had he eaten? Clothed himself? Kept from being killed by some wild animal?

And how wild had he become in the process?

Chapter 2

The ride back to Fairford Park seemed to take forever, with Grace offering reassurances to Her Ladyship all the way home. She had her doubts about the young man they'd collected at the dock, but she said nothing beyond a few subtle words of caution. It was up to Lady Sutton to decide whether he was her grandson.

They followed the other carriage all the way up the long drive, and finally stopped at the front of the mansion. Fairford Park had been in Lady Sutton's family for the past century, and this was where the countess had retreated after the death of her husband. Her son and grandson had lived here with her for the most part, for it was much closer to London than Sutton Court in Oxfordshire.

Grace was grateful to Lady Sutton for her post here. She loved the old house with its old-fashioned mullioned windows and high turrets, and she enjoyed discovering dusty old chambers that had gone unused for generations. There were three guesthouses at the far reaches of the property, and of course Lady Sutton maintained beautiful, extensive gardens throughout.

Grace wondered how life would change at Fairford if the man in the carriage in front of them was truly Anthony Maddox, Earl of Sutton. If Grace was lucky, it would not change at all. She was more than content with her life here, far removed from the difficulties of the city and the reminders of all she had lost. She and Lady Sutton had their shopping jaunts in London and enjoyed the occasional excursion to the opera. But Grace's greatest pleasure was in their visits to St. Andrew's Orphans' Home near Kingston.

Grace waited for the groom to unlatch the door of the carriage and assist the countess down the steps. Then she made her own exit, noting that Lady Sutton's shoe had barely touched the gravel of the driveway before she started giving orders to the servants who seemed to flow like lava from the front entrance. "Send for my physician, Faraday. And get some men to help with my grandson."

Lord Rutherford, an elderly friend of Lady Sutton, came out of the house just as they lifted the alleged grandson out of the carriage. Rutherford was a small man with thinning white hair and wispy white brows. At the moment, his pale gray eyes glittered with intelligence and excitement as he watched the servants lift the young man onto a wooden plank that one of the grooms brought.

It was an awkward business, moving the dead weight of the young man from the dock. His trousers were torn from waist to knee, displaying a scandalous length of his thigh. Even worse was the sight of his bare torso. A light dusting of black hair covered his chest, and his skin was a golden brown, darkened by the sun. One of his arms dropped to the side as they carried him. Even while limp, it was thick with clearly delineated muscle and sinew.

With such obvious strength, Grace could easily see how he'd managed to hold off the men who'd tried to subdue him. He had a formidable physique, which Grace realized would have been necessary to survive so long on his own in the jungle.

His eyes were closed, with thick black lashes lying in crescents over his high cheekbones. His nose was straight, but his well-formed mouth lay agape, most unattractively. Grace had the clear sense that this man would not often find himself incapacitated.

"He is a comely devil, is he not?"

"M-my lady?" Grace stammered. She would never presume to consider such a thing. It was entirely improper for her to have taken notice of the man's physique at all. But of course her indiscretion had been only for the purpose of ascertaining the man's condition. Self-consciously, Grace smoothed the skirt of her brown muslin morning dress and looked away from the men struggling to carry him.

"I would say he bears a distinct resemblance to my son—his father," said Lady Sutton.

"But we should not make assumptions . . ." Grace quietly advised. "Remember what Mr. Lamb said—"

"Where do you want him, my lady?" asked Faraday, for this happenstance had not been considered. They'd expected the young man to walk into the house like a civilized person and make his claim.

How wrong they'd been.

They could have forgone the trip into London that morning, but the countess had wanted a quick look at her alleged grandson as he alighted from his ship. Assuming the young man would arrive on his own two feet, Lady Sutton had planned to return home ahead of him and meet with him in the library. Clearly, she had not thought it would take much deliberation to determine whether he could possibly be Anthony.

"Put him in the yellow bedchamber, Faraday."

"Sophia . . ." said Lord Rutherford, touching Her Ladyship's elbow. "I would suggest you have him taken to one of the guesthouses on the estate."

Grace knew the ancient earl shared Lady Sutton's hope that Colin's long-lost son had been found, and understood Lord Rutherford's reticence to have the man taken into the main house, exposed to the scrutiny of the servants. Tales would be told of such a savage fellow. If he proved to be

Anthony Maddox, those rumors and stories would never leave him.

"But—" Lady Sutton stopped in the midst of her protest and gave a nod. "Yes, the Tudor cottage will do, Faraday. Grace, go with him until Tom Turner can be found."

Grace's jaw dropped. "But my lady—"

The countess squeezed her hand and spoke quietly. "Dear girl, I cannot trust his care to just anybody. Stay with him until Dr. MacMillan or Tom arrives."

Grace blinked at Lady Sutton's unconventional request, but knew she could not refuse her.

"Once he's settled," Her Ladyship continued, "ask Mr. Brock and Mr. Lyman to meet us in the library."

"Yes, my lady," Grace said resignedly, looking after the men who had started to carry the unconscious man to the back of the house.

"Then come and find me when Tom arrives."

Grace nodded. Leaving Lady Sutton with Lord Rutherford, she hurried to catch up with the men. She skirted round them and led them to the Tudor cottage, a small, pleasant house situated at the back of the estate in one of the far gardens.

There were two small bedchambers, and Grace entered one of them ahead of the supposed grandson. She pulled down the blanket and watched as the men shifted their burden from the plank to the bed.

What clothes he wore were in tatters. There was a large scrape on his shoulder and one on his cheek. Dried blood matted the hair above his forehead.

The footmen carried the plank out of the room. As the bald man turned to speak to Grace, the other started unfastening the injured man's trews. "If you'll excuse us a moment, miss, we'll get him situated here."

Grace felt her face heat when she realized she'd been caught gaping at the man in the bed. "Of course," she said, and quickly left the bedchamber.

The sitting room had recently been redone in a wholly feminine decor. Floral prints covered the settee and chairs, and a delicate carpet lay beneath a finely carved table. It was an incongruous setting for the man who lay unconscious in the bedchamber.

Grace wondered how long it would take for Lady Sutton to determine whether he was her grandson.

"He's had a bad blow to his head, miss," said one of the men as they came out of the room. "Best send for a doctor."

"Yes, it's already been done," Grace replied. "He'll be here soon."

"Never seen a fellow fight for his freedom the way he did."

The bald man shook his head.

"How did you get him to come here?" Grace asked.

"There was sickness in the village where we found him," said the man. "He was weak, so it was not too difficult to get him to come along."

His words did not answer all of Grace's questions, but she was not the one to ask them. "Lady Sutton awaits you in the library of the main house," she said. "Just follow the same cobbled path, which will lead you to the back of the house. One of the servants will let you in."

She stepped out of the cottage behind them and looked for any sign of Tom Turner. Sighing, she saw no choice but to return to the bedchamber where the jungle man lay insensible, covered to his neck with a fine linen sheet. Grace knew she should feel flattered that Lady Sutton trusted her with the young man who could very well be her grandson.

But it was so irregular.

Deciding to make herself useful, Grace poured water into a pretty porcelain basin and dipped a clean cloth into it. She then went to the injured man's side and gently blotted the dried blood from his forehead. Even in repose, he appeared a man of great strength, from his jaw to his straight nose and wide forehead.

Grace balanced herself on one hand and leaned closer, easing his hair away from the dried blood.

"Oh!" she cried as the man suddenly locked her wrist in his iron grip. His eyes opened and he turned his fierce gaze upon her.

"*Uko mazuri tiku*," he said, his voice raspy and uneven, but forceful and demanding, nonetheless.

Grace tried to pull free, but his grip was unrelenting. She did not know what harm he intended, if any, for his expression was inscrutable. Somehow, she managed to find her voice, shaky though it was. "Unhand me."

He released her and she took a step back, feeling unsteady as she rubbed her wrist, yet unable to look away. His eyes boldly raked over her, and Grace felt naked under his intense perusal. She swallowed thickly and tried to think of an appropriate set-down when he fell insensible again.

"Eh, Miss Hawthorne," said Tom, coming through the door. Grace felt overly warm and strangely unsettled, and Tom's words barely penetrated her consciousness. "Ye're wanting me here?"

The jungle man lay perfectly still, his face a deceptive mask of tranquility. No one had ever looked at Grace in such a manner, causing her to feel as though she were standing in the midst of a coal fire with her knees as mushy as porridge.

"Miss?"

"Oh yes. Tom." Grace turned away from the man in the bed, her breath feeling tight in her lungs. "Will you wait here with the . . . gentleman from Africa until Dr. MacMillan arrives?"

"Aye, lass. So he's the one? Her Ladyship's grandson?"

"Er, perhaps. Lady Sutton has yet to question him."

Tom came round to the side of the bed. "What happened to the lad? He's all banged up."

Grace gave a puzzled shrug, giving her attention fully to Tom. "He tried to escape the men who brought him here."

"Escape? 'Tis a mite odd, is it not?"

"Yes. You're right. Quite odd."

Grace felt oddly hesitant to leave the cottage and the captured man now. She did not know what to make of his strange words or his heated stare. She pressed a hand against her breast and wondered if her touch would rouse him again, and what he might do when he was fully awake.

"Did ye want me t' stay with him, miss?"

"Oh . . . yes," she said, ordering her thoughts. Staying here was out of the question. Besides, she was wanted by Lady Sutton at the house. "Thank you, Tom."

Hurrying out of the cottage, Grace decided she should feel relieved to be away from those piercing green eyes. When the man awoke again, she intended to be engaged in some wholly appropriate activity at the main house.

She got back to the house a few minutes later and encountered Faraday, who told her the countess and her visitors were in the library.

Lady Sutton's solicitor, Mr. Lamb, as well as Mr. Hamilton, the manager of her accounts and investments, were present. Hamilton was also the trustee of the Sutton estate, and would have much to do with the acceptance or rejection of the young man who lay unconscious in the Tudor cottage. Grace was quite familiar with these men, as she'd accompanied the countess on many a visit to London for meetings with them.

However, she was taken aback at the sight of the auburn-haired gentleman who sat on a chair adjacent to the settee. He was just as tall and handsome as Grace remembered, and he seemed not to notice her as she entered the room.

Grace's thoughts scattered like the fuzz of a dandelion caught in the wind. She had never expected to see Preston Cooper again, and the sight of the suitor who had abandoned her when her mother had become ill was so disconcerting, she tried to think of an excuse she might use to justify her quick departure from the room.

"Ah, Grace, there you are," said Lady Sutton, oblivious to Grace's distress, for she had met Mr. Cooper only once, briefly. "Come and sit by me."

"My lady, you seem well-attended here . . . I'll

just take my leave, if I may," Grace said, anxious to put some distance between herself and her greatest disappointment.

But Lady Sutton reached up and took Grace's hand. "Child, I need you with me. You know how poor my hearing can be, and my memory is just as faulty."

Disinclined to argue, Grace lowered herself to the settee, her posture straight and stiff as she forced herself to ignore Mr. Cooper's presence.

Mr. Hamilton remained standing while Preston Cooper put on his pince-nez once again and took up a pencil and tablet of paper. He began to jot notes as a clerk would do, but Grace could see that he was a lowly clerk no longer. He'd been well into his career two years before, when he'd told her their courtship was over. His status had obviously improved since then.

The countess placed her hand over Grace's to still it, and she realized she'd twisted a corner of her skirt into a tight knot. She pressed her lips together and reminded herself she had made a perfectly satisfactory life after Mr. Cooper's betrayal. That was long past, and she'd adjusted.

So had he, by the look of him.

"Did you get a good look at your alleged grandson?" Mr. Hamilton asked the countess.

Lady Sutton nodded, tightening her lips against a quiver that was entirely uncharacteristic of her. Grace gave Lady Sutton's hand a reassuring squeeze, and focused her attention on the proceedings, rather than on her own irrelevant past.

Hamilton paid no heed to Lady Sutton's distress as he walked to the window and pushed aside the lace curtain to look outside. "I take it you saw a family resemblance?"

Lord Rutherford reached over and patted Lady Sutton's shoulder. " 'Tis difficult, Sophia. But all will be well. I saw Colin in him, too."

"Mr. Lyman," said Hamilton, "you say you found your captive in an inland village?"

The bald man nodded. " 'Twas in a valley some hundred miles inland. We came across a nomadic tribe that had made a fairly permanent camp because of illness."

Mr. Cooper leaned forward to look at a map that lay open upon a table before him. He spread out his long, elegant fingers to smooth it, and Grace remembered the one time she'd danced with him, when he'd taken her hand in his.

"We were, frankly, quite astonished to see a white man there, in uncharted territory," said Brock.

"Was he ill, too?"

"He had been, which was the only reason we were able to get close to him. He was still weak."

The native tribesmen told Brock and Lyman that the white man had washed up on the shore of the river many years before, half dead.

Grace thought the story quite convenient, but remained silent and turned her thoughts to the man in the Tudor cottage. Whoever he was, he did not seem inclined to go along with Brock and Lyman's scheme. Yet why would they bring back an impostor whom they would have to force into posing as Anthony Maddox? It didn't make sense.

She wondered if Mr. Hamilton entertained the same question. "You believe this man is that child?" he asked pointedly.

"It stands to reason, sir. Don't you agree?" Lyman said.

"The Tajuru are nomadic," Brock remarked. "They would have moved camp by the time the elder Lord Sutton reached the spot. And once the boy recovered from his ordeal, the tribe would have sent him away to strike out on his own."

"Oh dear!" the countess whispered. "On his own in the wilds?"

"Yes, my lady."

"He stayed with those people, though? The Tajuru?"

"Our understanding is that he spent most of his time on his own, though we think he might have visited one of the small coastal villages from time to time," said Lyman.

"Did he have any possessions?" asked Mr. Lamb.

Brock gave a small laugh. "Hardly anything. A pair of woven shoes. An old Bible. His knife."

"Clothing?"

"Only a breechclout, sir. We purchased some clothes for him when we reached Pointe Noire."

"But he owned nothing to identify him as Sutton's heir?" Hamilton asked.

"We make no certain claim that this man is Lord Sutton," said Brock. "Only that it seems a very good possibility."

"Was he willing to accompany you to England?"

"He was still feverish when we took him."

"*Took* him?" Lady Sutton queried.

"Er, even the Tajuru said he should go and find his own people," Brock said. "But he did not wish to leave."

Silence ensued. Mr. Cooper's pencil paused, and as Grace kept her eyes trained on the two explorers, she felt her former suitor's gaze settle briefly on her before returning to his clerical task.

"So . . . with no actual evidence to prove it," Hamilton said, "you were so convinced that the young man is Anthony Maddox that you saw fit to abduct him and bring him to London?"

"*Abduct* is a harsh word, sir," said Brock. "We brought him here because we have no doubt at all that he is the missing Sutton heir. But we realize it will be difficult to prove."

"We thought his family would welcome the opportunity to determine that for themselves."

Mr. Hamilton came and stood over the two explorers. "Let me be perfectly clear, gentlemen.

There will be no reward, no release of funds until we—and the House of Lords—are convinced that this young man is truly Anthony Maddox."

"We understand, sir."

"Can you offer no further information about him?" Mr. Lamb asked. "Anything he might have said, or other objects in his possession that you might have disregarded?"

Brock shook his head, but Lyman replied, "No, sir. Nothing more but the timing, and the story told by the Tajuru."

"All right, then. Thank you," said Lamb.

Brock rolled up his map and the two men rose to go, but Lady Sutton stopped them. "Was it malaria?" she asked. "His illness, I mean. I understand it is common in the Tropics."

"No, madam," said Lyman. "At least, not in the opinion of the ship's physician."

"Then that will be all, gentlemen," said Hamilton, but the countess interrupted their departure once again.

"Just one more question," she said. "Although perhaps I shouldn't mention—"

"Please go ahead, my lady," said Hamilton.

"What is a breechclout?"

Anthony's head ached as badly now as the time he'd come down with the *gonjwa* fever in the Tajuru village. He closed his eyes to shut out the light, and wondered how long it had been since he'd seen

Dawa—his Tajuru mother—and the others. Many weeks, he was sure.

"Did you see, Grace?" he heard a soft, female whisper. "His eyes are green."

"Yes, my lady, he . . . Yes, I saw," answered the one called Grace.

Anthony had had a glimpse of her—the first Englishwoman he'd seen since being trussed like an oryx and thrown onto the Portuguese ship that had taken him far from home. She was exquisite. Small and brown with a froth of white at her throat, she reminded him of a small African bird that led badgers and humans to rich nests of honey. A pretty honeyguide.

He wanted to touch her hair and see if it felt as soft as it looked.

"He's taken a good knock to his head," said a man, his voice low and unemotional. "And his ankle is sprained. Not broken, I think. He'll need crutches."

It was strange to hear the language he had spoken only to himself over the years. Many times had he read the old, battered missionary's Bible that had been in the Tajuru's possession. The tribe had been mystified by his explanation of the book and the translations he had given them.

But Anthony was no churchman. He was a jungle hunter who lived by his wits in the wild. He had complete and utter freedom, visiting the Moto Dambia village when he felt the need of human company, or hunting with the Tajuru, the people who had taken him in and cared for him when he was nothing but a lost child.

Which was exactly how he felt now. He had little energy, and even less will to do anything more than lie still and let the fates decide his destiny.

The man poked and prodded Anthony's neck, pushed open his mouth, and pressed down his tongue. He slipped his hands across his head and found a particularly painful spot, but Anthony could not rouse himself to do more than make a small sound of protest.

"Keep him still for a day or two," the man said. "The ankle will bother him, and he's had a concussion from the blow to his head."

"Will he be all right, Dr. MacMillan?"

"I would be very surprised if he were not," MacMillan replied. "When he comes round, put him on a light diet. Broth, eggs, tea and toast. Nothing more until tomorrow. I'll bring crutches when I come tomorrow morning. But of course, send someone for me if I'm needed sooner."

Anthony felt starving, but did not have the energy to protest such weak *chuzika* food. He heard quiet voices at the edges of his consciousness, felt his stomach rumble, and then drifted into darkness once again.

It was clear to Grace that Lady Sutton had never had greater need of her support than now. Grace

could not say she was happy to be stranded here in
the Tudor cottage with the wild man, but at least
she'd been able to stay away from Mr. Cooper. She
wanted no embarrassing confrontation with the
man who had deserted her at the most dire time
of her life.

Unfortunately, at the moment, he was in the
other room of the cottage with Mr. Hamilton and
Mr. Lamb, waiting to hear the doctor's verdict.

Grace glanced in the mirror above the washstand and saw that her chignon was still neatly
pinned at the nape of her neck. She was dressed
in an unpretentious walking dress of light brown
muslin, with a simple, white button-down collar
and small white buttons marching from her throat
to the fitted waist of her bodice. Everything was in
place but her poise.

Smoothing skirts that were already in perfect
order, Grace summoned all her self-control and
composed herself. If Mr. Cooper had become
an associate of Lady Sutton's business manager,
then Grace would likely encounter him again.
And each encounter would surely become easier.
Preston Cooper was her past, she reminded
herself.

Lady Sutton gave a small cry of dismay, and
Grace turned to see what was amiss. "Did they
need to be so rough with him?" the countess asked
as she gently touched a bruise on the jungle man's
cheek.

Grace cast a cynical eye in the countess's direction. "My lady, he was rather rough in his own right, I think." And she hoped he remained unconscious for the duration of Grace's presence there.

"You're right, of course. But . . ."

As Grace looked down at the unconscious brute in the bed, Mr. Brock's description of a breechclout loomed large in her thoughts. The very idea of it was offensive, and Grace knew a true Englishman would never abandon his own civilized customs, his language and standards of dress, no matter where he found himself. But in the African wilds, this man had seen fit to dress himself in a brief draping of cloth that would just cover his . . .

She swallowed thickly and wished she could make an exit from the bedchamber. But the cottage was small, with only two bedrooms and the sitting room with its adjoining dining area. She could not bide her time in the second bedroom, and she was not about to join Mr. Cooper in the sitting room.

Lady Sutton took hold of Grace's hand, and she could feel the older woman trembling. The countess had been ever so supportive during Grace's mother's illness, visiting often, and even sending Dr. MacMillan to offer his opinions and assistance. Grace could do no less for the lady now, when so much was at stake.

"Keep his leg elevated. And you'll need to put ice on this lump," the doctor said, turning Anthony's head to the side, and lightly touching the injured area. "Get the swelling down. Once he comes round, he'll be just fine."

"Grace, Jamie is waiting outside. Send him up to the house for a bowl of ice."

"Of course," Grace said, keeping her voice deceptively calm. But when she stepped out of the bedchamber, she stood still in the hall. She closed her eyes and took a deep breath to compose herself.

It was one thing to come upon Mr. Cooper by surprise in the library. Now . . . She wished her hands would stop trembling. Her former suitor was likely married by now, with a family of his own. It had been two long years since they'd meant something to each other, and he'd made it plain that he intended to wed.

She lifted her chin and walked brightly into the main area of the cottage where the three men sat. They stood as she walked past, but Grace did not give them a glance, nor did she speak to them before going outside. She went down the cottage step and followed a cobbled path a short distance to where she found Jamie, a young boy employed to perform light housework and run errands. He was a cheerful lad, always happily willing to do what was asked of him. Grace saw him throwing stones into a puddle.

"Hello, miss." He grinned at her and dropped the rest of his stones.

"Jamie, I want you to go up to the house and get a bowl of ice. Tell Mrs. Brooks it's meant for the injured man's head."

The boy touched the brim of his hat and nodded, then hurried across the grounds to the house. Once he was gone, Grace had no choice but to return the way she'd come. But as she reached for the door, it opened and Mr. Cooper came out. Grace's posture turned rigid.

"Miss Hawthorne," he said, giving her a polite bow. He was as handsome as ever, with warm, cocoa-brown eyes and wavy auburn hair. He was well-dressed, as was fitting for an associate in Hamilton's prestigious firm. Grace had noticed no gold ring on his finger when he'd been taking notes in the library, but she believed many a married man did not wear one. The thought of a pretty infant with the same red-tinged hair gave her pause. Grace tamped down a rising feeling of utter betrayal and tightened her features into an expressionless mask. That child, and more like him, would never be hers. Mr. Cooper had seen to that.

She moved aside so that he could walk past her, but he made no move to leave. Grace felt tongue-tied and awkward in his presence, and chided herself for allowing his improper advances during their courtship. She'd believed his kisses had been heartfelt, and yet she'd learned they'd been anything but sincere. "Yes, Mr. Cooper. How do you do?" she said with utter politeness.

"I was surprised to see you here," he said.

Her mind seized up like a rusty key in a frozen lock, and she stated the obvious. "Yes, I . . . I became Lady Sutton's companion after Mother died."

"I saw the notice of Mrs. Hawthorne's passing," he said quietly. "My sincerest condolences."

Grace felt a sudden lump in her throat. He offered his sympathy very cavalierly, she thought, considering that it was her mother's illness that had brought their courtship to a close. He'd told Grace that, though he was anxious to marry, he was in no position to take on a wife as well as an ailing mother-in-law who needed her daughter's care round the clock. It was during that brief discussion that Grace realized she lacked whatever it took to achieve and retain a man's devotion. For surely, if he'd loved her, he would never have abandoned her.

Grace was aware that she had not changed in the past two years. Her hair was still an unremarkable brown, and the freckles on her face had not diminished in the least. She knew she was not ugly, but she possessed none of the conventional attributes that would cause a woman to be called beautiful.

"I came to the church service," he added.

"I don't recall seeing—"

"I did not think you'd have wished to see me. So I remained at the back."

Grace gave a brief nod. "It would have been . . . uncomfortable. Worse, perhaps, than it is now."

"Miss Hawthorne . . . Grace . . ."

"You seem to have done very well, Mr. Cooper, on becoming Mr. Hamilton's assistant. My congratulations on your success." She took her skirts in hand and started to move past him. "If you'll excuse me, I really must return to Lady Sutton."

"Of course." He stepped aside and Grace went back into the cottage, relieved to have that encounter done. And it had not been as bad as she had anticipated. In the future, should the occasion arise, she would surely be able to face Mr. Cooper with indifference.

When she reentered the cottage, Mr. Lamb was coming out of the bedchamber, but he turned back to speak to Lady Sutton. "I hope you'll consider what I said, my lady. Circumspection should rule your decisions in the matter."

Returning to the bedroom, Grace found Dr. MacMillan studying the countess with a critical eye as he packed his medical bag. "You look about done in, my lady. I don't want you overtaxing yourself."

"No, I won't," she said, but to Grace, she looked fragile and troubled. The week of anticipating Anthony's arrival had been wrought with stress, and this morning's events had been beyond disturbing.

For Grace as well as Lady Sutton.

"Perhaps you'll have a short lie down before supper," MacMillan suggested.

Lady Sutton looked at the young man in the bed, clearly torn with wanting to stay, but aware that her physician would accept no refusal. "Stay with him, Grace," said the countess. "I'll rest awhile and return shortly."

Grace realized the countess could have no idea that she had already suffered enough trauma of her own that day. She did not care to be left alone with the barbarian who'd torn up the docks that morning, and whose heated glance had so disturbed her.

She chewed her lip and looked at the man in question. He was covered to his neck by a fine linen sheet, but it was quite obvious he was not properly clothed beneath the cover. It was too much for the countess to ask. "My lady, I have not finished your correspondence . . . Perhaps a footman. Or one of the grooms—"

"No, dear. I'll have no servants who will go about telling tales." Lady Sutton grasped Grace's forearm. "You are family, Grace. I can trust you to be discreet."

"Of course," Grace said, humbled by Lady Sutton's confidence in her, yet discomfited by the task given her.

She was grateful that at least Mr. Cooper would be gone.

"Get some rest," Grace found herself saying, "and maybe he'll have awakened by the time you return." *Hopefully, not before.*

The countess beamed a grateful smile. "You are a gem, Grace. I knew I could rely upon you. We'll keep young Jamie out here to be available in case you need anything from the house. Old Tom will return to take your place when he is finished with his chores."

"I shouldn't worry about dealing with the young man, Miss Hawthorne," said the physician. "He's likely to be out for hours."

Grace swallowed her trepidation and smiled stiffly at the countess, who left the cottage on Dr. MacMillan's arm. She sincerely hoped no one ever discovered her present circumstances. It was most improper to remain out here, so far removed from the house, alone with the savage man in the bed.

Chapter 3

The bedchamber was not a restful one. Rose-patterned paper covered the walls, and there were numerous paintings of various sizes on every wall. The bed itself was a large four-poster from another era, with a recently added striped skirt and canopy to match. There were two patterned chairs; a small, round table with a white, lace-trimmed cloth over it; and the washstand Grace had already used.

What might have been a cozy window seat in other circumstances was bracketed by a large bay window that overlooked a pretty garden. Grace forced herself to stop pacing and thinking about Mr. Cooper. She pushed open the bay windows to let in some fresh air, then started to pace again. Thinking of Preston Cooper was entirely nonproductive, so Grace turned her thoughts elsewhere. She was concerned about Lady Sutton.

So much excitement was not good for her, nor would be the disappointment she suffered if they determined that the man in the bed was not her grandson.

How could a boy of eleven years have survived alone in the wilds? And if he had somehow done it, what would the experience have made him?

A savage, apparently. Grace had never seen anything vaguely resembling the altercation at the dock that morning. Such barbarism . . .

She wondered what the jungle man would have done if he'd had to overcome only Lyman and Brock for his freedom, and not an entire horde of stevedores. Where would he have gone? What had he intended to do?

More to the point, why hadn't he wanted to come to Fairford Park and claim his inheritance?

Perhaps he wasn't Anthony Maddox at all, but just an angry man, furious to have been brought to London against his will. But if he turned out to be the true heir, Grace wondered how the next-in-line cousin at Sutton Court would take the news. She speculated on whether Mr. Hamilton's firm would find itself keen to relinquish its guardianship over the estate.

The young man remained insensible, and Grace made a mental comparison of his features to the paintings she'd seen of Colin Maddox, the late Earl of Sutton. There was a distinct resemblance, just as the countess had said. They were both extremely comely men with dark hair, untouched by even the slightest curl. A slight cleft dented his square chin, and his eyebrows were thick and only vaguely arched.

But many men possessed good looks. It was one's behavior that determined whether he was a true gentleman. Grace had not seen the slightest hint of good breeding in him.

Jamie returned with the requested bowl of chipped ice, then went back outside, leaving Grace alone again with the jungle man. She wrapped some of the ice into a towel, then approached him warily. Taking care to touch him as little as possible, she parted his hair slightly to reveal the nasty bump, and positioned the ice carefully against it.

He gave a slight wince, but remained unconscious, and Grace could not bring herself to withdraw her fingers right away. She realized she pitied him. From all accounts, he'd been dragged away from all that was familiar, and carried off, against his will.

Gently, she slid her fingers across his scalp, through the dense hair. It would have to be cut, though doing so would be a shame. She drew back and noticed that the lower half of his face was a lighter tone than the rest. It seemed likely that he'd only recently shaved, and Grace realized there would be no reason for him to groom himself in the jungle. She touched the back of her hand to his jaw. Through the rough hint of beard, the skin was smooth.

Appalled at her own lack of decorum, Grace left the ice resting against the bump on his head and retreated to the window seat. A warm summer breeze brushed past her cheek as she considered the life the young man must have had. Rough. Brutal. Primitive. It would take him some time to adjust to society again.

No doubt Mr. Lamb's advice to Lady Sutton regarding circumspection was correct. In case the young man turned out to be the true Earl of Sutton, it would be best if no one witnessed his coarse behavior when he came round. Word would spread about the "wild earl," and Grace knew the gossip pages could be ruthless. Anthony Maddox would never be able to live down a scandalous reputation, even after he gained a gentleman's refinement. The House of Lords might even reject his claim to the earldom, based solely upon what they'd heard or read about him.

The man's return was clearly a matter best kept private, at least until Lady Sutton determined whether he was actually her grandson.

With the earldom being dormant since the death of Lady Sutton's son, restoration of the title was going to be a complicated matter. Mr. Lamb would surely be involved in the legal maneuverings, and of course Mr. Hamilton's firm would also have an interest in the result.

It meant that Mr. Cooper would likely need to spend more time at Fairford Park.

Grace rested her forehead on the windowsill and changed the direction of her thoughts. It was comforting to know that Lady Sutton considered her "family," but she knew it was true only to a point. She might not be a servant, exactly, but she was employed by Lady Sutton. Her livelihood . . . her survival . . . depended upon the countess's satisfaction and goodwill.

Grace had the utmost respect for Sophia. Like Rose Traynor, Grace's grandmother, Sophia was the third daughter of an earl. But unlike Rose, Sophia had inherited a sizable property of her own. And she'd made a very advantageous marriage, to a man with titles and estates.

By contrast, Rose had wed a gentleman in Chelsea and had borne only a daughter. There was no family fortune, although they'd been comfortable. And happy, just as Grace's own parents had been.

But there the parallels ended. Grace was penniless and had no prospects for marriage. She was a woman who had to make her way alone, and she could never forget it.

"*Majiri.*" The word was just a whisper that sent a chill down Grace's back. She turned toward the bed, hoping she'd imagined the sound.

Then the young man shifted slightly. "*Majiri,*" he repeated.

Grace rose to her feet and took one step toward the bed. Surely he would not attack a woman, but she knew he could be unpredictable. As unpredictable as an animal in the wild.

She garnered her courage and moved a little bit closer. "Do you speak English? Wh-what do you want?"

He opened his eyes, training their pure green hue upon her. "Water," he said clearly.

It was one thing to sit with an unconscious invalid. Now that he was awake, Grace was unsure what to expect. Yet she did not call for Jamie, but went to the washstand and poured him a glass of water. Lady Sutton had put her trust in Grace's experience in dealing with invalids, and in keeping her grandson's nature confidential. She would not betray that trust.

"Can you sit up?" she asked, moving to the bedside.

As he pushed himself up onto his elbows, his bare shoulders bunched with dense muscle. He looked at her as though her question was the most ridiculous thing he'd ever heard.

Grace drew her lower lip through her teeth. She'd assisted her mother in this same situation numerous times, but she could not imagine slipping her arm under this man's shoulders—at least, not while he was conscious—to support him as she put the rim of the glass to his lips.

The linen sheet dropped to his waist as he reached for the glass. Startled by the sight of his broad, bare chest with its dusting of dark hair,

Grace took an abrupt step backward, splashing cold water onto him. He reacted quickly, throwing the sheet aside and coming to his feet.

Grace stood as if paralyzed, though her pulse raced and her breath caught somewhere deep inside her chest as she wondered if he would attack. She kept her eyes straight ahead, focusing them on the hollow of his throat where his collarbones met the muscles of his neck. Away from the dark breech-clout draped about his waist.

"I promise not to eat you, *uzuri toi.*"

But Anthony would not mind a taste. He did not remember Englishwomen looking quite so delicious.

"The d-doctor said you are not to have more than a light meal tonight . . . Oh!" she said, obviously realizing the absurdity of her response to his remark.

She backed away from him, blushing from the edge of her high collar, all the way up to her forehead. It was remarkable. Anthony took a step forward, but stopped at the fiery pain in his ankle.

"I-I did not mean that you were thinking of eating me, exactly," she stammered. "Only th-that you . . ."

She continued to retreat until the backs of her legs bumped into a bench under a wide window. It was open and the sun shone in. The scent of rich dirt, cut grass, and wildflowers was strong—not at all the way he remembered England. He could hear the baying of dogs in the distance and smell wild birds in the brush nearby.

Where was the rain he recalled so clearly? He could not even smell it on the air. He moved closer to the blushing female, supporting his weight on a nearby table as he approached her.

"You should sit down," she said. She made a quick sidestep and put a good arm's length of space between them. "You're swaying."

He did not doubt it. His ankle throbbed mercilessly, and he felt as light-headed as the day he'd come down with the *gonjwa* fever. He moved forward and took hold of the back of a chair. "What happened? Where am I?"

"You're at Fairford Park." It seemed that she'd tried to eradicate every hint of her feminine figure, binding herself in some strange, tight garment beneath the drab brown dress she wore. But she had not been entirely successful, and Anthony appreciated the view.

"And my head?" He reached up and carefully touched the sore spot.

"You don't remember the . . . difficulties on the wharf?" She asked the question with distaste, crossing her arms over her chest.

"Of course I remember. Some idiot struck me with a staff," he said. She continued to back away from him, but he did not allow her to get very far. He moved closer, using the various pieces of furniture for balance.

"Why do you pull your hair so tight? Does it not hurt?"

"My hair is not the point at hand, sir."

" 'Tis brown like the feathers of a honeyguide," he said, reaching to touch the few curling tendrils that had sprung free at her forehead and at her temples. "And very soft."

She pulled her head away from his reach, clearly insulted. But he was not put off. He enjoyed ruffling her pretty brown feathers.

"Please return to the bed. You are in no condition to—"

"I am in very good condition, I assure you." In spite of the headache and painful ankle.

"But Dr. MacMillan said you were to rest."

"And eat a light meal." He approached her again. "I heard the physician's words. But I am hungry. Do you deny your prisoner decent food?"

"Prisoner? You are not being held captive."

"Then I am free to leave?"

Her eyes fascinated him. They were deep, deep blue, just like the waters of Lake Periba. Amazing. And her skin was not altogether white, like the other Europeans he'd seen since being taken onto the ship. Her face was dusted with tiny brown spots . . . the word was *freckles* . . . Lovely.

"You may have noticed that your ankle is sprained, sir. You will not get far on it. And besides, you cannot go anywhere without proper clothes."

"What is proper?" he asked, following her in a strange dance of advance and retreat about the room. For every one of her steps back, he stepped forward, supporting himself on a table here, a bookstand there, the back of a chair. "A necktie to choke me? A stiff shirt and jacket to bind my chest and arms? Trousers to smother my legs?"

"Smother—? Of course not!" Her indignation braced her spine, made her taller. Thrust out her chest. She slipped behind a chair and held on to its back like a shield. " 'Tis only proper to cover yourself appropriately."

Keeping his weight off his injured foot, he spread his arms and looked down. "My African attire does not meet with your approval, then."

"Good heavens, n—" She bristled, so stiff, she was as unyielding as the trunk of a quiver tree. He could not imagine how her man would ever approach her. "You are having a joke at my expense, sir. You know you are at Fairford Park, therefore you are unsuitably dressed."

The woman's scent caught his attention. It was flowers—quite familiar—but mingled with something else. A vague recollection of laundry day came to him . . . of the pleasant smell of . . . *starch*.

"Do all Englishwomen cover themselves from neck to toes?"

"Of course." She fingered the sharp, white collar of her homely gown. "I suppose you are accustomed to much more . . ."

He watched her creamy white throat move as she swallowed, and wondered how that soft skin would feel under his fingertips. His tongue.

"On the contrary," he said. "I am accustomed to much *less*."

She bristled, her feathers ruffling. "You should not say such things, sir. 'Tis wholly inappropriate to speak in such a manner."

"'Tis merely the truth," he said, thinking her elaborate skirts and concealing bodice might be even more enticing than the loose sarongs worn by Tajuru and Moto women. He thought of the soft delights concealed by this Englishwoman's tight wrappings.

"This is an absurd conversation. Please return to the bed and rest until Lady Sutton returns."

"The old woman?" he asked, raising his eyes from her waist to her chest, then her face. "Is she the reason I am here?"

"Not entirely, sir," she said. "If you are Anthony Maddox, then this is where you belong."

He nearly laughed at her absurd statement. If he truly belonged here, then his father would have stayed in the Congo and searched for his son. Lord Sutton would never have left without him.

Anthony caught sight of his *gunia*, lying on a table near the foot of the bed. He picked it up and looked inside. "You are wrong," he said, more casually than he felt. "I belong in Ganweulu." Where he'd learned to live on his own . . . where no one ever got close enough to betray him.

"Africa? That is very likely true," she said as though it were an insult. "But in the meantime, will you please return to the bed and put that pack of ice on your head?"

Every step caused him pain, but he'd had worse injuries than this one. As soon as he found a walking stick he would be able to make his way back to the dock. It could not be too difficult to find a ship bound for Africa.

But there was something he had to do, first. He drew his sharp *kisu* from the bag and slid it into the loop at his waist.

When he looked up at the woman, her face had gone white, but for the freckles that stood out against her pale skin. "M-must you?"

"Must I what?" he asked, puzzled by her sudden pallor.

"That knife," she said. "You will have no need of it here."

The *kisu*, given him many years before by Dawa's mate, had served him well. He was not about to part with it now.

"Outside," he said.

"I beg your pardon?"

"I cannot breathe in this room. Give me your arm and walk with me."

She crossed both arms over her chest. "I will not, sir."

He shifted his weight and moved toward the door without her help, bracing himself on the bed as he moved.

"What are you doing?"

"Leaving."

"Wait! You cannot!" Grace could not believe this was happening. Why couldn't he have remained unconscious as Dr. MacMillan had predicted? Now he stood before her, half naked, with the most wicked-looking blade attached to his waist that Grace had ever seen.

He stopped at the door and turned back to her. "I am no small lad for you to order about."

That was obvious, Grace thought. Not with the way he towered over her. But she braced herself anyway, and held her ground. "I am certain that is true. But in England, you cannot go about without clothes."

"I will rest outdoors."

"You will wait here until I find you some clothes."

"The day is warm—I have need of nothing more."

She gritted her teeth with annoyance. Impossible man. "This is not Africa. You will dress properly, so as not to embarrass Lady Sutton when she returns." Grace had no idea how she would enforce such a decree. She wished she could leave him here to his own devices, but Her Ladyship would expect Grace to manage the situation.

"If you will not return to bed," she said, keeping her voice calm and level, "then please take a seat on one of the chairs. I'll cover you with a blanket—"

He stood still, crossing his arms over his broad chest, and Grace felt the oddest sensation that she was trapped inside by a very large, frightening beast. A sharp knock at the door startled her from that ridiculous, fanciful notion, and she welcomed the opportunity to slide past him and leave the room.

She opened the door to Tom Turner, the elderly servant who'd been groom to Lady Sutton's husband many years before. The man doffed his hat with his free hand. In his other, he held a wrapped bundle. "The countess would like to see ye up at the house, miss. Sent me back here to keep watch over the young gentleman, she did."

Grace did not hear the jungle man come into the front room of the cottage, but she felt a frisson of awareness, a certainty that he was just behind her. She did not turn, did not acknowledge that prickle of consciousness, but nodded to Tom and walked past him, hoping the old man would somehow manage to exert control over Lady Sutton's folly.

The long walk through the garden did much to improve Grace's mood. Obviously, it was much more appropriate for a groom or footman to see to the man in the cottage. To get him dressed, to teach him proper behavior. Grace was glad to have been relieved of her odious duty.

When she arrived at the house, she went directly to the countess's private rooms. She found her benefactress sitting near an open window, gazing outside.

During these quiet moments together, Grace felt closest to the countess and appreciated her employer's kindness to the marrow of her bones. She did not know what she would have done had this situation not arisen. Probably hired herself as a governess somewhere, for her education was good and she loved children.

"I wish I had never allowed my son, Colin, to go to Africa with that horrible Mungo Park."

"Who?" Grace asked.

"The Scot who took it upon himself to explore the course of some river or other. I can't remember what it's called. In Africa, though."

"And the earl went with him?"

Lady Sutton rubbed her forehead. "Only a few survived the trip, and Colin was one of them, thank God. But that journey put the spark of adventure, of restlessness, in him. Never again was he content with the grand hunts and shooting parties at home. He wanted adventure. Danger."

"Do you need a headache powder, my lady?"

The countess lowered her hand and shook her head. "No, it's nothing."

"Are you sure? You look pale. Should I send for Dr. MacMillan again?"

"No, no. Don't worry about me. It's just these old memories have put me out of sorts."

"Then let us speak of something else." Grace did not understand how anyone would give up a secure position in society to go wandering to the primitive lands of Africa, or any other continent, for that matter. She enjoyed the calm predictability of life here at Fairford Park.

"That Mr. Cooper looked familiar," said Lady Sutton. "Do I know him?"

"I believe you met him once when you were visiting Mother and me."

The countess narrowed her eyes. "He was your young man? The one who . . ."

"Yes. Who jilted me when Mother became ill."

"The young scoundrel. And to think he has such a position of responsibility with Hamilton."

Grace shrugged. "It's been two years since he moved on, my lady. I'm well over my disappointment now."

But Lady Sutton's scrutiny did not end there. She pursed her lips and clasped her hands together.

Grace stood. "I'm content, my lady. You have given me a home and a purpose. I . . ." She swallowed. They'd been over this before, when Lady Sutton had pressed Grace on her intentions regarding marriage and a family. She was twenty-five years old—well beyond the prime age for marriage. She knew she was no catch, lacking a dowry and any particular talents to attract a husband. "I could not be happier."

It was true. When life had come crashing down on Grace, Lady Sutton had paid for Helene Hawthorne's funeral. She'd given Grace a situation that suited her well, for Grace loved the older woman like her own grandmother.

She did not want to see her hurt by a charlatan's ploy.

Lady Sutton turned back to the window. "Mr. Lamb tells me that the process of reinstating Anthony as Earl of Sutton will not be an easy one."

"But we do not yet know if the man in the cottage is actually your grandson."

"True. However, if I determine that he truly is Anthony, we may have a long and difficult road ahead of us. My satisfaction in the matter will not suffice to convince Mr. Hamilton or the Lords' Committee on Privileges."

"What will you do?"

"I'm not sure, my dear," said the countess. "But I would like him to have every advantage. Mr. Lamb says that if word of his barbaric behavior gets out, Lords will hardly be inclined to accept him as one of their own."

"I'm sure Mr. Lamb is right," Grace said, and realized that barely a thought of Preston Cooper had crossed her mind in the past hour. The brute in the cottage had fully occupied her attention.

The countess looked back at Grace. "I sent Old Tom out to the cottage, because I can trust him. But Tom is a simple man. I'm sure he cannot read, nor does he understand the nuances of society. Of politics."

Grace was certain that was true.

"He was brilliant with my husband's horses," she said. "He bred racers, you know. As did Colin. And they both trusted Tom with their precious stables."

Grace nodded. As a child, she'd heard about the Sutton stables. She'd even gone to the races a few times with her grandmother as Lady Sutton's guests. "Does Mr. Thornby keep the stables up at Sutton Court?"

Lady Sutton shook her head. "Not that I've heard. I don't believe Mr. Hamilton is inclined to gamble with horseflesh and races when he is entrusted with keeping the Sutton estate intact."

"Has Mr. Thornby been notified that your grandson might have been found?"

"As trustee of the estate, Mr. Hamilton saw to it, of course," the countess replied. "But I will not expose Anthony to him yet. I'd rather be sure of my grandson . . ." She looked up at Grace. "If that man in the cottage is my grandson, I want to know that he's civilized, presentable, and *knowledgeable* . . . before that happens."

Grace could see Lady Sutton's point. Gerard

Thornby sat in Sutton Court, with all the resources of the Sutton title—if not the actual power.

It had been an odd twist of luck that Thornby had become the heir-apparent. His elder half brother should have become Colin's heir, yet he'd died, soon after Colin. The only impediment to Thornby being made earl was that Anthony's death could only be presumed. There was no body, no actual proof.

Still, Gerard Thornby wielded a great deal of influence. And if the man in the cottage was actually Anthony Maddox, it would be unfair to pit him against Thornby, unprepared.

"We must be certain Anthony is capable of reading, of writing. He must be apprised of the discussions and debates in Parliament, meet Wellington and learn of Napoleon. He will need to learn to dress, to walk, talk, and eat. The social graces— polite behavior, dancing, and social discourse— will all be foreign to him."

Grace suppressed a sigh. It would have been so much better for them all if the jungle man had not been discovered. "You still need to talk to him, my lady, to see if you really believe he is your grandson."

"True," Lady Sutton replied, deep in thought. She looked up at Grace suddenly. "How could he not be? He looks to be the right age—Anthony will be thirty-four before year's end. His eyes are green and he has his father's straight, dark hair. And he was found in the same general region as where he was lost."

"Yes, but—"

"I will question him."

"He is not quite . . . civilized, my lady." Grace did not give her the bare truth: that her grandson was a wild man, a primitive barbarian with absolutely no sense of decorum, or courtesy.

"Of course he isn't, Grace," Lady Sutton retorted. "He's been living among savages and wild beasts for two decades!"

"All the more reason to take care . . ."

"I think I'd better get Jamie away from the cottage. He'll talk to his aunt in the kitchen, and I don't want her carrying tales to every other house in Richmond."

"I'll send for him, my lady."

The countess nodded absently. "Anthony will need a tutor."

"Shouldn't we establish that he actually *is* Anthony Maddox before you hire a tutor?" She did not want the countess to get too far ahead, leaving herself open for disappointment and regret.

"Why Grace, I don't plan to hire an outsider." Lady Sutton looked over at her. "I've decided that *you* will be his teacher."

Chapter 4

Anthony knew he would not get far on his bad ankle. He remembered enough about the distance between Fairford Park and the big English city to know that even with a walking stick, he would have difficulty returning to the docks. And he didn't even know where he might find Gerard Thornby.

He needed money and a horse, information, and some time to explore before he set out to find a ship to take him home.

But in the meantime, he had no intention of following the dictates of the woman who'd just left, her expression as alarmed as though a horned buffalo were about to charge on her. Anthony had never been compared to a buffalo. The Tajuru said he reminded them of a wild ape in his treetop nest. The Moto said that while he was hunting, he was like a wild, stalking cat. But never a buffalo.

An old man came into the house, but Anthony stayed at the door, balancing on one foot as he watched the woman disappear round the curve of the path. She was gone by the time he realized he had not learned who she was.

Or why she thought she was in charge.

"Here now, let me have a look at that foot," said the man. He set down the package he carried, drew up a low stool, and sat on it, gesturing for Anthony to take a seat in front of him. Then he pulled Anthony's foot into his lap and squeezed the heel. "That hurt?"

"Some."

"I'm Old Tom, by the by. Been in service to the Maddox family since I was a lad. Sat with you here when you first arrived." He pressed on the side of Anthony's ankle, and Anthony gritted his teeth against the pain.

"Not too bad, then," said Old Tom. "I've some liniment and a tight wrap that will put ye to rights in a few days. Bring it back later."

Anthony studied the old man as he examined his foot and ankle, fascinated by his face, his voice, and his mannerisms. Tom's head of dense, white hair lay in sharp contrast to his skin, which was darkened by the sun. He'd allowed the whiskers to grow down his cheeks, stopping before they reached his mouth. His chin and upper lip were clean-shaven, his face crinkled with lines of age. But he looked as robust and fit as the elders of the Moto Dambia tribe.

The old fellow flapped one derisive hand toward

the frilly furniture and decor in the room. "Bet this place gives ye the willies. Never could stand all this fuss, m'self."

Tom reached for his package and untied the thin, white string that held it together. Inside was a bundle of clothes, and he took out each piece. "This should all be obvious enough. Get dressed and I'll help ye outside."

Anthony did as Old Tom bid, pulling on layers until he was dressed much like Tom himself.

"Had to borrow what I brought," Tom said. "Not too many round here as tall as ye're, and no time to have anything made."

"Who is the woman?" Anthony asked.

"Which?" Tom asked, wrapping some ice into a cloth and tying it together. "Miss Hawthorne, who was just here? She's Lady Sutton's secretary. Been here nigh on a year, since her mum died. Come on now, lean on me and we'll go out to the chaise."

Anthony did so, and they went through the door and out to a small, cobbled area ringed by low brush and many layers of lush, colorful flowers. The sun was shining and there were several chairs and a table arranged in a neat setting.

"Here. You take this one."

The chair was part bed, long and cushioned, with heavy, ornate arms rising up from its sides. Anthony would not dream of getting onto such a contraption. He limped past the clearing and stepped off the path, where there were numerous old, venerable trees, with wide, sweeping limbs. The grasses had been mown much too short, but merely standing there gave Anthony a much-missed feeling of peace. He yearned for the thick canopy of trees of his valley and the quiet familiarity of all that he knew.

This place could not have felt any more foreign.

He reached up to a sturdy branch and swung himself up, as he was accustomed to doing at home. Here, he knew, he need not worry about snakes dropping down on him, or wild beasts chasing him through the wide savannah. It was the one advantage to this place.

Tom tossed the package of ice to him. "If you're going to stay up there, you might as well wrap this round yer ankle."

Most every part of Fairford Park was well-groomed. Stately old trees towered over beautiful flower beds and strategically placed paths. The three guest cottages were kept in ready condition for Lady Sutton's overnight guests, should there be too many for the house.

In spite of the careful grooming of the estate, there remained, in one far corner of the grounds, a run-down, old building that had been a private study and retreat for the last Earl of Sutton, Colin Maddox. Grace had heard that this was where the earl had pored over his maps and planned his expeditions with his traveling companions. It was there that he'd hung the skins and pelts and mounted heads of the exotic animals bagged on his travels.

But as the earl had been gone for many years, Grace believed the countess should have had it demolished. The old building was visible from the path that led to the cottages, even in the falling darkness. She could not imagine what the countess's guests thought when they saw it on their way back to their quarters.

"I hope he's awake," Lady Sutton said, holding Grace's arm as they made their way toward the Tudor cottage.

What Grace hoped was that he hadn't given Old Tom too hard a time of it. "He was awake when I left him."

"But his concussion . . ."

"He's had plenty of time to rest, my lady. It's been hours."

"Grace, why are you so set against him?"

"I'm not set against *him*, exactly," Grace replied. "I just don't want you to be too disappointed if it turns out that he is not Anthony."

"We'll soon see who he is, won't we?"

"If he were your grandson, wouldn't he have said so?" Grace asked.

"Perhaps. Or maybe he has a reason for keeping his identity to himself."

"What possible reason would he have for remaining anonymous?"

"I don't know."

"What if he's a criminal? Such a man would be loath to be discovered by the authorities, wouldn't he?" Grace had given it a great deal of consideration throughout the afternoon, and she could think of no other reason that the stranger would not want to admit to being heir to the Sutton estate.

"Oh dear, Grace, do not frighten me."

"I'm sorry, my lady," Grace said, truly regretful for alarming the countess. "He's likely not so bad, but we should be wary, I think."

The man in the Tudor cottage bore a resemblance to the portraits of Lady Sutton's son and daughter-in-law. But such a resemblance was not proof. Grace was sure there would have to be a great deal more, and a thorough examination by the authorities might very well expose his true identity.

Grace had yet to work out how the young man in the cottage would have arrived in Africa and been left behind—unless he were truly Anthony Maddox. But on the docks, the behavior of the two explorers had been rough, even brutish—

"I trust those two men from the African Study Society," said Lady Sutton.

But they had strong motivation to try to dupe her. "You will reward them handsomely if the young man is proven to be your grandson, will you not?"

"Yes, but—"

"It would really behoove them to substantiate their story in any way they can, whether the young man is your grandson or not."

"Grace, when did you become such a suspicious girl?"

"I hope it's not mere suspicion," Grace replied, "but prudent doubt. If he's truly Lord Sutton, then we'll soon know."

They'd almost reached the cottage when Lady Sutton stopped. "Oh dear heaven."

Grace followed the countess's line of vision, and her breath caught. Lady Sutton's purported grandson lay high upon a branch in a massive oak, leaning against the trunk, watching them like a beast of prey.

Lady Sutton tapped her cane on the pebbled path. "Come down from there, young man! Immediately!"

After a heartbeat's hesitation, he swung down to the ground. The countess turned to Grace. "Go and help him. He should not stand unaided on that injured ankle."

"He managed to get into that tree . . ." Grace grumbled, but she obeyed Lady Sutton, leaving the path to walk in his direction.

Grace approached him as a shiver of unease fluttered up her spine. He looked very different in conventional clothes, even more dangerous than when he was nearly naked, if that were possible.

He eased his injured foot down, bracing his weight evenly in a wide stance.

Grace refused to be intimidated by his size or his attitude. "You fancy yourself a monkey of some sort?"

"More like a great cat. Always alert, always ready."

"The countess wants you to lean on me," she said. "Feel free."

"Free? I will not be free until my ankle is healed."

Grace looked down at his feet. They were bare, and she glanced away quickly, embarrassed at the sight of them. Decent people did not leave their feet unshod for anyone to see. "Come along," she said rigidly.

They caught up to the countess, who'd gone on ahead of them. "Where's Tom Turner?" Grace asked.

Her alleged grandson shrugged. "At the cottage, of course. Was he not sent to guard me?"

"Guard you?" Lady Sutton's tone was indignant.

"I understand that I am not to leave this place."

"Perhaps you can explain why you're so anxious to go," Grace said.

"I told you. I do not belong here," he replied easily.

They continued on their way to the cottage. Once inside, the barbaric man had the audacity to sit down cross-legged on the floor, leaning his back against the settee. Even worse, he'd done so before the countess had taken her seat. Grace looked over at Lady Sutton, to gauge her reaction to his egregious breach of etiquette. But the countess appeared unruffled as she sat down in a chair across from him.

"I am Lady Sophia Sutton. My husband and son were earls of Sutton." She gestured toward Grace, who busied herself lighting the lamps against the gathering gloom and opening the windows to freshen the room. "This is Miss Grace Hawthorne, my companion."

The wild man tipped his head slightly in acknowledgment, and his long hair fell like a dark, silky curtain against the side of his face. "I am Kuabwa Mgeni of the Ganweulu Valley. I met Miss Hawthorne earlier. Although not formally."

The countess turned to Grace. "See? He is not irredeemable."

Undaunted, Grace crossed her arms against her chest and faced him. "Were you born in the Ganweulu Valley?"

"I do not recall where I was born."

"Obviously. None of us can actually *remember* our birth." Impudent man.

"I have some questions for you, young man," said the countess. "And you will answer without prevarication."

"Of course," he responded, and Grace resisted

the urge to tap her foot and roll her eyes. It was not like Lady Sutton to be so naïve.

"Do you remember how you arrived in Africa?" Her Ladyship asked.

He looked directly at the countess as he replied. He enunciated every word clearly, but his inflection was slightly foreign. "I was just a boy when I went on safari with my father and his friends."

"Tell me more."

"We went deep into unexplored territory," he said. "My father was quite proud of it . . . of going farther than any other white man."

Lady Sutton made a nearly imperceptible nod, and Grace tried to imagine the wild region in which Anthony—the *real* Anthony—had found himself. There would have been wild beasts, and none contained behind bars as they were in the Regent's zoo. The only people in such unexplored lands would have been savages, unschooled in civilized behavior and customs. Grace shuddered. She was more than content to keep the mantle of modern culture wrapped round her.

"We set upon the river in a *dhombo*—a small sailing boat—when the rains suddenly came. The storm was unlike anything my father or any of his companions had ever seen. They fought to control the *dhombo*, but it rocked and swirled uncontrollably." He paused, and Grace saw him swallow tightly at the memory. His dark hair shone in the soft glow of the lamps, and he shoved one thick lock behind his ear. The shadow of his beard darkened his jaw. "You cannot imagine the violence of the downpour and the resulting mayhem on the boat. In the chaos, I . . ." Grace saw the flexing of a muscle in his jaw as he hesitated. ". . . I fell overboard."

"But you survived the fall," said Lady Sutton. "And?"

"The water carried me many miles downriver," he said quietly. "I do not remember climbing out of the water. I don't know exactly what happened, or how I managed to survive the river."

How convenient, Grace thought. "We understand that someone found you and nursed you back to health."

He nodded. "Dawa. My Tajuru mother."

"And you have lived with these Tajuru people ever since?" asked Lady Sutton.

He shuttered his eyes and gave a shake of his head. "The jungle is my home."

"How does anyone live that way?" Grace asked.

"How does a father leave his son to the wilds?" Anthony asked quietly.

"Then you believe you are my grandson?" asked the old woman. Anthony was chagrined to see how she'd aged. In his memory his grandmother retained more dark hair than white, and she'd seemed youthful. Agile and sharp.

Now she looked like a small bird he should draw into his arms and protect.

Anthony shook off that impossible notion. He was responsible for no one, and had learned never to trust his countrymen—not even his own family. "I might be your grandson, but I do not belong here. I stay only because I have questions for my father."

Lady Sutton shrank a bit more, and Grace Hawthorne stepped behind the countess's chair and put one hand on her shoulder. Protective and affectionate. Sophia had all that she needed.

The younger woman looked over at him. "Are you saying you are Anthony Maddox?"

He shrugged. "I have not used that name for many years. I'd forgotten it until the *eupe* men came to the Tajuru village and questioned me."

"Can you prove it?" the Hawthorne woman asked. "Is there something personal, something unknown to anyone else that you would know?"

He rose to his feet, his patience gone. "I would speak to my father."

"Oh dear," said his grandmother. "You are so much like Colin, it . . ."

He saw pain in her eyes and regretted being the cause of it. But events that he could not control had been set into motion. He was here, and he would have answers before he left.

"A great deal has happened since you were lost," said Lady Sutton. "Your father . . . my son, Colin

. . . stayed in Africa for months, searching for you."

Her words sucked the air from Anthony's lungs. This could not be true. Colin had abandoned him in the most dangerous place on earth. His only son. "He searched?"

"Of course," said his grandmother. "You can't possibly think he'd have left the continent without his only child."

"But I . . ." His mouth went dry. "He . . ."

"When Colin came home, he was heartsick. He could not concentrate on work. He took no pleasure in anything at all. Not when his son was gone."

Anthony felt the blood drain from his head when he realized what his grandmother was telling him. "He's dead, then."

She nodded and her chin trembled. "He died inside a year after you were lost. He came down with a cold on his chest, went to bed and never got up."

Anthony felt a burning sensation at the back of his throat. This went against everything he'd come to believe. He'd languished for days after washing ashore, vacillating between illness and fear in the primitive Tajuru hut as he recovered from his injuries. At the time, he had not known whether the natives were healing him in order to eat him later, or if they meant him no harm.

He had needed his father desperately in those

early days, yet Colin had never come for his son. And Anthony had received his first lesson in the harsh realities of life. He could rely only upon himself.

"What of Thornby?" he asked.

"Of course he stayed in Africa with your father and helped him search for you."

No doubt he'd been certain they would find only a corpse. "Where is he now?"

"He lives with his wife at Sutton Court."

Sophia must have taken notice of his furrowed brow, for she clarified her statement. "With you gone, he became the presumptive heir to the earldom."

Anthony sank down once again to his place on the floor. How could his father have been so blind? "This changes nothing."

"What do you mean?" asked Lady Sutton.

"England is not my home." He preferred the isolation and freedom of the jungle. And the *predictable* vipers of Africa. Once he dealt with the one that resided at Sutton Court, he would be free to leave.

"Lady Sutton," said Miss Hawthorne, "this man has said nothing to prove that he is truly your grandson. Anyone might learn the history of Anthony Maddox—how he was lost, and this very feasible story of his escape from the river."

"Grace . . ." the countess said uncertainly.

The Hawthorne woman turned to him. "What

school did you attend before your journey to Africa?"

"St. Paul's."

"Who were your friends?"

He hesitated for a moment, forcing himself to remember the boys who'd been his closest chums. They'd come to stay at Fairford Park on occasion, and there had been adventures . . . "Daniel Bryant and Hugh Christie."

"They are now Lords Rothwell and Newbury," Lady Sutton interjected.

Grace resumed her interrogation. "Who was your favorite teacher?"

"Mr. Carlson. James Carlson."

She took on a studious expression, each of them aware that anyone who had done enough research could have discovered these facts.

"Your best subject?"

"Mathematics."

"That's true, Grace," said Lady Sutton. "Anthony always did have a head for numbers. Languages, too."

"My lady, it is he who should answer the questions." Miss Hawthorne turned back to him. "What was your favorite pastime?"

"Taxidermy."

"There!" said Lady Sutton. "No one but the family knew that Colin preserved his own birds and things. And Anthony loved to spend time at his father's lodge, stuffing all those animals of his."

The man in question looked at his grandmother. "The old lodge . . . it still stands?"

She nodded. "I could not face having it taken down, though it's an old shell of a building these days."

"I spent many hours puttering there with Father. He always let me choose the glass eyes," Anthony said, pushing those soft-hearted memories from his brain. They served no purpose but to make him weak-minded. "It was there that he planned our trip with the others."

"I am satisfied, Grace," said Lady Sutton, her voice quiet and slightly tremulous. "He is my grandson."

The countess reached for him again, but Anthony leaned back and avoided her touch. He braced himself against the wave of sympathy that threatened his intention to leave. His grandmother had all that she needed—money, influence, friends . . . and here stood a companion who looked after her interests. Nothing was going to keep him from returning to his life of freedom in Ganweulu.

The countess retreated, striking her cane once lightly on the floor. "You will begin your lessons tomorrow."

Grace took note of Anthony's closed expression and was outraged on Lady Sutton's behalf by the man's utter indifference. How could he behave so coldly toward his grandmother?

Surely they'd have been better off without this barbaric grandson who had no consideration for his elderly relative. Had Lyman and Brock left well enough alone, the countess's loss would have remained a quiet grief that barely troubled her anymore.

Tom Turner came in through the door and doffed his hat, giving Lady Sutton a brief bow. "Must have dozed off on that chaise. Your young fellow here wouldn't lie on it, and I saw no sense in letting the thing go to waste."

Lady Sutton was tolerant of the man's dereliction, sending him to the house with orders for supper to be brought out to the cottage. She'd already admonished Faraday that she wanted no other servants hovering about.

Grace sat down near the countess. In her opinion, the questions they'd posed to Lady Sutton's grandson had not been personal enough. They had decided nothing. He could be any random fellow of the correct age and coloring, tutored in the Maddox family history, and brought here to make claims on the earldom.

But Lady Sutton was satisfied. Perhaps there was some subtle element of his personality that she recognized, or a long-remembered mannerism that convinced her. Grace had to admit that he moved in a particularly unique fashion. Even with his injury, he was powerful and agile—like a great cat, as he'd said.

She took a deep breath. Regardless of whether he was authentic, or how nimble he might be, she had no intention of trying to tutor him. She was not suited to such a task.

"I assume you'll need to refresh your writing and reading skills," said Lady Sutton to Anthony, as though he had not just snubbed her.

Anthony did not reply, but Grace noticed a tightening in his sculpted jaw, and she wondered at his reaction.

The countess addressed Anthony again. "Your English is good. Did you ever have any use for it after . . . the accident?"

"I used it."

"Really? There were other Englishmen present?" Grace asked in a mildly sarcastic tone.

He shrugged. "There was an English Bible. The Tajuru had it from some long-dead missionary. They . . . they liked the stories."

"You translated it for them?" the countess asked.

Anthony gave a brief nod, obviously not pleased with sharing this personal information. It had become perfectly clear that he intended to keep his distance from his grandmother.

" 'Tis quite commendable, is it not, Grace?" said Lady Sutton. "Teaching the savages?"

"You mistake me," said Anthony. "I taught nothing. I merely translated some of the more amusing stories for them."

"Well," said Her Ladyship, unwilling to think any less of her grandson. "Your English is quite satisfactory."

"My lady, he was eleven years old when he left England," said Grace, contrarily. "Surely his language skills were solid by that age."

She felt unwilling to give the man any credit for his accomplishment. He was rude, he showed absolutely no consideration for his grandmother's feelings, and he was not forthcoming with information about his lost years.

A light knock at the door changed the direction of Grace's thoughts, sending them scattering when she looked through the window and saw Preston Cooper standing outside.

"Grace?"

She remembered herself and went to the door. Mr. Cooper doffed his hat. "May I?"

Grace realized she was gaping at him when the countess spoke without the slightest touch of welcome or warmth in her voice. "Mr. Cooper. Do come in."

He entered the room, standing until Lady Sutton gestured to a chair near her own. "To what do we owe the . . . Surely a single jaunt to Richmond in one day is sufficient?"

" 'Tis not so far, my lady."

He'd changed from his more formal business attire into a lightweight frock coat over his linen shirt and dun-colored trousers. He was perfectly attired for a warm spring evening.

But Grace was wearing the same gown she'd had on all day. She felt self-conscious and wilted when Mr. Cooper looked briefly at her. Thankfully, he quickly turned his attention to the countess, and Grace took the opportunity to smooth back the tendrils of hair that had come loose from her chignon.

"Mr. Hamilton sent me with a list of questions for . . . for the, er . . ."

"My grandson," Lady Sutton said dryly. "I'm satisfied that this young man is Anthony, but you are welcome to ask whatever you like."

"Lady Sutton, your quick acceptance may be premature," said Mr. Cooper. "Mr. Hamilton believes there are many more issues that need to be resolved before it can be stated that this man is truly Anthony Maddox."

"Yes, yes, I know," said the countess. "But Miss Hawthorne and I have already asked all the pertinent questions. I have no doubt that this is Anthony."

"My lady," said Mr. Cooper, leaning a little bit forward in his chair, and Grace was struck by the notion that he looked like an earnest schoolboy. And yet his betrayal had cut her deeply. "It will take rigorous questions and even more meticulous answers before this man can be instated as Earl of Sutton."

"Go ahead, then. Ask."

Grace barely heard the questions, but Mr. Cooper's voice restored many a tender memory to her heart. So many times had he called for her at home and taken her walking in the park. There had been the occasional outing to a favorite coffee shop, and he'd once invited her to a lovely soiree, hosted by his employer. Grace had had a new gown made for the occasion, and they'd danced. She'd been sure he would propose that night, but it had not happened. And then her mother had become ill.

". . . any unique markings on your skin? Birthmarks? Scars that would identify you as the grandson of Lady Sutton?" Mr. Cooper asked.

The countess shook her head, her dislike for Mr. Cooper evident in her posture. "Not that I recall."

"No," Anthony replied simply and with a decided lack of interest that Grace found unsettling. In spite of his injured limb, he rose from his place on the floor and prowled to the dining table, where a bowl of fruit had been artfully placed. He dug through the offerings and chose a peach, which he sliced in half with his wicked-looking knife.

He pulled a chair out from the table and sat down on it, facing its back as he threw one leg over the seat to straddle it. Dangling his hands over the back of the chair, he tore the pit from the peach and tossed it back to the table, then bit into the fruit.

Juice ran down his chin, and he wiped it with the back of his hand.

Grace turned away, unnerved by the sight of his unabashedly primitive behavior. Did he remember nothing of civilization? Was there any possible hope of rehabilitating him? Grace would have to speak to Lady Sutton again about her role in such an endeavor. Surely she was not the one to undertake such a daunting task.

Mr. Cooper asked several more questions, but none of Anthony's answers was definitive. Grace did not believe he had a prayer of being accepted as the Earl of Sutton. The House of Lords would never count such a raw and elemental man as one of their own.

"Lady Sutton, Mr. Hamilton would like to present"—Mr. Cooper tipped his head in Anthony's direction—"our findings to Lords in two weeks' time."

"We'll be ready," she said, then turned to Grace. "You have your work cut out for you, my dear."

"But, my lady," Grace replied, attempting to keep her voice calm, "what about your correspondence, your outings? Who will help you to organize the—"

"Grace." The countess stood, as if to emphasize her words. "As I said before, I will not bring in a stranger at this juncture. You are a well-educated young lady, and Tom Turner is my most trusted servant. Between the two of you, my grandson will learn all he needs to know to get on in society."

Grace had not noticed the color rising in Mr. Cooper's face until he spoke. "Lady Sutton, such a task will require a great deal of private . . ." He cleared his throat. "Is it entirely proper for Miss Hawthorne to spend so much time—alone—with . . . with . . ."

"With my grandson?" Lady Sutton asked, drawing herself up into a formidable force. "I can assure you that every propriety will be observed, young man. And by the way, he is to be called Lord Sutton henceforth."

Mr. Cooper seemed to deflate with the countess's reproof, and Anthony abruptly stopped eating. Peach juice dripped from his hand to the floor, and his expression was no happier than Grace knew her own must be.

"Lady Sutton," said Cooper. "Do you truly believe your grandson will be ready to appear before the Lords' Committee on the date Mr. Hamilton has chosen?"

Grace held her breath, and it seemed that Anthony did the same while they listened for his grandmother's response. She was nervously fingering the head of her cane.

"No," she said, finally. "I've decided we shall need a full month."

Even then, Grace knew she would be hard put to make Anthony presentable. She did not understand what the countess could possibly be thinking.

Mr. Cooper scratched the back of his neck and looked over at the would-be earl. "I must say that I have yet to hear anything that would convince me without a doubt that this man is your son's heir, my lady." He turned to Anthony. "Do you claim to be Lady Sutton's grandson?"

"I make no claims," Anthony replied, causing the countess to stand more abruptly than she had ever done in Grace's memory, and she worried again about Lady Sutton's nerves.

"We are finished here, Mr. Cooper," she said brusquely, leaning heavily on her cane. "If you and Mr. Hamilton have any further questions, be so good as to send them by messenger. Now, if you will excuse us . . ."

Grace knew that Mr. Cooper was only performing his job to the best of his ability. There was a precedent here, and Mr. Hamilton—as trustee of the Sutton estate—must be wary of making a grievous error.

She only wished Mr. Cooper—*and* Anthony Maddox—had shown some consideration of Lady Sutton's distress in this matter. The day had been long and trying for the countess, and she was an elderly woman, unaccustomed to such agitation, such controversy.

Grace turned her back on Anthony, who looked more like a common navvy than a peer of the realm, and helped Lady Sutton to the dining table. If there had been confusion as to his identity before, it was worse now. He had spoken to the countess as though he were her grandson, yet he would not make that claim to Mr. Cooper.

She did not understand him.

Mr. Cooper gathered his notes into his portfolio and said his good-byes just as Jamie and Tom arrived with a cart laden with trays of food from the house.

"If you would like to eat, *Lord Sutton*," Grace said, grinding out his title, "kindly turn round and sit properly in that chair."

Anthony decided the meal was a great success. In spite of the physician's orders that he sup lightly, he ate his fill of food he had not had to catch, kill, or pick from a branch. When he was finished, he sat back in his chair and spread his hands across his belly as all tribesmen did, and belched his satisfaction with the meal.

Adding to his enjoyment was the relaxation of Grace Hawthorne's stiff formality. She'd become as rigid as a pane of glass when the pale Englishman had arrived looking a great deal too impressed with his own importance. Now she was fiercely angry. It made her come very close to losing the prim and distant demeanor that she wore about her like a shield.

She was overheated, with a hint of moisture

on her forehead and high cheeks that was reflected in the candlelight. When she turned those magnificent eyes upon him in challenge, he could not help but wonder how intense her passion would be.

He knew she would not welcome his touch, but the urge to move in close and test the limits of her temper was strong. He shifted in his chair to ease his savage arousal.

The night was nearly as warm as his tropical home, yet Grace Hawthorne did not dress accordingly. Her clothes were tight and all-encompassing, with layer upon layer. While she and his grandmother conversed, Anthony imagined himself removing those layers, one by one, revealing the pale, freckled skin underneath. He did not believe she would be a passive lover, but would touch him, would kiss and lick—

"Anthony, your table manners are abominable," said his grandmother, shaking him out of the most intense fantasy he'd ever entertained. "Though I do not suppose it would be fair for me to admonish you just yet."

Anthony banished the lingering images from his mind and looked at his plate, at the bones he'd sucked clean. The meal had been delicious, and so had his imaginings. But he would not be staying in England long enough to sample much more of either. He had no intention of wasting his time learning the intricacies of an English table.

Or on the mating preferences of a stiff and starched Englishwoman.

"I'm going back to the house, to bed," said the countess. "Grace, perhaps you can stay and give Anthony his first lesson. I do not wish to be subjected to such a display again."

"My lady, I . . ." Grace sighed visibly, clearly dissatisfied with the arrangement.

"Tom will walk me back to the house."

The look of pure aggravation in Miss Hawthorne's face prevented Anthony from protesting any lessons. When Old Tom came into the cottage and escorted Lady Sutton out, Anthony surveyed the small white buttons that marched up the front of Miss Hawthorne's gown, and returned his thoughts to peeling that drab, brown cloth from her shoulders, and pressing his lips to the soft skin beneath.

He took a deep breath, inhaling her scent. "So you are to be my honeyguide?" he said to her.

She whirled on him, her blue eyes flashing with fury. "Honeyguide? How dare you?"

"How dare I what? Compare you to a very obliging bird?"

"I don't care anything about birds! Your grandmother has anticipated this day ever since we received the letter about you. Ever since the day your father returned home from Africa without you. And you . . . !"

He took a defiant stance, even though he felt a sudden burning in the pit of his stomach. "What about me?"

"Would it have hurt you to be a bit more kind to her?"

"Kind?" he asked harshly. "I answered her questions."

"And no more." She stormed over to the table and started picking up plates and putting them on the service cart with more clanking and clattering than was strictly necessary.

"She appears to have coped," Anthony said more casually than he felt. "My grandmother should understand that all this is . . . I will never fit into her society the way she intends."

"You are an insufferable savage."

He lashed back at her. "And you are the most buttoned-up excuse for a female I have ever seen."

"Buttoned—!" Her chest filled with air, and Anthony did not know where it could all go, not when she kept herself bound so tightly. He could loosen those ridiculous bindings for her and teach her how to breathe. With him pressed against the breasts she kept so well-hidden.

She came closer, but waggled one finger in the direction of his face. "Since you are quite obviously *ignorant* of correct and modest fashion, I will inform you that I am most properly attired. 'Tis you who have need of improvement."

He leaned toward her, and she lowered her hand. But she held her ground, placing her hands upon her hips and glaring up at him.

There were flecks of gold in her eyes, and she was as fierce as a lioness protecting her young. Yet she was not a cat, but the most alluring human female he had ever seen. "Your grandmother has spent the past twenty-two years grieving for your loss and the death of your father. She prayed every day that you would eventually be found."

"I am not the person she thinks I am."

"You are Anthony Maddox, are you not?"

He hesitated long enough for her to move away, returning to her task of clearing the table.

"Yes," he finally said. "I'm Lady Sutton's grandson."

She glanced at him with exasperation. "Yet you would not say as much to Mr. Cooper."

"Cooper. Ha. What is he to you?"

Her hands stilled. "What do you mean?"

"I saw the change in you when he arrived."

She returned to her task of clearing the table. "I did *not* change."

"You became as stiff as a hedgehog's quill when he came in." Something had gone on between them, and Anthony wondered if he'd been a lover or an adversary.

"I most certainly did not!"

He shrugged, although he found the thought of

Cooper's cool, pasty white fingers on Grace's warm skin irksome. "Whatever you say."

"I merely observed the proprieties, which, of course, you do not know, having been away from society for so long."

"Proprieties? I've never seen anything so ridiculous."

Grace slammed a piece of flatware onto the tabletop. "The first thing you will learn is that a gentleman—*you*—shall remain standing until all the ladies in the room are seated."

"Neither the Moto nor the Tajuru people would bother with such foolishness."

"You believe it is foolish to show common courtesy?"

He looked genuinely puzzled by her question. "After the men have hunted and brought meat to the women, it is for the women to remain standing while the men sit and take the choicest parts."

"This is going to be impossible," she muttered.

"What else?" he asked. He seemed to be having little difficulty getting round the room on his injured ankle, following her so closely she could feel the heat radiating off his body. He was absurdly handsome, but his primitive behavior negated any outward comeliness. Grace refused to acknowledge the strong pull of feminine interest and reminded herself that even the devil could make himself physically appealing.

"A gentleman assists a lady into her chair, then takes his own seat. He waits until the ladies are served before partaking of his own drink or meal, or what have you."

He shook his head, and his long hair shifted so that it brushed his shoulder. He laid one hand on the table right next to Grace. His clear green eyes bored into hers as he spoke in a low, quiet tone. "I would take my woman onto my lap and feed her the best morsels."

Grace swallowed. "Perhaps a . . . a native woman would allow such treatment, but I can assure you that no Englishwoman . . ."

He touched her cheek, drawing one finger from its crest, down to her chin. Her breath caught in her throat, and she could not move.

"No Englishwoman?" he prodded.

"N-no Englishwoman . . ."

"Likes to be touched by her man?"

"You are not my . . . my m-man." She pushed his hand away and moved sharply from his disturbing touch.

"Who is, then?"

"I haven't— Not that it's any of your concern," she said, "but I am not entertaining any suitors just now."

"Suitors." He looked genuinely puzzled. "Men in suits?"

"No. Men who court ladies to see if they suit one another."

He sat down and put his injured foot up on a chair. Grace blew out a puff of air in exasperation. Who ever heard of a gentleman going about in bare feet?

"You and Cooper do not suit, then." He leaned forward and started to rub his ankle.

"'Tis rude to ask such a thing." Whatever had been between her and Mr. Cooper was none of his concern.

"I do not remember England being so warm," he said.

"What *do* you remember . . . besides the time spent with your father in his lodge?"

"Snow. I remember snow in winter . . . There was a holiday . . ."

"Christmas, most likely."

"Yes. Christmas. It snowed in Oxfordshire at Sutton Court at Christmas, and my father took me up on his horse. We rode . . ."

He closed his eyes, and his face relaxed into an expression of simple wistfulness. Grace did not like to feel any softening toward the savage who sat quietly nearby, but she could not help but think he must have been badly wounded by the thought that his beloved father had abandoned him in the African wilderness.

"I remember my bed at school."

"Your bed?"

"I did not like to be away from home, so I kept a box of 'home things' under the bed." He opened his eyes and leveled his gaze at Grace. "Childish things. Things I quickly outgrew."

Like his need for his father? Grace wondered.

Anthony was relieved when she changed the subject. His English father had been dead to him for many years. He should not feel sorrow now, at this late date.

"You are not dressed as a gentleman should be. But I am sure Lady Sutton will have a tailor sent to you on the morrow."

He leaned forward and slid his fingers over the swollen joint of his ankle, annoyed by his infirmity. He hoped Old Tom was right and it would not keep him crippled for long.

"I have no wish to fit myself into my grandmother's idea of where I belong."

Miss Hawthorne's hands stilled. "You jest. You would turn your back on an earldom for the savage existence of the Congo?"

"Do not scorn what you do not sunderstand."

She had the grace not to argue, but completed her task of gathering the plates and serving pieces in silence.

"There can be no place on earth like my valley."

"You called it what? Ganulu?"

"Ganweulu. It means . . . fertile. Beautiful. Wild."

"All those things?"

He nodded. "It is not so easy to translate, but yes. Ganweulu is all those things. Perfection."

"How do you survive there?"

His days were spent in a perpetual cycle of hunting and resting. He'd taught himself to fish and hunt with a spear, and felt great satisfaction in providing his own food. He'd learned to climb the tallest trees and took pleasure in running with the small apes. Of swimming in his own glorious lagoon and visiting the tribes that provided him with simple companionship when he wanted it.

"By hunting and fishing," he said simply, for he could never describe the wonders of his life in Ganweulu. "By keeping my dwelling safe and secure, and far enough off the ground to prevent attacks by predators."

"Was it not dull?" Miss Hawthorne asked.

Indignation nearly choked him. "Dull?" He would have gotten up from his chair for emphasis, but his ankle had only just stopped throbbing. "How could it possibly be dull?" he growled.

"What do you do there?" she asked, pushing the supper cart toward the door. "Besides killing your food."

"I run free," he said tightly. "I manage myself, woman. There are no . . . no special clothes . . . no fashions to abide by. No stiff manners to restrict, no tidy rules, no absurd . . . What is it called? No *decorum* to follow."

She stopped abruptly and looked over at him. "And *that* is what you prefer?"

"Of course I prefer complete freedom. What man would not?" Even Cooper, with his fitted trousers and neck cloths and jackets would likely relish the opportunity to run free in the high grasses of the valley, eating the fruits he found, the meat he killed, relying upon no one. Being responsible for no one but himself.

It was with a breath of relief that Grace left the cottage and the man who evoked such vivid and objectionable images in her mind. She did not care to hear any more tales of Anthony Maddox, barefoot and wearing just a breechclout as he climbed trees and hunted dangerous beasts. Civilized Englishmen were difficult enough.

Jamie met her on the path to say that the countess wished to see her before she retired for the night. Grace was weary after her long day, but she walked through the darkness up to the house. Judging by the peaceful breeze that blew through the trees, one would never know of the disruption taking place here.

She went up to Lady Sutton's bedchamber and found the countess dressed for bed, her white hair plaited in a neat braid down her back. She arose from her dressing table when Grace came into the room, and Grace helped her to the bed, which had already been turned down. Twirling her rings round her fingers, the countess was obviously upset.

"Did you see how he ate? The way he dropped to the floor when he wanted to sit? He may be my grandson, but he is a savage!"

Grace would not disagree. Anthony Maddox moved like a predatory animal and behaved like a barbarian with no sense of decorum or of etiquette, which he had fervently denigrated.

"He is so much worse than I ever thought possible." Her Ladyship lay down on the soft mattress, and Grace covered her with a light blanket. If only that letter had never come . . . Lady Sutton might have enjoyed peace and contentment in her last few years, even as she pined for the boy Anthony had once been.

And Grace would not be required to rehabilitate the beastly man.

"I'd hoped it would not be necessary to put you out so severely, Grace. But I just cannot allow him to be seen in such a state." Lady Sutton shuddered. "I know society. He would be the subject of ridicule for the rest of his life. No one will ever give weight to his thoughts or opinions."

Grace sighed, unable to see any way out of this assignment. Nor could she tell the countess that it would likely all be for naught. If Grace was correct, Anthony had no intention of staying in England.

"Basic etiquette, my dear," said Lady Sutton. "That will be your first task."

Grace gave a resigned nod.

"There is so much to do, so many plans to make. Anthony must be ready for society in a month. I will introduce him at my charity ball."

Grace nearly choked. She managed to compose herself, then patted her benefactress on the shoulder. "Sleep now and we'll discuss it tomorrow."

The countess seemed to settle down, and Grace left her bedchamber and headed for her own room, where she intended to try for a few moments of peace before she retired for the night.

But it was quite a long interval before she was able to find her own rest.

Chapter 5

❦❦

"I will not!" Grace's indignation rang out loud and clear the following morning, as she glared at the tailor and the butler in turn.

"Miss Hawthorne," Faraday countered, "it is the express wish of Lady Sutton that you obtain the young lord's measurements and relay them to Mr. Crisfield, here."

"Where is Tom Turner? Surely *he* is the more appropriate—"

"There is a mare in foal and Tom is needed in the stable." Grace knew that Faraday was being spiteful only because he'd been forbidden to attend—or even meet—the young lord in the Tudor cottage.

"If only Lord Sutton were not in seclusion . . ." Crisfield suggested, and his prying curiosity—along with Faraday's gleeful attitude—grated on Grace's nerves.

She gritted her teeth and snatched the measuring tape from the tailor. "Show me what to do."

Crisfield used Faraday as his model to demonstrate how she was to obtain the measurements he would need. With a dark look toward the butler, she took the marked tape and marched out to the cottage, where she found Anthony sitting on the stones of the terrace outside his cottage, rolling a slice of ham into a sugar bun with his fingers. Wearing the same dark trousers and blue shirt he'd worn the day before, he looked up at her and shoved the entire thing into his mouth.

Grace had a suspicion that he chose to display his coarse behavior just to rile her, and she considered it the ultimate irony that such a comely man could be so disgusting.

"Would you care to join me, Miss Hawthorne?" he asked in the most refined manner possible, then gestured to the ground beside him. Grace huffed audibly in response.

"What?" he asked in feigned innocence, but Grace heard the mockery in his tone. "Is it incorrect to invite a newcomer to a meal?"

She had never known such an exasperating man. He knew he was behaving badly, and he was enjoying it. "It looks as though you are finished."

"It so happens that I am." With the assistance of the crutches that Dr. MacMillan had left on his earlier visit, Anthony came to his feet in one swift move, and stood directly in front of her.

"Lord Sutton, you are standing much too close. It is not proper."

Just to be contrary, he leaned closer, bent down,

and inhaled deeply right next to Grace's ear. She jerked back and dropped the items in her hand. "Lord Sutton!"

He bent down and picked them up. "Do you intend to measure something, Miss Hawthorne?"

Anthony extended the marked tape between his spread hands, and the heat that infused Grace's face had nothing to do with the bright sunshine. She wished her complexion weren't quite so reactive to everything he said and did. She was no schoolgirl to be embarrassed by such antics.

"Give me that tape and turn round," she said in as stern a voice as she could muster. "I have no intention of sparring with you today, Lord Sutton."

"Anthony."

"Lord—"

"If you must use my English name, then call me Anthony."

She sighed with exasperation. Would he ever learn proper decorum? He was clearly no fool, but merely recalcitrant. "Stand still, then."

"What are you going to do?"

"I've been charged with the task of measuring you for a suit of clothes," she replied. "Your grandmother will not even allow the tailor to witness your lack of proper etiquette. And since she is my dearest friend—"

"My grandmother? *She* is your dearest friend?"

"Yes. Turn your back to me and extend your arms, please."

The stretch of his arms was impossibly wide. The sleeves of his borrowed shirt did not quite reach his wrists, and he'd rolled them to the elbows. Grace measured his full wingspan, but could not avoid touching his bare skin as she did so. Her breath hitched in her chest. She stood at eye level with his shoulder blades and the dense black hair that nearly brushed them. She pressed the tape against the center of his back and he shifted slightly, his thick muscles tightening under her hand.

The number she noted flitted from her mind.

"Seems odd that your closest friend is an old woman," he said. Grace blinked and the moment passed, though his voice sounded as strange as Grace felt. "You have no friends nearer your own age?"

Regaining her businesslike manner, she remeasured his arms, frankly uninterested in delineating the dismal state of her social life. Lady Sutton was more socially engaged than Grace, but she was not about to tell him that.

"Of course I have friends." She wrote the measurement on the tailor's scrap of paper. "Now lift your arm." She stuck one end of the measuring tape under it, then drew it down as far as his waist. "It's just that Lady Sutton is . . . well, she is a very special woman. I like her very much."

Her words probably sounded like a warning, but she did not make any clarification. She memorized his measurement and moved round to the front of him.

"You're too close, Miss Hawthorne," he chided in a mocking tone, echoing her words.

"Try not to be so difficult. You know I must come near you to accomplish this."

He seemed to grow taller as she stood before him, and the rhythm of his breathing changed. The air seemed thicker somehow, and Grace felt the warmth of the sun on her shoulders and head. She raised herself up onto her toes and draped the measuring strip round the back of his neck. "Raise your chin."

He did as she bid him, and his throat moved as he swallowed. Her hand brushed against the rough underside of his jaw, and she drew back.

"Have you never felt a man's whiskers before, Miss Hawthorne?"

"Of course not." She did not go round touching men's faces, yet the urge to test the texture of Anthony's skin was strong. She reminded herself of the task at hand, sliding her fingers through the hair at his nape. It was as silky as she'd imagined.

"Miss Hawthorne?"

Grace realized she was standing still, and quickly pushed his hair aside to press the measuring tape against his skin. Next, she slipped her finger under the tape at his throat and took a measurement there.

He exhaled roughly when she withdrew the narrow strip and wrote down the measurement. "What's next?" he croaked.

Grace hesitated, eyeing his midsection. "Your waist. Raise your arms."

She slipped her arms round his waist, and came very close to pressing her cheek against his chest. Barely successful at avoiding that personal contact, she connected the two ends of the tape behind him.

He startled her by touching her hair. "Lord Sutton!"

She pulled away, but it was too late. Her chignon came loose and her hair tumbled in disarray down round her shoulders. She reached up to grab it, but when she caught sight of Anthony's eyes, her hand stilled.

"You mustn't . . ."

A wave of heat slid down her back and pooled within her womanly core, and she felt an elemental awareness of this man, of all his masculine power. Her heart beat faster than it should, and her breasts tightened, tingling impossibly. " 'Tisn't—"

"—proper," he finished, but he did not appear contrite. Grace sensed the deep, primal facet of his character that he kept barely leashed. Yet she did not believe he would harm her.

On the contrary, she feared he might wish to introduce her to dark and impossible pleasures.

Grace forced herself to walk calmly to the table, where she set down the measuring tape and wrote down the circumference of his waist. Keeping her back to him, she salvaged a few hairpins and twisted her hair together, quickly securing it into some semblance of order. She felt unsteady and unbalanced, as though something fundamental in her world had shifted.

Yet nothing had changed.

Chewing her lower lip, she gathered all her fortitude and turned to face him. Remaining impersonal yet pleasant, she would get through the task Lady Sutton had set for her, and return to the sanctuary of her own bedchamber, where she could put herself and her world to rights.

"Are we finished?" Lord Sutton asked, his voice husky and low.

"One more," she said, averting her eyes from his face. "Spread your legs."

He cleared his throat.

"Believe me, I do not like this any more than you."

She knelt in front of him and placed the measuring tape on the ground next to his bare foot. She should be accustomed to seeing it by now, but she was not. It was all too intimate. She raised the tape, moving it inch by painstaking inch, up to his knee, and then higher.

"Ah, but I do not mind," he said, his voice sounding gruff and raw.

Grace clenched her teeth and strove to keep from chucking the whole lot—the measuring tape, the paper and pencil—into the shrubs and walking away.

"Your touch, Miss Hawthorne, is . . . more than I could ever have imagined."

If she went any higher, she was actually going to brush against his private parts. Yet the thought of it did not quite cause the abhorrence she expected.

"'Tis good enough!" she said, drawing away abruptly. She rose to her feet and retreated to the table, grabbing her paper and turning on her heel. "I'll just take these measurements to the house. Good day to you."

Grace kept her head down as she hurried to the servants' entrance, where she knew Mr. Crisfield was waiting. She was mortified.

With trembling hands, she returned his tape measure and the paper with the measurements, then quickly made for the staircase and the privacy of her room.

The situation was untenable, yet Lady Sutton had made her wishes quite clear. No one was to have any contact with her grandson besides Grace and Tom, until he was presentable to society.

All propriety prohibited the humiliating task she'd just performed. Next time she was asked to do something so wholly inappropriate, it would have to wait until Tom Turner was on hand to deal with it. Tom would just have to make himself much more available, for such familiarity with Anthony Maddox was absolutely unseemly, and Grace did not intend to repeat it.

She blanched at the memory of his hard chest beneath her cheek, her arms round his waist. She had never before embraced a man—not even the one she'd planned to wed. And when she'd measured the inside seam of his trousers . . . Anthony had most decidedly reacted to her touch. He'd made a light quip, then gone utterly still, not even breathing as she'd raised the measuring strip against his leg.

Grace could not claim she'd had the presence of mind to give up the task and merely estimate the last few inches. She'd only been anxious to escape the unnerving situation and quit his company as soon as possible.

"Miss Hawthorne," said Faraday, stepping into her path. "You have a visitor."

"Not now, Faraday. I've—"

"There you are, Miss Hawthorne!" Grace's heart sank when Edward Bridewell came from the small parlor into the hall. Faraday slipped away and Grace had no choice but to greet the somber gentleman, a man who had indicated an interest in her.

"Hello, Mr. Bridewell . . . I, er . . . This is not the best time—"

"I happened to be in the neighborhood," he said, "and decided 'twould be a good opportunity to take you for a drive."

"I am truly flattered, but—"

"I'm sure Lady Sutton would spare you for a short carriage ride," he said in a vaguely edifying tone.

Grace knew she must be gracious. Mr. Bridewell's suit was not entirely unwelcome, although she had misgivings about marriage to a man so stern, and so many years her senior. He was a widower with four children, the eldest of whom, an adolescent girl, did not seem entirely pleased by the prospect of a new mother.

In the wake of her distressing morning, it was difficult to gather her thoughts and sort through her mixed and tumultuous emotions.

Lord Sutton—*Anthony*—had likely enjoyed her embarrassment at the cottage just now, and a good wardrobe was not going to change his character. Grace doubted that any amount of teaching on her part would be a great help, either.

She did not want to give him even the slightest opportunity to breach the boundaries of propriety again. Such situations led to familiarity, which gave rise to forbidden intimacies. It was far better to avoid the kind of odd sensations that had come over her when he'd loosened her hair.

Fortunately, such an unseemly interlude would never occur with Mr. Bridewell. She looked up at him, at his high forehead and neat, blond hair, at his perfectly pressed suit and polished Hessians, and decided that an hour away from the house—and the Tudor cottage—would not be amiss.

She drew her lips into a pleasant smile. "If you'll give me a few minutes, Mr. Bridewell . . ."

"Of course."

Forcing herself to a calm and sedate pace, Grace went up to her room and put her hair back in order. She smoothed a few wrinkles from her skirts, straightened the lace edge of her collar, then put on her bonnet and considered her predicament.

Perhaps one of Her Ladyship's friends had a relative or a trustworthy acquaintance who could tutor her outrageous grandson. Grace decided to suggest it to the countess before the fiasco progressed any further.

Such an option made sense, for the diversion of Grace's attention to Anthony Maddox would result in the dereliction of all her other duties. And there was much that Grace needed to do at the moment, with the countess's charity ball approaching so quickly. There were many details to take care of, not the least of which were the invitations Grace needed to write, soon.

Taking a deep, restorative breath, she descended the servants' staircase and went to the library in search of the countess, encountering her just inside. A neatly dressed lady, perhaps ten years older than Grace, stood beside Lady Sutton, so tall she towered over her. It was clear that the woman was not a servant, but as she wore no hat or gloves, she could not be a visitor, either.

"Grace, dear," said Lady Sutton. "Are you going out?"

"Yes, my lady. Mr. Bridewell came to take me for a drive. I hope you don't mind . . ."

"Of course not," the countess said, smiling. "The air will do you good. Oh, but before you go, here is Miss Geraldine James."

"How do you do?" Grace said with a slight bow.

The woman's polite response was lost in the countess's enthusiasm. "Miss James is Lady Wentworth's secretary, and she has agreed to help us this month!"

"Help us?" Grace asked, her stomach sinking.

"Yes. While you work on your . . . *special project*," Lady Sutton said, quite visibly pleased with her euphemism. "Miss James and I will finalize the details for my charity ball."

"Oh, but I—"

"I know you are completely devoted to St. Andrew's Orphans' Home, Grace," said Lady Sutton. "And we will certainly need your opinion on very many of the arrangements for the ball. But your other project is most important to me, and I would like you to devote your entire attention to it."

Grace hesitated for one heartbeat, but knew she would not change Lady Sutton's mind. She tipped her head to give Lady Sutton a compliant nod. "Of course, my lady. I've already begun."

"Wonderful!" said the countess. "Miss James and I will start on the invitations. The list is in the right-hand drawer of the desk, is it not?"

"Yes," Grace said quietly, her disappointment palpable. "That is where I left it."

"Very good. Enjoy your drive, dear."

Lady Sutton and Miss James turned their attention to the papers in the desk, leaving Grace in the hall. The countess gave Grace a cheerful smile, making her wonder how she would possibly manage to get through the next few weeks.

In spite of Grace Hawthorne's absence for a full day—after she'd nearly unmanned him taking his measurements—Anthony had dreamed about her. Not about his idyllic territory in the Congo, or about the dwelling he'd made for himself high in the boughs of a majestic acacia tree. His night had been filled with Miss Hawthorne.

She had aroused him even in sleep, wearing a filmy sarong that clung to her unfettered body. Her beautiful hair curled round her face and shoulders, and her scent haunted him. As he watched her slip out of her sarong, Anthony had never wanted anything more than he wanted Grace Hawthorne. She'd reached up and brushed her lush mouth against his lips, tasting like sweet berries.

He'd touched the tips of her breasts as he kissed her, and felt her nipples harden in his hands. She'd made a soft sound of arousal, and Anthony had felt close to bursting. He took one of her hands and placed it on his erection, and his moan of arousal woke him abruptly.

He sat up, rubbing a hand across his face, banishing his image of Grace, lying bare, beneath him. He had to get out of there.

He pushed himself up from the bed and grabbed his crutches in order to escape the close confines of the cottage. He lived without ties, and would continue to do so. Autonomy suited him, for as long as he maintained his independence, no one would ever be hurt.

He took himself outside and breathed in the fresh morning air, remembering that the swimming pond was not too far away. A hard swim would do him good.

For all Grace's resolve, sleep had not come easily to her the night before. She found herself tossing and turning, and finally leaving her bed to sit by her window, gazing out at the star-swept gardens. She wished her restlessness had been caused by enthusiasm over Mr. Bridewell's courtship, but Grace knew that was not it.

She was going to have to return to the Tudor cottage and hope that the measuring incident had been forgotten. Lord Sutton had reacted to her touch. She might be inexperienced, but she knew he'd been aroused.

When morning came, Grace took her usual care in dressing properly, then ate a solid breakfast. She was going to make it quite clear that Lord Sutton was not to touch her or speak inappropriately to her. They were going to conduct their lessons in an organized, respectable manner.

Swallowing her trepidation, she started out for the cottage, carrying a newspaper as well as two books that dealt with the most recent era of British history. Lord Sutton could do some reading on his own time, while Grace would work with him on matters of protocol and etiquette.

She knocked at the door, but no one came, and she heard no one stirring about the cottage. Tapping her foot impatiently, she wondered if he might still be asleep. It was early, and with an injury to his head only a few days before, perhaps—

The creak of his crutches in the garden caused her to turn round.

Grace dropped the books when she saw him, dripping wet, with his hair soaked and slicked back. Leaning against his crutches, he wore nothing but the dark trews Tom Turner had found for him.

"Miss Hawthorne," he said, then murmured a few exotic words Grace could not understand.

Looking intently at her, he seemed unaware of the water dripping down the sides of his face from his hair, or the soaked patches on his trousers. He was creating a puddle on the stone floor of the terrace, and when Grace raised her eyes from that small pool, she could not help but notice the way the trews hung on his hips, or the hard, rippled surface of his belly.

In spite of Grace's resolve, the same trembling awareness she'd experienced the day before came over her. Her breath stuck in her throat, and she was powerless to move, to think.

He came to her and bent down to pick up the books she had dropped. "Your books."

"I . . . Thank you," Grace managed to say. "Lord S—"

"Anthony."

"Anthony," she said stiffly. She must regain her equilibrium and set some proper limits. She knew the kind of pain that resulted when boundaries were improperly breached. "Perhaps you would be so good as to dress yourself appropriately and then return here for our lessons."

"Do you swim, Miss Hawthorne?"

"Swim?" The proper façade she'd just recovered crumbled at the thought of him spearing through the water of Fairford's pond. It was clear he had not worn the trews for his swim, for they bore only a few wet patches. "Not in years."

"Why not? The pond is just as good as I remember it . . . with clear, deep water. 'Tis available for your use, is it not?"

"I'm sure 'tis very refreshing, but I prefer to bathe in private."

"My lagoon in Ganweulu is very private." His voice was quiet and deep as he handed the books to her. "In my valley, I would take you bathing in the moonlight."

She swallowed.

"Without clothes."

"You should not say such things to me," she said. "Such talk is . . . unseemly." But it intrigued her. That much was clear to Anthony.

When she bit her lip and pulled it through her teeth, he could think of nothing but tasting that plump morsel with his tongue to see if she was as sweet as she'd tasted in his dream . . .

His body reacted predictably and he squelched it. This was not a woman who would react well to a mating dance, at least not with him. Perhaps with that skinny, pasty-faced Cooper.

Anthony doubted she realized the way she thrust out her chest when she was annoyed, but he appreciated the view.

"We have work to do." She took a step back in retreat. Or perhaps it was disdain.

Anthony approached her cautiously, just as he would a skittish hare in the long grasses of the savannah. When Miss Hawthorne had backed into a tree, he cupped her cheek with his free hand. She smelled of flowers again, and he inhaled deeply of her scent. "You are very soft, Miss Hawthorne."

She bristled and drew away from his hand. "I believe 'tis a characteristic most women share."

"And your eyes are the same color as a very deep and dangerous lake near my valley."

"I assure you that I am neither deep nor dangerous," she said, skittering away. She escaped to the opposite end of the terrace and set her books on the table. "I am simply your grandmother's companion, attempting to perform a service for her."

"My rehabilitation?"

"Yes. Now, please—"

"You know I have no intention of staying." It was a good reminder both for himself as well as for Grace. No matter how badly he wanted to taste her mouth or touch her soft skin, he knew better.

He closed his eyes and drew in a deep breath as he thought of returning to Ganweulu. There he enjoyed a perfectly self-sufficient life without fancy clothes or mind-numbing rules. He'd learned to take care of himself, to survive, to rely upon no one. He had companionship when he needed it, for Dawa and her family allowed him to join them whenever they happened to be traveling through his valley. Sometimes he stopped in the Moto Dambia village or visited one of the small towns near the coast. Anthony needed nothing more.

But he was here in England—if only temporarily—and the opportunity for vengeance had presented itself. Learning a few English ways would only help him achieve it.

Anthony went into the cottage and quickly donned his shirt. He looked forward to spending the day with Grace Hawthorne more than was good for his peace of mind.

* * *

The morning progressed decidedly better than Grace would have thought, given the way it had started. She could not have anticipated encountering Lady Sutton's grandson in such a manner, half naked and soaking from a dip in the pond. Who ever heard of such antics at Fairford Park?

Grace had never known of anyone bathing in the pond, yet perhaps Anthony and his father had done so. By all accounts, the two had been very close, and Colin had been anything but a conventional man.

His son had certainly broken the mold.

When he returned to the terrace fully covered, he took a seat at the small table across from her, and picked up the newspaper.

"Where shall we begin?" he asked. "Shall we read?"

His hair was still damp, and he had not shaved, so there was a dark shadow of whiskers on his jaw.

"W-we'll get to that later." She cleared her throat and turned to the lesson she had planned. "Right now, I'd like to concentrate on basic etiquette."

He slouched back in his chair, extending his legs forward, crossing them at the ankles.

"Good posture is the stamp of a well-bred gentleman."

"Or lady?" he said as he straightened, drawing his legs—and bare feet—back to where they belonged. He cupped his hands together on the table and looked up at her.

"Of course." Grace forced herself to remain still, for there was nothing at all wrong with her own posture. "First of all, you must always present yourself properly dressed. Shoes, for example. A gentleman always wears them."

"I have none."

"Nor do you have any other wardrobe, so your attire will wait."

He'd rolled his sleeves to the elbows again, and the smattering of crisp, dark hair on his arms called to mind the dark, wiry hair she'd seen on his impossibly broad chest.

"Miss Hawthorne?"

She tore her gaze from the hollow beneath his throat and looked up. "Y-you must always remember to stand until the last lady is seated."

"Yes. So you said last night."

Grace realized he'd caught her gawking, and quickly gathered her thoughts. "Keep your elbows at your sides, and never resting on the table."

He lowered his arms, and Grace noted his sardonic expression. But she did not care what he thought. If she did her job well, he would soon be prepared to meet the official committee that would decide whether to grant him his father's title and estates. His decision to stay in England or leave was not part of her equation.

"You must never come too close to another person. It is—"

"I remember. Not proper," he said. "Why?"

"Because— Well, because it's just not done."

"Then 'tis a custom, not a law."

"Oh, but it is a law of sorts. The law of appropriate behavior. And another thing. Touching."

He raised a brow.

"You shouldn't have touched my cheek . . . or my hair yesterday when I was measuring you."

"Ah, but Miss Hawthorne, *you* were touching *me*," he said, "in a most intimate manner."

"But we were not in a social situation. I was performing the tailor's task—"

"This is not a social situation, either, is it, Grace?" He leaned closer to her.

Grace's heart sped when she considered what he must mean. "This is . . . No. It's not exactly a social situation, but we must behave with decorum. Touching is not acceptable. Nor is using my given name."

A muscle in his jaw tightened as he sat back. He suddenly stood and took his crutches in hand.

"Another thing—"

"No, *Miss Hawthorne*," he said as he strode away from her. "Nothing more today."

Anthony remembered where the stable was located, and he headed for it. He had no patience for any more of Grace Hawthorne's stipulations or regulations. Worse, he had an irresistible urge to do exactly what she'd told him he could not, and take her hair all the way down. His fingers itched to slide into that soft, fragrant mass. He longed to see her as she'd been in his dream, her body freed from the bindings that held her so tight. He wanted to bury his face between her breasts.

"*Mbaya*," he muttered, disgusted at his own lack of discipline. Far better to get up and away from her than to give in.

"Eh, m'lord," said Tom Turner as he came out of the stable carrying a bridle in one hand and a tool in the other. "Fancy ye're up and movin' on your feet today."

"Thanks to your liniment and the physician's crutches."

"How's the swelling?" Anthony lifted his bare foot so that Tom could see it. "Looks better, I'd say. How's it feel?"

Anthony shrugged. He'd had worse injuries than this and managed to get by.

"You ought to get off it, m'lord. Put it up." Tom led him to a simple wooden bench in the shade. "Here. Take a seat and raise your foot."

Anthony did so, while Tom pulled up a three-legged stool and sat down across from him. "What do you think of the place . . . Fairford Park, I mean. Is it the same as you remember it?"

"I suppose so," Anthony replied. "Miss Hawthorne is new."

Tom gave a short chuckle. "Aye, that she is. Been with us nigh on a year or more. Came just after her mum died when she had no money and nowhere to go."

Anthony would never forget his own abandonment and being left to fend for himself. "It makes you stronger."

"You may be right," said Tom. "But I fear a lass might see it different. The servants up at the house say Miss Hawthorne was to be married, but the man let her go when he learned her mother was ill and dying."

Anthony frowned, dismayed at the thought of Grace being left to fend for herself. "Why? I don't understand."

"Nor do I, lad. I suppose an ailing mother-in-law would put some men off."

"*Wajinga* man."

"What's that?"

"Cooper," Anthony replied, shrugging as he tried to think of the English word that would best describe him.

"Oh aye. The swell what came up to the cottage when you first came? Some would call him a milksop."

"Indeed." But Anthony was not mistaken in thinking the man still had an eye for Grace Hawthorne. She had not exactly admitted what she and the milksop had been to each other, but Anthony had sensed it. And he hoped Grace had better judgment than to allow him back into her affections after his desertion.

"But Miss Hawthorne and my grandmother were . . . friends?"

" 'Twas Miss Hawthorne's grandmother who was friends with yours as girls. Both were daughters of earls."

Now it began to make sense to him. "Did you know her—the grandmother?"

"Oh aye. A pretty lass she was in those days. She married a gentleman down Chelsea way. And after, she didn't much travel in yer grandmother's circles anymore."

"I don't remember you being such an old gossip, Tom," Anthony said with a wry grin.

Tom laughed. "Oh, but I was. Talk of every kind passes through the stable yard, don't ye know."

"And what are they saying about me?"

"Not much to say," Tom replied. "And Her Ladyship would like to keep it that way. So ye'd better hie yerself back to the cottage and stay out o' sight afore any the grooms come back to the stable."

Chapter 6

With the old, battered King James at hand, Anthony had done plenty of reading through the years, never realizing how much he missed books. Other books, other subjects. Before Africa, he'd been a good student and an avid reader who had barely scratched the surface of his academic subjects. He greedily eyed the stack of books Miss Hawthorne had brought from his grandmother's library while she paged through the old King James Bible.

"Whose name is written here?" she asked.

"Robert Kelson."

"Who was he? What happened to him?"

Anthony shrugged. "The missionary who owned it, I suppose. And I have no idea what happened to him." Survival was difficult in the Congo—it was unlikely the priest still lived.

"There are pages missing." She bit her lip as she looked at the tattered pages, and Anthony felt a hard punch of arousal.

He let her scent swirl round him like the rich, black velvet of an African night. It enticed him, tempting him to taste of her, but he knew better. Rules dictated Grace Hawthorne's life, and touching was forbidden.

She abandoned the Bible and began to discuss current political affairs while Anthony studied her clothing. Her gowns could not be more different from the loose African dresses he was accustomed to seeing, but they were superbly feminine, concealing yet strangely taunting. While she spoke of Corn Laws and Emancipation Rights, he thought about divesting her of each one of her layers, slowly, enticingly, until they were each panting for more.

And her hair . . . He knew how little effort it took to release that soft mass to let it slide down her back like the waterfall at the end of his lagoon. He also knew how she'd react if he did so.

"There is much that you've missed in the past twenty-two years. Good heavens, you must not even know about Waterloo. Or Wellington. We'll have to be certain your lessons include a history of the—"

"I prefer this." He reached for the book he'd been reading and considered Miss Hawthorne's neatly hidden curves.

"Mary Shelley's silly gothic? You may feel free to read it when I am not here to tutor you."

He could not help but smile at the stern words from the soft, womanly creature before him. She wore a more attractive color today, a deep rose that suited her coloring perfectly, though the stiff lines of every gown she wore concealed her natural figure.

He did not understand why the woman should be so shy of her own skin. "What do you wear beneath your clothes that binds you so?"

Miss Hawthorne gaped at him, incredulously, then snapped her mouth closed. "Have you . . . Did you not hear . . ."

She pressed her fingers to her temples and got up to head for the door, then turned back. Anthony left his book on the table and rose to face her, balancing on his crutches.

"Lord Sutton," she said crossly, "I am certain that by now, you understand how unacceptable it is to mention anything that I might wear."

He moved closer. "I like it, though. Your waist is trim, but you've got luscious hips. And here . . ."

He started to brush his fingers against her breast, but she gave out a strangled sound and stepped back as though he'd scorched her.

"If you please!" She flushed a deep scarlet color, from her neck all the way up to her forehead.

Anthony drew away, giving a shake of his head as he frowned with puzzlement. He'd seen Tajuru men do exactly this with their women and have an entirely different result.

"Men do not touch women in England?"

"Of course not!" Miss Hawthorne retorted

harshly. "And the only remark you might make on another's attire is how well they look in it. Or how nicely the color goes with their hair or eyes, or whatnot."

Fingering the buttons at her collar, she eyed the door, clearly considering whether she might leave. She let out a deep sigh, then turned in resignation, and went to the dining table to sit down. "Let us try writing."

Anthony stood still, using all the willpower he possessed to remain there in the cottage. The social strictures here did not suit him in the least. He was a solitary creature who wanted no truck with this complicated English society.

Or this complicated Englishwoman.

He knew where he belonged, and he would return there happily, as soon as he dealt with Thornby.

He eventually took his seat at the table and began the process of writing. The pen felt strange in his hand, and he splattered ink on the page before he wrote anything. Miss Hawthorne took the pen from him.

"Not so much ink. Like so." She dipped the pen into the bottle and handed it to him.

Feeling as untutored as a schoolboy put him even further out of sorts. He put pen to paper and started to write. First his own name, then his grandmother's, then that of Grace Hawthorne. It felt awkward, but he managed to jot the first sentence that came to mind, and felt immediate satisfaction in doing so. *Ganweulu Valley is the finest place on earth.* He turned the page and showed it to Miss Hawthorne.

"Perhaps that is because you have never been to the Lake District."

"I have no interest in the Lake District."

"Do you intend to pine for Africa for the rest of your days, then?"

"No need."

"Because you intend to return there." Her eyes sparkled with interest.

"Miss Hawthorne, nothing can hold me here in this cold, foreign place."

"What about your grandmother?"

Sophia had done well enough without him before, and he did not doubt she would continue to do so after he left. Anthony would certainly be better off in his valley, with no one to worry about but himself.

Not even a pretty woman with freckles that beckoned to every masculine bone in his body.

He changed the subject. "Your pink gown looks well with your eyes."

"That is quite correct, Lord Sutton," she replied. "It is a pleasant but impersonal remark."

Anthony turned the writing paper toward himself once again. "Is that what you want from life, Miss Hawthorne? Pleasantness and impersonality?"

She looked at him intently for a moment, her clear eyes unblinking, but unsettled. "What of you? Isolation in your remote valley is what you most desire?"

" 'Tis far safer than your complicated world, Miss Hawthorne."

Tom Turner arrived just then, pushing the cart he'd used the night before to bring supper to the cottage. Miss Hawthorne rose and went to help him bring in the meal, and in so doing, their discussion ended.

"Here is luncheon," she said. "We will share the meal and work on table etiquette, Lord Sutton."

Grace feared her complexion was going to be permanently altered from her time spent with Anthony Maddox. He had caused her to flush pink so many times that morning, she could hardly keep track. At least their luncheon went well, with no more inappropriate, personal remarks.

She had heard his question. And of course the answer was that she preferred the courtesy and impersonality of good society. It was that imperturbable propriety that had held her together at Preston Cooper's abandonment, just when the truth of her mother's condition had come crashing down on her.

But Anthony's assertion that Africa was safer than England? Absurd. The man could not possibly prefer a secluded life in his Congolese valley.

They finished their meal, and he set down his knife and fork, following Grace's example. "Very good, Lord Sutton," she said. "It appears you have mastered the protocol."

He rested his hands upon his knees and leaned forward. "There is a particular protocol which is followed in the Moto Dambia village."

"Do tell," she said pleasantly, encouraging social discourse, for surely he would stay long enough to allow his grandmother to introduce him to her friends.

"Visitors are always served first."

Grace gave a slight nod. "As is the custom here."

"But the meal is served *after* the guest partakes of a ritual bath."

"A bath?" She gave him a dubious smile. "Here in England, we can usually assume a guest has bathed *before* coming to the table."

"I'm not speaking of cleanliness," he said, "but of ceremony. Protocol."

"I stand corrected," she said pleasantly. "Go on."

"The Moto village stands beside a wide but shallow river with a rocky bed. When a guest comes, he is taken to the water with the chief of the tribe and his wives."

"Wives?" She managed to keep all but a hint of scorn from her voice.

"You do not approve, Miss Hawthorne?"

"Of course I do not. Polygamy is a barbarian custom."

"I assure you that Jahi would not agree," Anthony said with a grin. "He is quite content with his three wives."

Grace supposed Jahi was the chief. An abominable man with three women to serve his every whim. She returned to their subject. "Then what happens? The ritual bath, I mean."

"I think you may not want to hear the rest."

"Why ever not? Of course I wish to hear it."

He put his elbows on the table and tented his hands together, but Grace did not correct him this time. She noticed an ink stain on his finger, but it did not detract from the appearance of those big hands. His nails were trimmed short, his fingers long and blunt-tipped, and there were thick veins snaking across the backs of them. Altogether, his hands looked strong and capable.

"The wives remove their clothes—the women of Moto Dambia wear only a thin, loose sarong, so 'tis not a lengthy procedure."

Grace's smile faltered slightly.

"Then they invite the guest into the water with them. When he agrees, they help him with his clothes."

"Help him? You mean, they remove the visitor's clothing, too?"

He gave a nod and his green eyes sparkled with mischief. "But in Africa, we are not quite so fond of layers as you are here in England."

"No," she mouthed. Grace did not doubt it

would take but a tug on the cord at the waist of his breechclout and it would fall to the ground. She swallowed as he continued, his voice a fraction deeper than it had been before.

"Then the chief joins his wives and the guest—or guests, as the case might be." Grace's eyes dropped to his mouth as he spoke. "Everyone submerges completely. And when they rise from the water and walk onto the shore, the chief and his wives bow to the guest, and he bows back."

Grace was speechless. Bathing unclothed among strangers? "You jest."

" 'Tis true, I assure you. In my valley"—he leaned farther forward—"you and I would have disrobed before our meal. We'd have bathed together and bowed graciously toward one another."

The image of such an event came much too easily to Grace. She felt her pulse in her throat, and did not trust herself to speak, or even to move. Anthony watched her intently, his green eyes sharp but hooded.

Grace's palms became itchy, and she suppressed the urge to check and assure herself that all her buttons were correctly fastened.

"There are many more customs of which I could tell you."

"Uh . . ."

"But you are not ready to hear of these things."

He stood and picked up his crutches, and Grace slumped unattractively in her chair, feeling more dazed than she wanted to admit. She remained at the table as he hobbled out of the cottage, and pressed a cool hand to her hot cheek, putting aside a mental image of the man greeting his guests naked.

Anthony needed to get out of there before he made an arse of himself. Thinking about standing naked with Grace Hawthorne—in or out of water—had aroused him far too quickly, and much too acutely.

Her naïveté drew him like a honeyguide to a sweet nest, but he sensed that her tame conversation hid a fiery temper kept carefully submerged. Anthony suspected she feared her passions, hiding them well, under her cloak of respectability.

She was likely unaware of the way her warm gaze rested upon his lips; or how her eyes lingered on his hands, as though she knew what pleasures they could teach her. She could not know of Anthony's reaction to her interest.

Anthony knew better than to test the softness and the heat of her full lips, but he'd had to leave the cottage to maintain control over his own passions.

He wanted her. And if he did not take care, he would have her.

He followed the path away from the cottage, without any destination in mind, only knowing that he needed an escape. He'd been an idiot to speak of the Moto Dambia custom, for it had only made him imagine sharing such a ritual with Grace

As he walked, he swore at his own pathetic lack of discipline. Only a fool allowed himself to depend upon another human being for his happiness or his welfare. There wasn't a woman on earth whose charms could make him forget that. Anthony had managed very well on his own these past twenty-two years, and he would resume his unfettered life once he returned to his valley.

He moved on and stopped short when he found himself at the doorstep of his father's lodge.

Standing in the shade of a huge linden tree, he looked at the old place, its sagging roof and mossy shingles. It had deteriorated in the years Anthony had been away, fallen into ruins since his father's death.

He could still remember the excitement of planning their expedition to Africa. They'd pored over maps and lists of supplies, had conferences with Thornby and the rest of Colin's adventuring friends, and told tales of past excursions to faraway places. Colin had lived for such adventure, and his thirst for excitement had been infectious.

There was no point in going inside. Every hope and wish that had been dreamed in that building was long dead. Why would he want to enter?

Yet he found himself pushing open the door and stepping inside.

The windows were dusty, so very little light

penetrated the large, one-room interior. Anthony found a box of matches on the thick oaken table in the center of the room, and lit some candles. He discovered that the interior of the lodge was as decrepit and shabby as the outside.

Dirt, debris, and cobwebs were everywhere. Water marks streamed down the walls, indicating that rain had gotten in. Some of the wooden furniture had rotted, the stuffing pulled out by rodents. The maps and papers strewn about the table crumbled in his hands when he touched them.

So many plans had been laid here.

He wondered if Thornby had decided his own devious course while they gathered companionably there, or if he'd acted on the spur of the moment.

It hardly mattered, for the bastard would soon pay for his actions.

Anthony wandered through the room, touching the feathers of a mallard duck he and his father had preserved and mounted together. He gazed at the other birds, the stuffed squirrels and foxes, and the head of a bongo, mounted and hanging over the stone fireplace. The beautiful antelope was not often seen in the wild, and Anthony marveled that his father had managed to bring this one home. He hoped the members of Colin's expedition had feasted on the meat and not just wasted the majestic creature.

He sat down on a low stool near one end of the room and opened the glass door of his father's bookcase. Taking out a thick tome on northern Africa, he let the book fall open to the place his father had marked with a strip of leather. It was obvious it had not been touched for twenty years.

In all this time, Anthony had never once considered that Colin might be dead. After his near-drowning, Anthony had spent weeks on his own, wending his way alone through the dangerous jungle, retracing the path of the river that had carried him away. He felt lost and betrayed, and his trust in his father had faded. He'd begun to wonder if Colin had been complicit with Thornby, though he'd soon decided that could not be true.

The only conclusion he had finally reached was that his father had not cared enough to remain in the wild country and use his considerable influence to secure Anthony's rescue. And if his own father had not cared . . .

Anthony tossed the book to the table and reached down to the wide drawers at the bottom of the bookcase. He pulled out the one on the left and released the catch that kept it from coming all the way out. Drawing it the rest of the way out of the case, he carried it to the table and removed the notebooks, as well as the penknife and compass that lay inside. Tipping it over, he found the pegs underneath and pushed them in. The bottom of the drawer loosened, and Anthony reached for the penknife. There was little resistance when he pried open the hidden compartment to find the cache of money his father always kept there.

Anthony did not know why Colin felt the need to keep so much money hidden away, but there it was, and there it must have been for at least two decades.

There were coins and paper money, likely much more than Anthony would need for the task he'd set himself, and for his return passage to Africa. Colin had obviously stashed the money in case of some kind of trouble, but he could never have anticipated how Anthony would use it.

His father was much too trusting, assuming that everyone's motives and desires matched his own.

Anthony replaced the contents of the drawer and returned it to the bottom of the bookcase, then headed for the door without looking back.

Becoming maudlin served no purpose. Dawa had told him that every life moved in cycles. Anthony wondered if his return to Fairford Park meant that he'd come full circle.

No. When he returned to Africa—to the place where he'd become a man—only then would he have gone full circle.

Chapter 7

"'T is a warm evening, both inside and out," said Anthony to Grace Hawthorne as he pulled his collar away from his neck. Tom had helped him dress in all the layers of his new clothes, and he felt hot, irritated, and ridiculous. But dressed in this manner, he would be able to move freely through English society.

"Finally, you have your clothes," said Grace, looking at him with a distinctly approving gaze. She came much closer than was her habit and straightened his lapel, sending a shivering pleasure directly to the most sensitive region in his trousers.

"Properly attired, you actually appear the civilized Englishman," she said. He doubted she was aware of her supremely improper effect on him, or she'd have scurried out of the cottage with all the speed of a bush baby.

Anthony had seen her in candlelight before, but tonight, she was different, wearing a pale blue gown that left her collarbones and shoulders bare.

Above her neckline was just a hint of the silky feminine fullness she never failed to hide from the world . . . from *him*.

She was no longer his plain, brown honeyguide, leading him to the knowledge and information he needed to survive in England. Tonight, she'd become an elegant blue crane, taunting him with her loveliness.

"But I am not civilized, Miss Hawthorne," Anthony said, his voice a low rumble. He brushed the back of his hand against the soft curls at her temple. "And well you should remember it."

So should he, but he couldn't seem to help himself.

"L-Lord Sutton." Her delicate throat moved as she swallowed, but she did not step away. " 'Tis my duty to refine you."

His cravat felt like it was choking him and his trews were much too tight. He slid one hand round her waist and pulled her closer, bringing her skirts flush against his legs. "Are you succeeding?"

She looked up at him, and he saw uncertainty in her eyes. Curiosity, too.

Anthony wanted to kiss her. He wanted to feel her arms round his neck, her body pressing against his arousal.

The pulse in the side of her neck was racing, and Anthony was glad to know that his own heart was not the only one galloping.

"I'm not sure . . ." Her eyes alighted upon his mouth, and Anthony lowered his head.

"I am well dressed . . ." he breathed, his mouth close to hers.

"Yes." Her breath touched his lips.

"And I've mastered table etiquette."

He felt her tremble. "You have."

"You've taught me all about Napoleon . . ." His voice was but a whisper. She put her hands on his forearms and held him as though she needed his strength to steady herself. ". . . and Waterloo . . ." He brushed her mouth lightly with his own. "I've even read about the Corn Laws . . ."

He took full possession of her mouth. Grace made a small sound as her chest filled with air, her breasts pressing against him, rousing him mercilessly. With more finesse than he felt, Anthony drew her even closer, and the room faded away. He slid one hand up her back, and slipped her gown from her shoulder. Tasting her, breathing in her floral scent, he felt a desperate need to dispense with the layers of cloth that separated them.

He ran his fingers across the smooth, feminine skin of her back, and she drew sharply away.

"I . . ."

"You are exquisite."

She sidled out of his grasp, putting her gown to rights as she stepped away. "I . . . I must go!" she cried hoarsely. Her lips were moist and distended, and he thought about trying to convince her to stay.

But he knew better than to frighten her. Years of experience had taught him that the best way to capture his prey was to approach it slowly, obliquely, and with infinite patience.

Grace did not remember walking back to the house. She had dressed for Lady Sutton's small dinner party, but had made a short detour to Anthony's cottage before the guests arrived. Her intention had been merely to see if Tom had managed to get him dressed in the clothes Crisfield had sent. She'd expected to see him in a plain frock coat and trews.

But he had been unbearably handsome in his formal suit. The high, white collar and cravat contrasted sharply with the gold-brown hue of his skin, and the black coat and trousers emphasized his broad shoulders and narrow hips. He was the embodiment of all that was virile and masculine.

Grace had always believed she had better control and yet—

"Miss Hawthorne, are you quite well?" asked Reverend Chilton, who was seated at her left in the small, formal dining room.

"Oh yes! Quite!" Grace said when she realized she'd sighed aloud. "I-I was just thinking of . . . of the improvements you will soon be able to make at St. Andrew's."

"Yes, Her Ladyship's charity ball is certain to bring in a much-needed infusion of cash."

"I say 'tis brilliant to hold an auction during the festivities," said Lord Rutherford.

"Just so," said Chilton as the conversation continued. "And the African motif you've chosen for the decor. Very original."

But Grace could only think of Anthony, of the way he'd pulled his hair back into a queue in the fashion of a foregone age. Of the feel of his mouth whispering against hers, then kissing away her self-control.

"Miss Hawthorne, I do believe you are trembling. Do not say you are you coming down with something."

"Oh no, sir." She rubbed her bare arms. "Remember the chilly rooms at St. Andrew's last winter? Lady Sutton's ball will bring in a great deal of money for coal this year, will it not?"

"And for blankets," added Mrs. Drayton, the wife of a country squire whose property lay within Reverend Chilton's parish, quite near St. Andrew's. "Those poor souls seem never to have enough."

Grace could not think of the charity ball, or even the orphans, when the sensations she'd experienced in the Tudor cottage preoccupied her so. Anthony had crossed the line of propriety so frequently that Grace had finally called his bluff when he'd stepped so close to her, had touched her waist, and then her hair.

He never should have taken such liberties. A voice in her head admonished that *she* never should have allowed it to go so far. She was the teacher and he the student. It was her example that should instruct, and it ought to be flawless.

Yet she had not been able to walk away from the flood of sensations whirling through her at his touch. His kiss had set fire to her senses, making her breathless and dizzy. She'd yearned for more, and did not know how she'd managed to come to her senses.

Or how she would face him upon the morrow.

"No, no," said Lady Sutton in answer to someone's questions. "My kitchen staff will deal with all the refreshments, but for the pastries."

"Have you decided upon any particular decorations for your African theme, my lady?" asked Mrs. Drayton.

The countess gazed at Mrs. Drayton for a moment, giving the impression of considering the question. Then she spoke. "I am open to your suggestions, Mrs. Drayton."

The Africa theme was a surprise to Grace, though she should have realized Lady Sutton would decide to introduce her grandson to society in a grand manner. Everyone in society would, of course, have known of Anthony's history, and Lady Sutton was brilliant to bring it to the fore, rather than trying to ignore it, or pretend it never happened.

Grace had not thought Anthony quite ready to

join polite society, but after seeing him in his evening clothes, she was not so sure. Certainly no lady in his presence would find any shortcomings, and she could not imagine any gentleman would dare to cross him.

"How delightful, my lady," said Reverend Chilton. "I, too, have a few ideas I would be willing to share." Like all of tonight's guests, he was unaware of Anthony's presence at Fairford Park, nor did he understand the significance of the Africa theme.

"Perhaps after supper you all can jot down your suggestions," said the countess. "I plan to go into London with Miss Hawthorne on Thursday, and we will order the materials we'll need."

Grace was grateful for the reprieve. A day away from Anthony could not be more welcome. She needed to regroup, to regain her objectivity and a healthy distance before she succumbed to any more scandalous behavior with the wayward lord. Her acquiescence to his indecent advances was appalling. She'd been raised better than that.

Besides, he had no intention of staying in England. When he left, his grandmother's heart would be broken.

Grace had no intention of allowing the same to happen to hers.

Anthony had had enough of books and table manners. He'd moved well past desire for Grace Hawthorne and had progressed to pure obsession.

Everything about her intrigued him, but he knew how to put a stop to it.

His ankle was all but healed, and he put it to use on a quick walk to the stable. There, he found Old Tom, brushing down one of the geldings.

"How many horses have you?"

"Four geldings and three mares," Tom replied.

Anthony took note of several saddles, neatly stored beside a workbench that held numerous bottles of liniment and all sorts of tools and leather tack. "Choose one for me," he said.

Tom gave a nod. "Aye. 'Tis time."

The man picked out a black gelding, and walked Anthony through the process of saddling it. "Ye'll likely always have someone to do this fer ye, m'lord. But it never hurts to know how."

Anthony agreed. He had not yet decided how he was going to confront Thornby, so he wanted to keep all possibilities open.

He remembered his childhood riding lessons, how to keep a light hand on the reins, and to use gentle pressure with his thighs. Tom mounted one of the mares, and they took a slow ride down the bridle path that bordered the estate. "Keep yer heels down, m'lord," said Tom. "And lean a bit forward."

Anthony did as instructed, and the sense of the horse beneath him began to feel more and more familiar.

"Not too fast, m'lord," Tom admonished. "If ye

haven't ridden for some time, it can take its toll on yer arse."

They slowed to a walk and soon came to a road. "Is this the way to Oxfordshire?" Anthony asked.

"The start of it," said Tom. "Ye'll go north a few miles, then get onto the western road. That'll take you out toward Sutton Court if that's what ye're thinking."

"Gerard Thornby is there." And Anthony would corner him there. "What of his brother? The elder one. Was he made earl?"

"Nay, m'lord. No one is earl in your father's stead."

A frown creased Anthony's brow. "Then why is Thornby in possession of Sutton Court?" Not that Anthony wanted it, but it seemed impossibly wrong for Thornby to have reaped the benefits of the Sutton fortune, especially after pitching Anthony off the *dhombo* and into the raging river.

He remembered the last time he'd seen his father's distant cousin. Anthony had made a desperate grasp for Thornby's hand, for anything to hold on to. And then Gerard had kicked him hard in the chest, taking away his breath and causing him to slide over the edge of the boat.

No one must have witnessed his murderous action in the confusion and tumult of the storm, or Colin would have denounced and disowned Thornby.

"The elder brother, David, died," said Tom.

" 'Twas only a year or two after yer own father's demise. The two brothers were racing at Sutton Court . . . I'm not sure I ever learned exactly what happened, but David was thrown from his horse. Broke his neck."

"Another convenient accident," Anthony muttered.

Tom pointed to the right. "That's the road to London. It'll take you up through Kensington, but I wouldn't advise going until you've gotten used to it. Riding, I mean."

"Does Miss Hawthorne ride?"

"Oh, aye," said Tom, grinning. "I gave her lessons when she first came to us. She's a good seat, too."

It had been two days since Anthony had seen her, but she had never been far from his thoughts. He imagined her in the saddle, sitting straight and tall, and thought perhaps he could get her to come out riding with him.

Then cursed himself for a fool who could not abide by his own resolve to remain detached. Here was Old Tom who hadn't a care in the world. He lived above the stable and dealt with horses. He would never feel the pain of abandonment, of betrayal.

Anthony would do well to follow his example.

He could smell rain coming. A quick glance at the sky verified that heavy clouds were moving in.

Even if he could get Grace to come out riding, the coming weather would bolster his resolve to keep his distance.

"Ye look good, m'lord," said Tom. "Soon we'll have you out cantering in Richmond Park. Ye'll be a sight fer all the ladies who ride there."

The park was not where Anthony wanted to go, but if that's what it took to become a proficient rider, then he would comply.

It started to rain just as they reached Mr. Lamb's office in Fleet Street. The footman held an umbrella high over Lady Sutton's head as he assisted her from the carriage, and Grace followed, all too aware of Anthony dismounting beside the carriage. His understanding of etiquette and protocol had progressed to a great extent, but Grace was surprised his grandmother had invited him to this meeting. The countess had to realize that just because Anthony was well-dressed, he was not yet ready for society.

Not when he believed that amorous advances toward proper ladies were socially acceptable.

Grace hurried into Mr. Lamb's building behind the countess, then turned to watch Anthony through the open door as he handed his reins to the groom and stood gazing down the busy street. She realized she could not fault him entirely for his caresses that night or his mind-numbing kiss.

She'd been drawn to him by some unexplainable magnetism that robbed her—*momentarily*—of her good sense.

It would not happen again.

"Lady Sutton, come in, come in," said the clerk, taking cloaks from the ladies. "Mr. Lamb is expecting you."

When Grace felt Anthony's hand at her lower back, her resolve began to falter. Immediately, her better judgment returned and she straightened her spine and stepped away.

"My lady," said the clerk, taking note of Anthony, who towered over everyone in the reception area. "Will you . . . er . . . Is he . . ."

"Lead the way, young man," Lady Sutton said, shooing him ahead without explaining Anthony's presence.

Mr. Lamb opened his office door as the countess approached, and raised his eyebrows when he saw Anthony. The attorney quickly ushered the three of them inside, closing the door behind them.

"Well."

"I thought you should meet my grandson now that he's conscious," Her Ladyship said, taking the seat across from the attorney's desk.

Grace sat down beside Lady Sutton, but Anthony remained standing nearby, almost hovering. He crossed his arms against his prodigious chest in what seemed a protective stance, although Grace doubted he would admit to any such thing. He'd shown no desire for developing anything but the most superficial connection with his grandmother.

Mr. Lamb extended his hand to Anthony. "How do you do, my lord?"

Anthony hesitated for a moment, but when he took Lamb's hand and shook it, his body seemed to relax.

"Have you made any progress, Mr. Lamb?" Her Ladyship asked.

The attorney went to his desk and opened a folder, turning it so that Lady Sutton could read the contents within. "My lady, on your grandson's behalf, I've sent a writ of summons to the king for your young man's recognition as earl. In response, a special committee has been convened to review your claims for Lord Sutton."

"Lord Rutherford mentioned that he is to be part of this committee," said Lady Sutton.

"Yes, fortunately, he is. He will make a formidable ally." Mr. Lamb turned to Anthony. "What do you think of all this, my lord?"

Grace had come to believe that Anthony had merely been biding his time out at the cottage until his ankle healed and he could leave. She was chagrined to admit that their passionate interlude must have fallen into the same category. With a queasy awareness, she knew his seduction could only have been an amusing pastime.

Anthony Maddox was a man with his own schemes and plans, and he'd been alone so long he was unaccustomed to sharing them with anyone. Yet he spoke of Africa often, of the perfect climate and complete freedom he enjoyed. He needed— he *wanted*—no one, and nothing but his precious valley.

"What *should* I think of it, Mr. Lamb?" Anthony asked. "'Tis a complicated procedure?"

Lamb eased back in his chair and looked up at Anthony. "Not what I would call complicated. You must convince the committee that you are truly the son and heir of Colin Maddox, Earl of Sutton."

Anthony glanced at his grandmother, then back at Mr. Lamb. Grace felt her jaw drop at his next question. "What proof will satisfy them?"

"'Tis up to you to determine that, I'm afraid."

Grace was perplexed by Anthony's apparent capitulation. Could he actually be considering pursuing his grandmother's goal? It did not fit with anything he'd said to Grace, and if he still intended to leave England, he could not possibly care about the title. She waited for him to clarify his position, but he said nothing.

"What about Lady Sutton's testimony?" Grace asked. "Surely her opinion is relevant."

"Certainly Her Ladyship's opinion will be considered."

"What do you mean?" the countess asked.

Anthony turned to one of the bookcases in the office and seemed to peruse the titles he found on the shelves. But Grace sensed that his attention had not wavered from the discussion. He was listening to every word. She tried to make some sense of his inconsistencies, and could only conclude that he felt more attached to his grandmother than he wanted . . . or would ever admit.

"The committee will demand definitive evidence. Not just opinions," said Lamb. "And if I might be frank, my lady, the opinion of a sentimental lady whose only grandson was lost so many years ago might not be considered particularly viable."

"I don't see why not," Lady Sutton said indignantly.

"Who else would know him better than the countess?" Grace asked.

Mr. Lamb leaned forward and tented his fingers above the folders on his desk. "There are rules of evidence. The law does not operate on mere whims or opinions. Is there any hard evidence that this young man is actually Anthony Maddox?"

Anthony abandoned the bookcase to come and sit down beside his grandmother. Grace decided she could not be mistaken about Anthony's regard for the countess. She did not think he was even aware of the way he leaned slightly toward her, or their similarities of posture and attitude. Anthony had the same hint of a cleft in his chin, as well as Sophia's thick, black eyelashes. And there was that same stubborn tilt of his head . . .

"He bears the very likeness of his father's portrait," said Lady Sutton, and Grace had to look away from his stunning visage. He'd become somewhat civilized, but she could hardly stand near him without feeling his deeply primal alertness and a stunning physicality that was unlike any other man she'd known. He was fiercely male, and she did not believe any number of lessons would truly tame him.

She twisted her hands in her lap and focused on the conversation, not on the way Anthony Maddox could melt her bones with the slightest touch of his hand to the small of her back.

"His resemblance to the portrait will not be enough, my lady. I daresay many a dark-haired man will resemble your late son."

"But he knew about his father's lodge and spoke of the animals they preserved together," Her Ladyship said.

Lamb gave a shake of his head. "Anyone might have known this information and passed it on."

"Well! They will just have to trust my word on the matter."

"My dear lady," said Lamb, "the process doesn't work that way, especially when there is another possible heir who will dispute every piece of soft evidence you may present." He turned to Anthony. "Is there nothing concrete you can add, my lord?"

Grace saw his eyes flicker away from the attorney's. "No."

"Well, then. You must know that Gerard Thornby has protested our proceedings." Lamb pulled out a sheaf of paper and handed it to Lady Sutton.

Grace saw Anthony draw his hands tightly against his thighs as he and the countess quickly read it. The tension in his body was palpable, and she almost expected him to spring away from the office like the agile barbarian she'd first seen on the dock.

"I might have expected such drivel from Thornby," said Lady Sutton.

A muscle in Anthony's jaw flexed. "What has Thornby to do with it?"

"He is your father's heir . . . after you, of course."

"But he is not earl," Anthony said.

"Correct."

Anthony stood and walked to the window, but he said nothing more. Grace realized she'd been remiss in her instructions. She should have discussed his title as well as the difficulties Mr. Thornby would have had in claiming it.

"Mr. Lamb," said Grace, "do you believe the committee will be influenced by Mr. Thornby—a man who stands to gain by discrediting Lady Sutton's grandson?"

Lady Sutton did not give Lamb a chance to reply. "Only a fool would be duped by the kind of Banbury tale Thornby would tell," said the countess. "Once the gentlemen meet Anthony at Fairford Park, they will know who he is."

Mr. Lamb raised a questioning brow. "My lady?"

"I intend to gather some of the lords who sit on the committee at Fairford Park."

"Do you think that is wise, Lady Sutton?" Mr. Lamb asked.

"Of course, I will not invite them until my grandson is perfectly ready to present himself," said Lady Sutton. "And I'll include some allies besides Rutherford, I think."

Grace barely heard the conversation, not while Anthony stood nearby, clearly disturbed by the mention of Mr. Thornby and his claim. She wondered if his disdain for Thornby would be enough to make him stay and try to somehow thwart the man's ambitions, and she could not help but question the cause of such enmity.

"I hope you know what you are doing, my lady," Mr. Lamb said, furrowing his brow as he gazed at the countess. "'Tis a very sensitive matter."

"Naturally. But I am convinced that he is Anthony, and he will easily convince them, as well. They have but to meet him."

"Still, I would advise you to wait—"

"It will be an intimate gathering," Her Ladyship said, ignoring her attorney's advice. "And it will serve as a rehearsal for the role he will play at my charity ball."

Mr. Lamb sighed and sat back in his chair as he

laced his fingers together across his abdomen and listened to the countess's plans.

"First, a small supper party. Then, I intend to 'bring him out,' so to speak, at the ball at month's end."

"Lady Sutton, I realize that the season is well under way, but is there some good reason for your haste? After all, he has been gone more than twenty years. Surely he needs more than a few weeks to become reacclimated—"

"But *I* haven't that much time, Mr. Lamb. I will be eighty years old on the day of my ball. And I should dearly like to see at least one great-grandchild."

Lady Sutton's remark drew Grace up short. *Of course* the countess intended to see her grandson wed to a suitable young lady. She glanced at Anthony and found him looking directly at her. "He is so handsome," the countess added, and Anthony's gaze dropped down to Grace's lips.

She felt that same tight, physical pull that had occurred deep within her body when he kissed her. And yet he had not even touched her.

A tremor ran through her as Lady Sutton continued. "The young ladies will surely swoon at the sight of him. He will make a brilliant match."

"Even if he has no title?" asked Mr. Lamb.

The countess gave a hard look at the attorney. "The committee has not yet met, has it, Mr. Lamb?"

* * *

"You'll send word if there is any news, of course," Sophia said to the attorney as she rose from her chair and went out to the vacant anteroom.

"Naturally, my lady."

Anthony helped his grandmother with her cloak, satisfied with what he had learned. Thornby was aware of his return from Africa and had started his own legal proceedings.

The Sutton groom came inside with an umbrella to escort his grandmother to the carriage, as Anthony took Grace's cloak from the hook. He slipped it over her shoulders, allowing his hands to linger, giving him a chance to bend down and breathe deeply of her scent.

He'd thought he would be able to resist touching her, but had been drawn to her ever since seeing her that morning, climbing into the carriage with his grandmother. Her posture softened slightly at his touch, and she made a soft sound that emboldened him. He had to taste her again.

Turning her gently, he lowered his head as her eyes drifted closed, and she trembled, her desire obviously matching his own. *Mbaya*, how he wanted her. "Grace . . ."

The door opened and a burst of cool, damp air swept in. Along with it came Preston Cooper.

Grace quickly recovered and swung away to look up at her former suitor. Anthony could have throttled him.

"My dear Miss Hawthorne," Cooper said, taking Grace's hand and kissing the back of it. Anthony felt a very primitive urge to bare his teeth and frighten the fool away. "'Tis very good to see you again."

But Grace blushed to her ears, and Anthony touched her lower back, giving her a slight nudge. "We are leaving."

She dug in her heels and ignored him. "Thank you, Mr. Cooper. You are looking well."

He could not credit her words. The milksop's face was pale, and he had soft, white hands and an unctuous manner that brought bile to Anthony's throat.

Cooper looked up at him, as if noticing him for the first time. "Mr. . . . er, Lord Sutton. We meet again."

"Cooper," he growled, giving a quick nod in the man's direction. Grace would not dare fault him for his trifling greeting, especially in light of what he knew of the man. Abandoning his woman, indeed.

Cooper returned his attention to Grace. "Miss Hawthorne, I wonder . . . would it be possible for me to call upon you at Fairford Park? Surely your responsibilities allow you some free time?"

The Sutton groom returned, ready to raise the umbrella for Grace. She appeared torn between staying to visit with Cooper and going to join Sophia in the carriage. To Anthony, there was only one possible reply.

"Mr. Cooper, I—"

"Please do not go until you say yes, Miss Hawthorne."

"Well, I . . . I suppose . . ."

"You haven't the time to spare, Grace," Anthony interjected, his voice low and rough. He felt her react to his wholly improper use of her given name, but he'd used it intentionally. He wanted Cooper to understand . . .

Mbaya, there was nothing for Cooper to understand. Grace Hawthorne was not his concern. She could run off with the man if she chose.

"Of course I have the time," Grace said decisively. "Thank you, Mr. Cooper."

Chapter 8

❧

Anthony's tree fortress was still there, and its condition was nearly as bad as that of the lodge. But the floor appeared to be intact, and so were the walls that rose halfway up the sides. The ladder was gone, and the roof, a light canopy that was supported by narrow columns rising from the floor, had deteriorated so that large pieces of it were missing.

His father had called it Tony's Lodge, and joked that it was a replica of Colin's own retreat. Except that the enclosed platform they'd built in the tree together—with the help of a few Fairford carpenters—was a much more exciting place, where Anthony had battled fiery dragons and armies of fierce Picts. Colin had even allowed him to sleep out there on warm summer nights, when Hugh and Daniel had come to spend part of their school holidays with him.

Anthony had been raised with a fascination for faraway places. His father had told him exciting tales of the untamed places he'd visited . . . India, Siam, the West Indies, Africa . . . and taught him many of the skills he'd used to survive the wilds of the Congo.

As Anthony stared up into the tree, the sharp sting of loss hit him suddenly. His mother had died when he was a mere infant, so he'd never really known her. But his father . . . They had been closer than most fathers and sons.

Anthony could remember the shape of Colin's boot prints in the soft dirt ahead of him as they'd hiked together through the mountains in Wales. He'd learned to swim in the chilly waters of Lake Windermere with his father by his side, and Anthony could almost hear his father's laughter as he'd put his own hands to the task of building the tree fort. None of his friends' fathers would have dreamed of doing such a thing. But Colin—

"You drew many a treasure map out here."

Anthony turned at the sound of his grandmother's voice. Her hair was white now, and the wrinkles on her face an atlas of the years she'd spent without her family.

She approached him, using her cane for support. "I believe you spent the entire duration of your school holidays out here."

"I'm sure I was made to come into the house occasionally to bathe."

Sophia's dark eyes twinkled. "As I recall, you rather preferred bathing in the pond."

He wondered if Grace had spoken to his grandmother of his intention to leave England. He had not seen her since their return from London, sitting across from her in the carriage, desiring her with every drop of blood in his body.

Her instincts were better than his in this instance. She'd wisely avoided being alone with him since then, bringing Old Tom along when they'd had their lessons.

"I always worried you would drown out there, but your father assured me you were a very strong swimmer."

"Yes. I was."

"It was the reason Colin could not bring himself to leave the region where you were lost," she said. "He said you could not possibly have drowned."

He did not remember Sophia being quite so small. The top of her head would not even brush his chin if she came that close to him, and she was so frail a strong wind might blow her away.

When he was a child, though, she'd been strong and robust. His grandmother had never been a person to cross, yet it was into her lap he'd crawled when he was sleepy, or hurt. She had always packed something secret, something special, into his luggage when he'd left home to return to school. He remembered her lavish tales of her English father's avid courtship of her Portuguese mother, stories of how his great-grandfather had pursued his sweetheart all the way to Portugal and back, because he could not live without her.

Anthony looked away from the old woman before him and turned his attention to the tree fort above. There was no one he couldn't live without. He'd taught himself everything he needed to know, and had become completely self-sufficient. He had the friendship of the Moto and Tajuru people, but no dependence on either of them for his well-being. And he certainly had no need for any sort of social commerce here in England.

Not even with Grace Hawthorne, though arousal shuddered through him at the very thought of her. He could not deny that she intrigued him, and made him burn with need. But when the time came to go, Anthony would have no trouble walking away.

Grace must have misunderstood Mr. Cooper's request. Or perhaps he'd had second thoughts about calling. For surely he would have found time to come out to Richmond by now. Grace wished he would make his visit soon so she could get the unpleasantness over and done. She intended to tell him—as kindly as possible—that she could not possibly resume their courtship.

She wished Anthony had not been present for their chance meeting at Mr. Lamb's office. His words had goaded her into agreeing to see Mr. Cooper, when she knew better. She'd come to realize that Preston Cooper could never be trusted to deal with adversity. Marriage to him would have been disastrous.

Mr. Bridewell was an entirely different kind of man. Clearly, he took his commitments and responsibilities seriously. He was a man to be relied upon, a man who would never let her down.

And yet her impossibly intimate encounters with Anthony played out over and over again in her dreams, curling her toes and making her yearn for something she could not define.

For two days, Grace managed to stay away from the Tudor cottage and the confusion that always followed her interactions with Anthony. He'd progressed well in his lessons, and merely needed some uninterrupted time to read, to familiarize himself with recent history.

At least, that was the excuse Grace gave for avoiding him.

In the meantime, she stayed busy, for there was much to do to prepare for the charity ball. She spent time with the Fairford kitchen staff, discussing recipes for refreshments. She met with the carpenters, going over sketches of the decorations Lady Sutton had described. In the process, Grace tried not to concern herself with the reason Anthony had been so tense in the attorney's office. Something about Thornby had disturbed him . . . but there was more to it. Perhaps he was having second thoughts about leaving.

Such a notion was hardly productive. The life of a prodigal earl had nothing to do with her, beyond making him presentable to society.

She knew Anthony would be received well. He'd looked striking in his evening attire. He knew how to comport himself, was familiar with proper protocol and etiquette, and was unlikely to say anything embarrassing.

He would do even better at the charity ball.

Grace was not looking forward to it, for she did not think she would be able to stomach the feminine fawning that was sure to take place. Even if Anthony was never recognized as the legitimate heir to the earldom, he would inherit a substantial fortune from his grandmother. Coupled with the utter virility of his bearing, that would make the young ladies of the *ton* lap him up like a cat with a bowl of cream.

Two days of long, hard hours on horseback had not kept Anthony's thoughts in line. Far from enjoying his hours of solitude as he explored the Richmond region, he'd had to make a conscious effort to avoid riding up to the main house to find out whether Cooper had come to visit Grace.

His brain had fixed upon her. Her pretty blushes and sweet smiles occupied far too many of his thoughts. Even now, as she sat across from him in his cottage, wearing her plain, brown dress, he could not keep himself from wondering if the woman ever did anything with abandon.

Ever since Tom had told him she knew how to ride, Anthony had pictured her on horseback, galloping wildly through the fields with her hair trailing behind her. He'd imagined how she might laugh with delight when they stopped and dismounted and he reached up to take her waist in hand and lower her ever so slowly to the ground.

Anthony clenched his teeth and thought about bees' nests, rather than the freckle that lay at the corner of Grace's mouth, beckoning his attention.

"Lord Sutton," she said, and his eyes were drawn to her mouth once again. "A proper gentleman always wears shoes, unless he is . . . Er, when you are with me, I will expect to see your feet properly shod."

He knew where to find the largest honey nests in Ganweulu—thanks to the honeyguides that led him to them—and he knew how to baffle the bees in order to steal their honey.

He wondered if he could baffle Grace into another kiss. Perhaps after one more, he could stop staring at her mouth, and at the silken lock of hair that curled at her nape. Surely then he would be able to get her out of his thoughts.

"Lord Sutton?"

"You don't really mean to entertain Cooper," he said abruptly.

Her mouth dropped open and her back went rigid. "I don't see how 'tis any of your concern."

"Past acts proved him an unreliable suitor, did they not?"

She stood and walked across the room to the window. "We were talking about your shoes. Why don't you go into your—"

"He abandoned you."

Her throat moved as she swallowed, and she pressed her lips tightly together for a moment. "We were discussing your shoes—or lack thereof."

"You cannot want to encourage the man," he said, following her to the window. He felt torn between wanting to shake sense into her, and taking her into his arms. "He is a weak-kneed deserter."

"What transpired between Mr. Cooper and me . . ." She turned to face the window.

Anthony stood close behind her, and bent close to absorb her scent. "Why would he let you go?"

"He did not care to take on the responsibility of an ailing mother-in-law."

"But he'd have had you." He slipped one pin from her twist of hair and bent to press his lips to the side of her neck.

She skittered away. " 'Tis all past history." Her tone was casual, but she sounded breathless. "And that is what I've come out to discuss with you. Did you read the articles on Lord C-Canning's handling of the Greek revolt? 'Tis an ongoing matter that will surely be discussed in—"

"Canning achieved self-government for the Greeks, but under Turkish supervision," Anthony replied, although he did not wish to discuss politics or world events with her. "But Wellington seems to have other ideas with regard to Russia's involvement."

"Very good."

He came alongside her and touched her cheek with the back of his hand. "Did you come to Fairford Park when your mother died?"

She nodded, brushing his hand away. "Your grandmother was in need of a companion, and since we two have been acquainted since I was a child, it seemed natural for me to take the position."

He was glad his grandmother had seen fit to take her in and provide for her. "Your hair smells of flowers."

" 'Tis lavender."

She moved again, but Anthony stopped her, leaning close, putting one hand against the wall next to her head. This time, he was going to quench his thirst for her.

He moved slowly and deliberately, enjoying every feminine inch that made contact with his body as he bent toward her mouth. He drank in her nearness, and relished the tiny sound she made just before her eyes flew open.

She quickly ducked beneath his arm and grabbed one of her books, carrying it to the dining table. She opened it and gave a grand show of looking for the page she wanted to discuss with him.

It took Anthony a moment to recover. "I do not remember lavender."

" 'Tis nothing but a common flower," she said lightly, as though they had not just come within an inch of devouring each other.

"Do you bathe in scented water?" He asked the question quietly, from a distance.

She snapped the book closed. "Lord Sutton! I've—"

"Yes, I know." His gaze drifted to her mouth, to the freckle that fascinated him. The urge to taste her eroded his better judgment. " 'Tis too personal a question. But how am I to learn all I need to know if you do not answer my queries?"

He watched without breathing as her tongue slipped out and moistened her lips. "My soap is scented," she said, then turned and reopened their discussion. "What do you know about Waterloo?"

He took a seat at the table, in spite of the rule that demanded he wait for her to be seated first. "It was the battle that ended Napoleon's illustrious career. Why do you wrap yourself so tightly when we are together? Your blue gown shows your beautiful curves to advantage."

He could almost see the flush that would creep up to her cheeks, even though his back was to her.

"What was the most significant change made to criminal law by Sir Robert Peel?" she asked.

"You are very determined to browbeat me with dull facts, Miss Hawthorne."

"Your grandmother would like you to be pre-pared to take your seat in the House of Lords."

He snorted at the very idea, glad to be reminded of his one and only purpose for staying here. "I've already told you— "

"Right. You do not intend to remain in England. I know," she retorted, taking a seat across from him. "But Lady Sutton has given me an assignment to complete, and I have every intention of doing so."

Anthony tapped his thumbs together repeatedly, and considered mutiny. Why did he bother stay-ing here? He'd gone riding as much as possible, and was ready to go to Oxfordshire to confront Thornby. There lay his only reason for staying in England—not to make entanglements he had no intention of keeping.

Yet he leaned back and noted the row of little buttons that marched up the center of Grace's bodice from her waist to her neck. How easy it would be to unfasten them. His hands itched to touch her, to lay her shoulders bare and—

"Who is King of England?" she asked, deter-mined to return them to the task at hand.

"George the, uh . . ."

"George III was king when you left England in 1807," she said, surreptitiously hooking a loose curl behind her ear, and Anthony craved the touch of her delicate hand. "He went mad and his son, George, became regent. That George is now King George IV."

It was far too easy to imagine those hands slipping round his neck and pulling him close while she sipped from his lips.

Anthony dragged a hand across his face and stood. "I might go mad, too, if we stay inside any longer. Let us take our lesson outside, Miss Hawthorne. There, you can regale me with as much history as you like."

"But we—"

He didn't listen to her protests, but unwrapped his silly cravat and tossed it, along with his coat, onto the settee and headed for the door. He had to get away from their close quarters before he acted on his ill-advised attraction to his tutor.

He functioned better on his own. Life was simpler—happier—with no one to worry about, and that was how he liked it.

It was a short walk to his tree fort. He'd made a ladder to replace the one that had rotted away, but had only climbed to the top of it to look inside. He had not yet gone inside his old play place.

"Where are you going?" Grace called to him as he headed down the path in the opposite direction from the house.

Anthony turned slightly to see that she was following, but noticed that she came along with a distinct lack of enthusiasm. He was going to tell her to return to the house and mind her own business.

"Come and see," he said, his tongue clearly disconnected from his brain.

He followed the overgrown path to the fort and started up the ladder.

"What are you doing?" she asked.

He climbed all the way up to the platform and stepped onto it, disappearing from sight below.

"Lord Sutton!"

He moved round the trunk of the tree, testing the solidity of the floor.

"Come back down!" Grace called. Anthony looked out and saw her pacing back and forth as she looked up, tenting her hand over her eyes to see him. "Please."

Once he decided the fort was safe, he went back down the ladder, landing directly in front of Miss Hawthorne. Much too close, he was sure.

She stepped back. "What is that monstrosity?"

He placed one hand over his heart. "Miss Hawthorne, you wound me. Now you must pay a forfeit for such an insult."

"A forfeit?" she said as a frown creased her brow. "What do you mean?"

"You must join me in my fort."

She looked aghast, gazing past him at the fort that lay high in the tree. "Certainly not."

He was undeterred. "Come here. Put your arms round my waist."

"I have no intention of—"

"Miss Hawthorne, I have gone along with all your little lessons . . ." He moved closer, and she took her skirts in hand, ready to flee. "I've followed your directives at table and with my grandmother. But you just insulted my first attempt at building . . ." He stepped even closer. "You owe me . . . a forfeit."

The pulse in her neck was beating hard. He knew he was pushing the bounds, but he could not seem to help himself. He wanted her in his arms, and this seemed the only way to accomplish it.

He moved in quickly and slipped one arm round her waist, then lifted her off the ground, tossing her weight onto his shoulder. She squealed and he laughed, bracing one arm against the backs of her legs. He started up the ladder. "Hold on, Grace!"

She fought him as though her life depended upon it, but he started up the ladder.

"Be gracious," he instructed, mimicking one of her lessons.

"Let me down," she ordered, but Anthony ignored her. She squirmed in his arms, but he held her secure until they reached the platform, and he set her down just inside the opening.

Grace stood against him, hanging on to fistfuls of his shirt, trembling and breathing fast. Anthony felt exhilarated, but it had little to do with his climb, and everything to do with the woman in his arms.

He'd never felt stronger or more potent than he did at that moment.

* * *

Grace was afraid to open her eyes. Not because of the distressingly high place where they'd landed, or the manner in which he'd gotten her there. But because every need, every yearning, every one of her improper, unsuitable desires would be clear in her eyes. So she held on to Anthony and allowed him to believe she was angry and wholly unnerved by his escapade.

He touched her chin and raised her face to gaze up at his. "You can relax, little honeyguide," he said quietly. "I won't let you go."

"You m-must not—"

"The floor is sound, Grace. There is no danger."

The heat of his hand drew a fresh current of tremors from Grace. She swallowed when he slid it down her back and pulled her closer. His proximity, his touch, caused a torrent of tiny fireworks to go off just under Grace's skin. She felt hot and fiery, yet light and airy all at once.

She released her death-grip on his shirt and slid her hands up his arms, only to confirm that the heavy muscles under the fine linen of his shirt were real. He was far more powerful than anyone she'd ever touched, capable of carrying her to heights she'd never imagined.

She should be furious with him, but when she looked out past his shoulder, she felt dizzy with sensation, as though she'd been numb for the bulk of her life. She closed her eyes and did nothing but relish the luxury of these few minutes suspended in time, with Anthony Maddox's big hands sliding up and down her back. In a moment she would demand to be let down to solid ground once again, and she would return to the business of preparing him for society.

But she felt his fingers working at her hair, and suddenly her chignon fell and her hair was cascading down her back.

"Beautiful," Anthony whispered, sending shivers through Grace's body. "You should always wear it loose and flowing . . ."

It was all Grace could do to remember to breathe.

"Now you must open your collar," he said as he unfastened the first few buttons at her neck.

She stilled his hand when she felt his fingers slip down to her throat. "No. You cannot," she said, but her voice was much too quiet to hold a true ring of authority.

"In a tree fort, naught is improper." His voice was but a whisper that Grace could barely hear above the slight breeze that rustled the leaves of the tree.

He bent his head low, and Grace could feel his warm breath on her cheek. Her knees buckled with the caress of his fingers on her buttons, but he did not let her fall. She knew she should not allow this degree of intimacy, yet she seemed to have neither the wits nor the impetus to push him away.

The crisp hairs on the back of his hand brushed against her neck, raising goose bumps upon the sensitive skin there. He smelled of clean water and fresh air, and felt hard against her body.

"You are so very soft, Grace." His voice was low as it wafted through her, seducing rational thought away on the breeze. Grace found herself slipping her hands up his chest, tipping her head back, letting her eyes drift closed . . .

She should make him take her down to the ground. But when his lips grazed hers, the familiar excitement flared within her. Fever burned through her, and she found herself pulling his shirtfront again, drawing him closer until his mouth took full possession of hers.

He made a low sound and shifted, positioning his hands at her back, sliding them down to her hips and pulling the full length of her body intimately against his. She burned where their bodies touched, and Grace arched against him. He drew her tongue into his mouth to tangle with his own, and Grace encircled his neck with her hands.

He tipped his head slightly to deepen their kiss.

The strength and toughness of his body was unthinkably arousing, and Grace felt as though she were drowning in sensation. Hot, liquid pleasure swelled through her womb and coursed through her body to the tips of her breasts. She ached for more. For the raw feel of his rough body against hers.

Her head swam when he cupped her face and then moved his fingers down to her bodice. Grace ignored a niggling protest at the back of her brain, desperate as she was to feel his hands on her breasts, touching her nipples. She knew little of what was expected, but nature guided her to cradle his hot erection in the sensitive cleft between her legs. He made a low, rasping sound as he opened more of her buttons, and suddenly her shoulders were bare.

Her eyes flew open as rationality returned, and she broke the kiss. "No," she whispered. "Oh heavens! What am I . . ." She swallowed. "Anth— Lord Sutton, I cannot . . ."

Anthony appeared bewildered, but oh so handsome with his eyes hooded and aroused, looking at Grace as though she were the only woman in the world. But Grace knew better. The solitude of his African life called to him as no woman ever could. And if he did not leave England, he would be required to wed a young lady of the *ton*.

She broke away from Anthony's embrace and turned her back to him as she pulled her gown into place and started to fasten the buttons. Mr. Bridewell was a proper suitor, and she would not dishonor him with such wanton behavior.

Anthony remained silent, and when Grace turned her head to see what he was about, she saw a deep frown on his face.

It was with an unsteady voice that Grace spoke. "I

have t-taught you about our society. You must know that life is dictated by propriety. It is unseemly—"

"*Mbaya,*" he muttered, and though Grace did not know the meaning of the word, she understood the frustration in his voice.

She felt embarrassed and confused, and when a muscle in his jaw tightened and he turned away, tears burned the backs of her eyes.

But she was not in the wrong. He should never have carried her up here, kissed her senseless, and made her forget all but her own name. She looked down at the ladder and was unsure how to manage it. "I want you to take me down. Please."

He stepped away to the far side of the platform, and a dismal hollowness filled Grace. She tried to bring Mr. Bridewell's visage to mind, but could not.

"My father and I built this together three years before he took me on safari."

His abrupt change was disorienting. Grace knew she should not have allowed matters to go so far, and she accepted part of the blame. If only she weren't so deeply attracted to Lady Sutton's grandson, this would never have happened. She needed to get away from him. Now, before her resolve deserted her.

He crouched down and picked up a battered wooden case with rusted hinges, turning it to show it to Grace. "I hid my treasures up here, in this box."

"Can you open it?" she asked in spite of herself. She cleared her throat, for her voice had not quite returned to normal.

" 'Tis locked."

"I wonder what happened to the key?"

"Naught of value lies within. Just a young boy's meager prizes." There was a harsh rasp in his voice, but he returned the box to the floor—the most personal thing he'd shared with her yet.

Grace reminded herself that she'd done the right thing. And now she needed to get down from there, and away from him. A long walk or a ride through the countryside might succeed in drumming him out of her senses, for no matter how clear her purpose was, she was not immune to his potent virility. She needed to put some space between them.

Any further lessons would have to wait until she had figured a way to remain detached. Impersonal.

"I'd like to leave, Lord Sutton. If you would just help me down."

He looked across at her, and the deep green of his eyes burned into hers.

And then he laughed, a loud, thoroughly exultant laugh that brought a flush of embarrassment to Grace's cheeks and the sting of confusion to her heart.

"Take me down," she said firmly. "Now."

Chapter 9

G race hurried back to the house with every intention of putting her hair and clothes to rights before having to face anyone in the household. But her flight to her room was interrupted by Faraday, opening the door to a caller, just as she arrived in the foyer. She attempted to make a quick retreat, but she was unable to escape.

"Miss Hawthorne?"

Grace took a deep breath and faced Preston Cooper, whose voice held a tone of incredulity. She knew she must look a wreck.

"Oh, Mr. Cooper," she said, as though her hair were in place and her buttons had not just been hastily refastened. She refrained from looking down at them to be sure they were lined up correctly. "I was not expecting you."

Her heart fell to the pit of her stomach. It seemed her lot to be caught in disarray at the most inopportune moments. Straightening her spine, Grace drew herself up and pretended a degree of poise she did not actually possess. She gathered her hands gracefully together at her waist and gave him a wan smile. Somehow she had to collect the courage to say what needed to be said.

But she felt entirely at sea. Her behavior with Anthony Maddox had been beyond reckless. And now here was Preston Cooper to witness her fall from propriety. At least it was not Edward Bridewell.

She took a deep breath to calm herself. That unlikely interlude in Anthony's tree fort had been an aberration, and would not be repeated.

Mr. Cooper looked very lean and stylish, dressed in a suit much like the one he'd been wearing when she'd seen him in town, but he'd started growing a mustache. It was a thin, reddish affair that—Grace was ashamed to think—looked a bit like a rash on his face. "Will you come into the parlor, Mr. Cooper?"

She led the way into the room and sat down on the settee. Her former suitor sat across from her and leaned forward to take her hand. Grace avoided his touch and cleared her throat, unsure how to begin.

"You have done very well in business, I see," she remarked, although that was not at all what she wanted to say.

"Yes. Very well, indeed. And I've decided . . . 'tis time to take a wife." He had the courtesy to appear at least slightly abashed. "I've come to see if you will consider my suit once again, Miss

Hawthorne. I realize it's been two years, but after seeing you . . ."

Feeling extraordinarily ill-at-ease, Grace stood and walked to the window. She knew it would be much better to be straightforward than to draw out her rejection. But it was all so uncomfortable. "Mr. Cooper, I am not sure that that would be such a good—"

"Please don't be hasty, Miss Hawthorne. My career has progressed sufficiently, and I have enough put by to provide for you. We can make a very satisfactory life together."

"I do not think so," Grace said.

"Your mind cannot be so closed against me. Were we not the best of friends at one time?"

"Mr Cooper, I fear I must have misled you when we met in Mr. Lamb's office. I was not thinking clearly."

He came to her and took her hand in his. "I regret having surprised you there. But I cannot regret our encounter. It gave me hope that we might resume where we left off two years ago."

Grace withdrew her hand and walked to the fireplace. "Mr. Cooper . . . While I am flattered by your renewed interest, I'm afraid I will have to decline."

He was silent for a moment. "I realize what a grievous error I made two years ago when I . . . This is very awkward, Miss Hawthorne."

Grace had not thought the discussion would deteriorate into an argument, and decided it was time to end it. "Mr. Cooper, we must not deceive ourselves. You just happened upon me here at Fairford Park, did you not?"

He frowned. "I'm not sure I follow."

"You did not seek me out here; you did not even know I had come to live at Fairford Park."

He hesitated, and Grace looked directly at him.

"Miss Hawthorne, I must assure you that my intentions are—"

"I bear you no hard feelings," she interjected, and she meant it. The hurt of his abandonment had been supplanted by her mother's illness and subsequent death. Grace had managed to deal with it on her own, and she'd learned about placing her hopes where they would only be shattered. "But I am certain we no longer suit. My life has changed in many ways, and I am content with it."

Her life at Fairford Park was ideal—with the exception of her duties regarding Anthony. She did not know how she would face him again.

He had made a great deal of progress in a short time. He had devoured the books she brought him, as well as the London papers and periodicals. His skills at mathematics exceeded her own, and he'd mastered the principles of etiquette.

It was remarkable.

Yet his behavior that afternoon was no better than that of a man from the wilds of the Congo. He took liberties that no man should assume, that no proper woman should allow. Grace shuddered. His wildness must be contagious, for his words and deeds seemed to rob her of all rationality.

Preston Cooper startled her back to the present. "I am sure that if we see each other frequently, we can recapture our former friendship."

"I do not think so," Grace replied. She started toward the parlor door as a clear indication that their conversation was over. "It was very good to see you, Mr. Cooper, but I must bid good day to you."

"Miss Hawthorne. Grace," he said, a little bit desperately. "We should at least try."

She shook her head, feeling slightly annoyed by his persistence, and determined to be firm. "I am not the same girl you knew and cast off when I—or rather, my mother's illness—became inconvenient."

"Grace, I did not 'cast you off' as you say. It was with the greatest regret that I departed."

"And it is with regret that I must decline your offer to rekindle our association." Grace gave him a hard look. "Again, good day, Mr. Cooper."

Grace sat down beside Lady Sutton at breakfast the next morning. "I understand your Mr. Cooper called yesterday," said the countess.

"Yes."

"I hope you are not seriously considering seeing that fellow again."

"No, my lady, I declined his suit."

"Good. Mr. Bridewell is a much more fitting prospect. He is solid and reliable, although perhaps a bit older."

Grace returned a lame nod. "He is very nice."

Lady Sutton placed her hand upon Grace's forearm. "You are hesitant, my dear. Promise you will not allow yourself to rebuff him on my account. When the opportunity presents, you must not worry about me."

That was not the reason for Grace's reticence, but she gave Her Ladyship a pleasant smile. "Of course not."

Lady Sutton took a sip of tea, unaware of the turmoil in Grace's heart and her memory of Anthony's kisses. She could not imagine allowing such intimacies with her suitor.

"Mr. Bridewell's estate is not far from Fairford Park, Grace. We should still see very much of each other."

Grace swallowed. "Yes, he would make an ideal husband. But he has not yet spoken of marriage."

The countess patted Grace's arm. "He will. He would not come visiting Fairford Park after church every Sunday if he were not seriously courting you."

She knew Her Ladyship was right. She also knew she had to put thoughts of Anthony out of her mind and concentrate on securing the staid and proper Mr. Bridewell for her spouse.

"On another topic altogether," said the countess, "I've decided 'tis time to move Anthony into the house. It will make his remaining lessons much more convenient for you."

Grace looked sharply at Lady Sutton. Move him into the house? "M-my lady, are you sure?"

"Perfectly. We had supper together last night, and he could not have been more correct in his deportment. You have done an excellent job with him."

"Thank you," she murmured.

"He was so alone for all those years in Africa," Lady Sutton said, her expression growing somber. "I fear he still blames his father for leaving him."

Grace nodded, her thoughts racing. She was not sure she could succeed in her association with Mr. Bridewell if she had to face Anthony at every meal, walk past him in the corridors, sit with him in Her Ladyship's parlor. "He does not speak of Lord Sutton."

"No. Not even to me. One would think he'd want to know the details of Colin's return home. That he would wonder . . ."

"He does not allow himself to wonder," said Grace. "I think . . . It must hurt him very much to know he was wrong about his father for all those years."

"Yet he feels very sour about rejoining society. He does not wish to acknowledge that he belongs here."

Grace chewed her lip. "Has he said so?"

"He need not say anything, Grace. I know he still feels betrayed—by the very person who should have cared most for him."

"Yes, you may be right, my lady," Grace said.

"He told me of the tribe that took him in when he was nearly drowned, but I believe he remained an outsider even there."

"It was a difficult life, but he thinks fondly of it," Grace remarked, although she did not want to be the one to inform Her Ladyship that Anthony intended to leave England and go back there.

"And he will accustom himself to life here." The countess placed a sheaf of paper on the table beside her. "I've drawn up a list of eligible young ladies I'd like Anthony to meet at the ball."

Grace inhaled sharply, causing a crumb of her toast to go down the wrong way. She coughed and choked, scolding herself for being such a ninny. Of course Her Ladyship had women in mind for him.

"What is it, dear?" Lady Sutton cried. "Shall I pat your back?"

"No, no. 'Tis nothing." Grace shook her head and forced herself to stop coughing. Once all was well again, the countess handed her the list and pointed to the first two names.

"I think Lady Aubrey Kinion would be his best choice, although there is nothing shabby about Lady Theodosia Craddock." She looked up at Grace. "What do you think? You've met both those young ladies. I do not believe Lady Theodosia is in possession of a great fortune, but she comes from an excellent family, and her reputation is beyond reproach."

Grace could only nod, since she did not seem to be able to breathe. Or find her voice. The other names swam together as the prospect of living nearby as Mrs. Bridewell came to her, along with the awareness that Anthony—if he married— would be a frequent visitor here.

A bitter pang of longing struck her in the middle of her chest, a yearning she could not dismiss. She'd spent most of the past fortnight wanting to be rid of him, and yet now . . . She focused her attention on the list, although the names swam before her overly moist eyes.

Lady Aubrey was stunning, with gleaming blond hair and a figure any woman would envy. Anthony would surely find her more than attractive.

Or Lady Theodosia. She had beautiful, dark doe's eyes and the longest lashes Grace had ever seen, and she knew how to use them in coy flirtation. Grace would never measure up to such an accomplished coquette.

Not that she'd ever wanted to do so. She was going to become Mr. Bridewell's wife . . . and stepmother to his well-behaved children.

"Perhaps the Morgraves' daughter," Lady Sutton mused quietly, almost to herself. "She's only just out, but . . ."

Grace's throat started to burn. The Bridewell children had no fondness for Grace, and they'd shown it. "My lady, would you excuse me? I . . . I just need to . . ."

"Are you all right, Grace? Have you recovered from your choking spell—"

"Yes, quite," she replied hoarsely, although it felt as though her lungs were being squeezed together. She needed some air.

"All right, then. Go. I'll see you at luncheon. With Anthony."

Anthony knew Grace did not see him when she came into the deeply shadowed stable. She seemed nervous and agitated, very much the way Anthony felt. Wasting no time, she asked one of the grooms to saddle a horse called Posy, then went outside.

He took his time saddling his own mount, then waited for the groom to take Posy out to Grace so that the sight of him would not deter her from her ride. He knew she was displeased with him.

The last time he'd seen her was the previous afternoon when he'd indulged his cravings and kissed her. She'd fit against him perfectly, and he knew she'd been as aroused as he. Their kiss had dazed her and stirred him relentlessly. Even thinking of it now—

He walked his horse out of the stable and saw that Grace had already mounted Posy and ridden down the path toward Fairford's gates. She sat straight and tall in her sidesaddle, wearing a hat of straw with a light blue band that matched the gown she wore, another construction of high neck and concealing cuffs. And all those intriguing layers . . .

He cooled his ardor by shoving his hands deep into the horses' trough and splashing cold water on his face.

Then he mounted his own horse and started out at a walk. The path was deserted, and as Anthony hung back giving Grace a good head start, he wondered at her safety. Should she be out riding alone? He vaguely remembered an incident . . . One of his father's friends had been attacked on the road to Richmond from London by robbers. No, the robbers were called something else. *Highwaymen*.

He looked round to see if anyone else was in sight. *Mbaya*. She could be riding straight into danger.

He reminded himself that it was daylight and there seemed to be no one else on the path, but Anthony decided he would take issue with Grace riding alone. It could not be entirely safe.

She rode in a direction he had not yet taken on any of his rides, turning down a narrow path through a thick grove of trees. He stayed well behind her and tried to remember if he'd ever come here as a lad. 'Twas very likely he had, for once he'd learned to ride, he and his father had explored every acre round Sophia's Richmond estate.

It was his father's preferred home, located close to London and his friends, as well as the explorers' societies he so favored. Fairford Park had been the primary home Anthony had known, although he remembered Sutton Court well. He'd been born at his father's estate in Oxfordshire, and his mother had died shortly afterward.

Anthony had not thought of her in ages. He knew her only from the portraits that hung at Fairford Park and the few tales his grandmother had told, for it had saddened his father to speak of her.

He knew his mother had been an excellent horsewoman. She'd enjoyed parties and been a fine mistress of the Sutton estates, visiting their tenants regularly and providing for their needs. According to Sophia, Colin had loved her so well, her death had cut him deeply. He'd grieved for several years, and had never looked at another woman.

The path started on a gradual decline and curved round to the left. Anthony continued following Grace as he considered the kind of love his father had felt for his wife. And for his son. It had been so great he had not been able to continue living without them.

It was disturbing to ponder.

Anthony soon found himself at a low, grassy ridge, beyond which was a rapidly flowing river, but Grace was nowhere in sight. It looked as though she must have ridden over the grass to his right, so he pressed in his knees and headed in the direction he thought she'd gone, then slowed when he saw her.

She'd dismounted, and now stood at the edge of the rocky riverbank. Anthony watched as she took a seat on one of the larger rocks, surprised to see that her demeanor was not as stiff as usual. She allowed her back to curve, and her shoulders sagged uncharacteristically, as though she were bearing an indescribable weight.

He took a step forward, but stopped short when her shoulders began to shake and she covered her face in her hands. She was weeping.

Anthony had seen any number of African women cry, loudly and with passion, but no incident had ever shaken him the way Grace's quiet tears did.

What had happened to upset her so?

The last time Grace had cried was at her mother's funeral. She had not believed she'd had any tears left after that day, or would ever suffer another occasion that would frustrate and upset her so much that she would weep over it.

She did not even know why she was crying now. Her life had taken a surprisingly pleasant turn. If Lady Sutton was correct, Grace could very well be married shortly, to Edward Bridewell. She would have the family she'd always wanted, with an honorable, upstanding widower.

His estate seemed to be prosperous, and he was a most proper gentleman. Grace could not imagine that he would ever attempt to slide his fingers through her hair unless they were in a quite private place. Nor would he try to disrobe her, even after they were married. He would always act with complete and total propriety, respecting her privacy. He would never arouse those hot, wild feelings that Anthony Maddox's scandalous seduction so disturbed in her.

Leave those for the bride Lady Sutton chose for him. Let that young lady be the one to lose all sense of herself and melt at his touch. Such madness was not for Grace.

She blew her nose and wiped away her tears. Such an outburst was entirely unwarranted. Her life was beginning to progress just the way she'd hoped, with a man any wife would be proud of. Grace had reason to be jubilant, not morose.

Posy nudged Grace's shoulder, and she got up from her perch on the big rock beside the river.

It was clouding up. Grace realized it would soon rain and she should return to the house before she got caught in it. She took hold of Posy's reins and turned the mare, but stopped at the sight of the last man she wanted to encounter.

His deeply masculine bearing evoked an unwelcome response in Grace, which she stifled with sheer force of will.

Leading his horse, he came toward her, wearing boots that were shined to a fault, with his fashionable breeches neatly tucked inside, but he'd neglected to wear a waistcoat or cutaway. Nor was there a cravat round his neck. He wore a simple white shirt with gathered shoulders and full sleeves, and they were rolled to his elbows.

No one would ever consider him a worthy gentleman when he dressed in this manner.

Yet Grace swallowed thickly at the sight of the dark hair that curled just inside the open neck of his shirt. She tightened her hand round Posy's reins and did the prudent thing—she started to walk away.

"Is it entirely proper for you to be out riding alone, Miss Hawthorne?"

Grace could not believe her ears. "Pr-proper?"

"Or safe?"

She stood still, gazing up at his intense green eyes and the thick, black lashes that bordered them; at the uncut hair that brushed past his shoulders, and the expanse of densely muscled chest that was obvious through the fine lawn of his shirt.

And started to laugh.

It was not the kind of sweet, genteel laugh she would use in a drawing room, but a bright gust of mirth that seemed to burst from her, unchecked. And once she'd started, she could not stop.

To his credit, Anthony seemed to understand the irony and he laughed as well, until they both sat down together on the rocky bank and laughed until they could hardly breathe.

Grace gave not a thought to the dirt that must

be soiling the back of her riding gown, or the light drizzle that had begun to fall. She looked at Anthony, at his eyelashes as they separated and darkened in the rain, at his hair as rivulets of rainwater dripped down his face. Through the golden tan of his skin, his cheekbones took on a ruddy hue, and Grace noticed he'd stopped laughing.

He tipped his head downward and started to move in closer. As the heat of his body surrounded her, Grace felt his breath on her mouth. She started to tilt in for his kiss, allowing her eyes to flutter closed, submitting to that dark, primitive place inside her that—

Dismayed by her undisciplined reaction to him, Grace grabbed hold of Anthony's shoulders and levered herself up, scrambling away from him. She moved quickly, leading Posy to the shelter of the trees beyond the riverbank. But Anthony caught up to her and seized her by the waist, drawing her alongside him through what was quickly becoming a downpour.

She stumbled, but he held her securely, guiding her up the bank and into the trees with the horses right behind them. Anthony did not release her when they reached the canopy of the trees. He kept his hands upon her waist and backed her up against the trunk of a broad oak.

A hot and primitive thrill filled her from the tips of her breasts all the way to the center of her womb at his possessive touch. When he dipped down, taking possession of her lips in an all-encompassing kiss, her knees wobbled beneath her. He teased her mouth open and began a full-blown assault with his tongue.

The warm rain seemed to meld them together, the layers of their clothes disappearing with their soaking. Grace felt his hard arousal against her abdomen, and he deepened their kiss, swallowing her sigh of pleasure. His hand moved from her waist to her breast and he cupped it, then opened his palm and stroked her through her clothes, her nipples becoming erect in spite of the layers covering them.

Grace had never known such bone-melting pleasure. She skimmed her hands up his chest and through the long hair at his nape as she pressed her body against his, craving something more. Something beyond this wild, incredible passion he'd elicited from her.

The sound of a horse's snort on the path nearby barely penetrated Grace's awareness, but it was Anthony who broke the kiss. He pressed his forehead against hers. "Someone . . . I hear a horse."

Grace swallowed tightly. Her body still hummed with desire, even though she knew it was wrong. It was a mistake. That kiss, those caresses . . .

She stepped away from Anthony and attempted to press her hair back into some semblance—

And then realized it was pointless to bother.

She'd made a harlot of herself. She might as well look the part.

"There ye are, Miss Hawthorne!" called Tom Turner when she came into his sights. "I was worried when Jamie told me ye'd ridden off on yer own."

"I'm fine, as you can see," she replied, "if a bit wet. Lord Sutton came after me."

Anthony followed her, drawing the horses behind him. He held her hat out to her.

And Grace realized she hadn't even noticed she'd left it behind.

Chapter 10

"I prefer the cottage," Anthony said in reply to his grandmother's statement. He felt edgy and restless, and was not about to move into the main house. He had no desire to see his old bed-chamber, no interest in his father's library, or the small parlor where he'd sat upon his grandmother's lap and listened to her stories of passionate longing and love.

"Why, you are family!" Sophia said. "I won't hear of your remaining in a guest cottage while—"

"I believe I made myself perfectly clear, my lady. This cottage suits me perfectly." And by remaining out there, he would be able to come and go without alerting the entire household to his activities.

Because, one day soon, he was going to pay a visit to Sutton Court and meet with Gerard Thornby. Afterward, he was going to ride back to London and find himself a ship. He only needed a few more days to become conditioned to riding, and then he would be able to manage the distance.

"Meals, then," said Sophia. "You'll come up to the house for your meals. 'Tis time you learned to interact properly with the servants. As the Earl of Sutton."

"My lady," he said, clasping his hands behind his back, "I am not interested in becoming earl. Nor do I wish to stay in England."

She staggered slightly backward, and Anthony regretted his bluntness. "Not stay—? You don't mean to say you wish to return to Africa?"

"Please sit down," he said, taking her arm and leading her to an armchair in his sitting room.

"I cannot believe you," she said forcefully, although her color had gone pale. "You have only just returned, and you must know it will take time to readjust."

Anthony retreated to the dining area and poured his grandmother a glass of water from a pitcher on the sideboard. He was mucking up everything in a spectacular manner.

First Grace . . . He had not seen her since their passionate encounter in the rain. They'd ridden back to Fairford Park with only Tom Turner's conversation between them. She'd left the stable in a hurry, making a run for the house through the rain.

And now Sophia. He should have given her a few more hints before blurting out his intention to leave.

He returned to the sitting room and sat down

across from her, handing her the glass. "Have a drink."

"I do not care to drink, thank you. I want to discuss what you intend to toss away as though it were nothing."

"It *is* nothing to me."

"You only say that because you are unaccustomed to our ways. There is much that you do not understand—"

"No, *you* do not understand. I am more Kuabwa Mgeni than Anthony Maddox," he said forcefully.

Sophia sat still for a moment, looking at him intently. "What does it mean?" she finally asked. "Kuabwa Mgeni?"

Anthony had not thought about the significance of his name in years. "Stranger," he said. "And after I'd grown some, I was called Tall Stranger. That's what the words mean."

She said nothing, but pursed her lips and looked at him pointedly.

It meant nothing. He was no stranger to the people in those Ganweulu villages. He belonged there, in spite of what they called him. "The people often use descriptive names."

Sophia quirked her head slightly, but Anthony refused to be drawn into an argument. To his relief, she changed the subject. "Supper tonight is in your honor. We'll be having guests."

"I don't—"

Lady Sophia stood and started for the door.

"Seven o'clock," she said. "Full evening dress, if you please."

Anthony knew he should speak up now and repeat that he had no intention of assuming his father's title. But as he watched Sophia's retreat, her small form relying heavily on her cane as she left the cottage, he decided it would have to wait until another time.

He followed her outside and took her arm, placing it in the crook of his elbow. "You shouldn't walk all this way alone. I'll take you back."

Grace had nothing appropriate to wear but the light blue tulle gown she'd worn to Lady Sutton's last supper party. It was the same gown she'd worn the first time Anthony had kissed her.

She sat down at her dressing table and brushed her hair, deciding to arrange it slightly differently than usual. Instead of forcing her curls to lie flat, she arranged them to frame her face softly, and twisted the back into a more ornate style than she usually wore.

Opening the small box that held her few pieces of jewelry, she removed the long, gold chain that held her mother's locket, and slipped it over her head. Then she added a pair of small ear bobs.

One of the maids tapped at her door. "Miss Hawthorne, do you need my help getting ready? Oh my, your hair is lovely."

"I believe I'm all ready, but thank you, Maisie."

"Aye, you are," said Maisie with a giggle. " 'Tis a shame Mr. Bridewell will not be here tonight!"

But Grace could not manage to regret his absence. She caught sight of her reflection in the mirror and wondered at the woman who gazed back at her. She hardly recognized herself.

She'd changed since the previous day's adventure . . . or rather, *mis*adventure . . . and not for the better. Such intimacy was to be saved for a husband, not a barbarian who was on the road to becoming a rake. Grace realized that her actions had only supported such behavior.

Where had her common sense gone? Riding out without a groom had been her first mistake, one she'd never made before. Then going to that isolated spot on the river to weep her heart out, as though she had any legitimate complaints about her life.

She could hardly credit what she'd done, sacrificing her principles to fall into Anthony's arms again. And now she had to sit calmly with him at his grandmother's dining table and try not to think of how well he would suit Lady Aubrey.

Grace yanked on her long gloves and went downstairs, where she found Faraday, overseeing preparations.

"Has Lady Sutton come down?" she asked.

"Yes, miss. You'll find her in the small parlor."

She went to the other side of the staircase and entered the parlor where she'd last spoken to Mr.

Cooper. And discovered Edward Bridewell with Lady Sutton, dressed in his evening attire.

"My dear Miss Hawthorne," he said, bowing over her hand. "Lady Sutton has graciously invited me to join you for supper tonight, and to meet her grandson."

"I thought it only right, as Mr. Bridewell is our nearest neighbor," said the countess.

Anthony stood silent nearby, looking every bit as imposing as the Earl of Sutton should do.

"Oh yes," Grace said, forcing her attention from his striking figure, and turning to her suitor. " 'Tis lovely to see you, Mr. Bridewell."

Anthony wore black, with a crisp white waistcoat and shirtfront, and a white cravat tied expertly round his neck. He was freshly shaved, and he'd drawn his hair back into the neat queue at his nape. Grace did not understand how he could appear so composed, so very proper. Not after their uncontrolled interlude at the riverbank.

"You look quite elegant this evening, Grace," said Lady Sutton. "Do you not agree, Mr. Bridewell?"

Grace felt Anthony's eyes upon her, but did not turn to look at him. She could not trust herself to remain aloof as she should, as she must.

She smiled at Mr. Bridewell's compliments, determined to distance herself from Anthony. She should have known the widower would come tonight. And now he would think she had dressed especially for him.

As she should have done.

Grace wondered if Anthony knew the true reason his grandmother had invited Mr. Bridewell. While Anthony remained silent, Grace tried to settle her nerves.

It was a relief when they heard carriages coming up the drive. Grace knew Lady Sutton had invited Lord Rutherford and a few of the other peers who were members of the privileges committee. These were the men who would make a recommendation on whether to recognize Anthony as the rightful Earl of Sutton.

The noblemen entered the house with their wives, and servants set about taking the ladies' shawls and serving refreshments. It was a convivial group, and all the members seemed to know one another very well. Mr. Bridewell was introduced all round, and Grace noted that he mingled with ease.

Anthony did credit to Grace's lessons, greeting each guest very properly as they were introduced. But she felt all at sea with them, like a fraud who had succumbed to her darkest desires while being courted by the respectable gentleman who stood at her side.

Lord Rutherford arrived, entering the drawing room alongside a handsome and stylish dark-haired gentleman with deep brown eyes.

"Hugh?" Anthony said quietly, his expression incredulous. He took a tentative step closer to the young man and broke into a smile. "Hugh Christie . . . *Mbaya*. You have not changed in twenty years."

"Nor have you, my friend." He took Anthony's hand and shook it, warmly clasping it with his opposite hand. "I could not believe the news when I received your grandmother's note."

Another young man, this one fair-haired, came into the house with his wife, and when Anthony saw them, he grinned broadly. "Daniel Bryant!"

"Rothwell, now," the man said, returning Anthony's smile. They clasped each other in much the same manner as Anthony had done with his other friend, Hugh Christie, Lord Newbury.

The hard planes and edges of Anthony's face seemed to soften as he spoke to the two men. Grace felt her throat thicken with emotion at Anthony's unreserved welcome of Rothwell and Newbury. Perhaps now he would see how deeply connected he was.

"If there is any question about Sutton's identity," Mr. Bridewell said quietly, "no one could ask it now. How would he have known these two men if he were not Lady Sutton's grandson?"

Grace observed all the other gentlemen and tried to gauge their reactions to Anthony. Lord Rutherford, of course, needed no further convincing. He believed in Sophia's judgment. Lord Barrington stood back beside Viscount Nye and quietly watched. Lords Mattingly and Carlisle left their wives with the other women and joined Anthony and his two friends.

Rothwell's wife came to Grace and gave an artful bow, which Grace returned. She possessed lovely features, but most attractive of all was the sense of happiness that radiated from her. Her eyes seemed to glow from within every time they alit upon her husband, and Grace felt a twinge of envy over her obvious contentment.

She chided herself for such foolishness. All she really wanted—needed—was an honorable man who would marry her and treat her with kindness and respect. She was fortunate to have that man standing beside her.

"Miss Hawthorne, I understand you've been working with Sutton since his return," Lady Rothwell said.

Grace nodded. "Yes. It's been a very long time since he was in England. He needed a few pointers."

Lady Rothwell smiled broadly. "Well put, Miss Hawthorne. But you needn't worry about us. I can see that my husband is convinced he is truly Lady Sutton's grandson. I understand they were very close as children. I daresay Newbury will stand for him, as well."

Grace released a nervous breath. This was Anthony's first real test, and what happened here tonight would strongly influence the committee. She knew he had no interest in what they thought of him, but he looked incredibly handsome tonight, and as poised as the nobleman he was born to be.

"He does not care for all this, does he?" asked Lady Rothwell.

"Not really," Grace replied, unsure quite how to answer. "After so many years in the Congo, he was well acclimated to that life. He is not really comfortable here."

"Savage place, Africa," Mr. Bridewell remarked.

"Miss Hawthorne, do you think Sutton can be fully initiated into society?"

"Most certainly, Lady Rothwell," Grace said as Mr. Bridewell made a quiet sound of disbelief. She ignored his incredulity and looked at Anthony, standing together with Rothwell and Newbury. They were all of a kind, she thought, and she had no doubt that Anthony *would* acclimate once he renewed his friendships here. It had barely seemed possible before, but watching him now, she had to wonder if he might relent, and stay.

"I would not be too sure, Miss Hawthorne," said Mr. Bridewell. "Such an experience is sure to have changed him, fundamentally."

Grace let his remark pass, unwilling to open up such a conversation when so many of the lords on the committee were present. Besides, Faraday announced supper just then, and everyone followed Anthony and his grandmother into the dining room.

They took their seats and supper was served as Mattingly addressed the question that must have crossed everyone's mind. "What does Thornby say about all this? He cannot be happy with the situation."

"Heard he's been spending his blunt at the, er . . ." Lord Carlisle coughed into his handkerchief, then looked sheepishly at the ladies present. "Well, heard it was at one of the . . . clubs . . . in town."

Mr. Bridewell reddened beside her. " 'Tis too base a subject for discussion in mixed company, is it not?"

Grace took a swallow of wine and wished he had not interrupted. She was grateful when Lady Sutton ignored him and pursued the matter. Obviously, she wanted to know everything about Mr. Thornby's current activities, and Grace could not deny her own interest.

"Hamilton would not allow that bounder to squander the Sutton fortune," said Lady Sutton with indignation. "How is he able—"

"Perhaps I was mistaken, my lady," said Carlisle, regretting upsetting the countess.

"No, I've heard he's quite on the rocks these days," said Nye.

"Has it always been so?" asked Lady Sutton.

Grace was no expert on the comings and goings of gentlemen in London, but she'd heard of unsavory gambling clubs where fortunes could be won . . . and lost. And she feared that more went on in those places than gambling. Conversation stilled as the guests busied themselves with their food and drink.

"My lady," said Lord Rutherford in his frank manner, "Thornby has never been a model gentleman. However, he's been quite noticeably on the cut since word of your grandson arrived. Anthony's return has rattled him significantly."

Lady Sutton laid down her fork. "Thornby had better not be dipping into the estate's assets."

"The trustees would not allow it," said Barrington. "He must have some small fortune of his own."

"'Tis a complicated matter," Mr. Bridewell said.

Grace studied his profile as he followed the conversation. He was a decent-looking man, though his nose was a bit long in relation to his broad face, and his light hair barely covered the dome of his head. He was an opinionated man, though an honorable gentleman of substantial property, and Grace would be a fool to rebuff his attentions.

She had no intention of doing so. Yet when she felt Anthony's gaze on her, she allowed her own to drift toward his end of the table. He was seated at the head, with his grandmother right beside him.

His eyes smoldered with the same heat Grace had seen at the riverbank when he'd kissed her senseless. He did not allow his gaze to waver, and Grace stifled her frustration at the awareness that she felt Anthony's presence more keenly than that of the man right beside her.

Servants took plates and dishes away, and served the next course while Grace tried to ignore the tightening of her nipples and an intense quickening deep within her. She sipped her wine with feigned composure, and listened to Mr. Bridewell's conversation, even as a hot, carnal ache spread through the lower part of her body. She squeezed her legs together and wondered how she would get through the rest of the meal.

Anthony had no interest in supper. Not when all he could think of was tasting Grace again. He'd tried to keep his eyes from her and that pompous bore beside her, but she'd loosened her hair and worn the blue gown that displayed the delicate shoulders he wanted to kiss.

It was impossible to think of Ganweulu and his leisurely, tropical life when the lush curves of Grace's breasts taunted him with her every breath.

He wanted her naked. He desperately wanted more of her kisses, more of those small cries of arousal. Next time they came together, there would be no interruptions. They would not stop.

His course was clear, but there was naught to be done about it now. Later, when Bridewell and the rest of the guests had all gone, Anthony was determined to find her where she would most certainly be alone, in her bedchamber.

Anthony gave his attention to the dull conversation of the elder lords, answering all their questions about his life in Africa. He followed the protocol Grace had taught him, eventually turning his attention to Rothwell's wife for *pleasant* and *impersonal* conversation.

It was the last thing he wanted.

He felt raw and restless. He only vaguely heard the ladies' discussion of country houses, and city dwellings, and visits to Paris; Bridewell's remarks on the price of wheat. He listened to talk of a grand ball his grandmother would soon give at Fairford Park, but he was distracted by the long gold chain round Grace's neck, and the way its pendant teased the cleft between her breasts. He was captivated by that seductive freckle at the corner of her pretty lips and the soft curls that framed the delicate shell of her ear.

He would taste her there, then nibble his way down her throat as he unfastened her gown and laid her bare. He concocted many a plan for her seduction while the conversation droned round him.

When supper was finished, the men started for the terrace at the back of the house, for the night was fine. Anthony rose from the dining table and joined the men, who lit cigars and drank the brandy that was provided by the servants.

But Bridewell was conspicuously absent, and Anthony felt the hot flush of something dark and dangerous. The man was far too friendly with

Grace, and she had been flushed with the effects of the wine. Anthony excused himself and went toward the drawing room, but found himself sidetracked by voices in his grandmother's small parlor.

He found Grace there, with Bridewell looming over her, much too close to be proper. *Another suitor.* Anthony should have realized it from the way the man had hovered over her all through the evening. Now he stood ogling Grace's feminine qualities, and Anthony started forward.

"So, Miss Hawthorne," said Bridewell, "would tomorrow be agreeable, then?"

They noticed Anthony as he stepped into the parlor. "Agreeable for what?"

"Oh! Lord Sutton," Grace said with surprise, and Anthony gathered that she was not altogether pleased to see him.

Bridewell rocked up onto his toes and then down again, clasping his hands behind his back, clearly annoyed by Anthony's interference. "Suitable for an outing, my lord. A drive in the park."

"Mr. Bridewell, I am afraid Miss Hawthorne will be engaged all day tomorrow."

Grace looked up at him with fire in her eyes. "You are mistaken, Lord Sutton." She did not turn to Bridewell, even though it was he whom she addressed. "I would very much enjoy a drive tomorrow afternoon."

* * *

"Excellent," Mr. Bridewell said. "I will call for you at one o'clock."

Grace managed to rein in her anger when she spoke to Mr. Bridewell. "Perhaps you would like to join the gentlemen on the terrace," she said to Mr. Bridewell as evenly as possible. "I need a word with Lord Sutton."

"In truth, I must take my leave, Miss Hawthorne. My youngest daughter has had a slight fever all day, and I do not entirely trust the nursemaids to deal with her correctly."

"Oh, I am so sorry," Grace said as Anthony glowered nearby. As if he had the right to disapprove of her suitor. "I will pray for her swift recovery."

"Thank you," he said. "I will just bid farewell to the countess, and see you upon the morrow."

Grace waited for him to leave the parlor, then shut the door behind him, turning to confront Anthony.

"How dare you interfere?" she hissed, keeping her voice down so that none of Lady Sutton's guests would hear her.

Anthony had the audacity to cross his arms over his chest and glare at her.

"What I do with my social life—such as it is—is *my* concern, Lord Sutton. It is none of yours."

"He is an ass. He struts. Cooper was bad enough . . ."

The tone of his voice irritated her enormously.

He would engage in an illicit affair with her, would obstruct a legitimate courtship.

She turned her full fury on him. "I have every right to aspire to marriage and motherhood. And Edward Bridewell is . . ." She pressed one hand to her breast and took a deep breath. "Do not interfere with my affairs, *my lord*."

A distant, shuttered look came over him. He let his arms drop to his sides, and walked away.

A cold chill came over Grace. She might have had the last word, but she doubted she had won the skirmish.

Chapter 11

Anthony itched to get these ridiculous clothes off and dive into Fairford's pond. He wanted to swim in the cool water until his muscles screamed with the strain and he purged Grace Hawthorne out of his system. But the sight of Sophia's small, gnarled hand resting upon the head of her cane stopped him.

He had made her no promises. In truth, he'd made his position perfectly clear. He was Kuabwa Mgeni, and he did not belong here in high society with a cluster of men with soft hands like Cooper's, men who would not know how to wield a *kisu* if their lives depended upon it.

He wasn't going to remain here among them any longer than necessary. Soon he would have his revenge on Thornby and be done with it. His grandmother might appear frail, but he knew she was not. She had money and power and a hundred servants to see to her needs.

She had done very well without him and would continue once he was gone.

"How will you substantiate your claim as Anthony Maddox?" asked Lord Nye.

"Why should he have to?" Rothwell scoffed. "He knew Newbury and me without hesitation."

"Well, anyone might—"

"And how do you explain his appearance?" Rothwell added. "Look at the portrait of his father. Have you ever seen such a likeness?"

"There is certainly a resemblance," said Barrington. "But 'tis not proof, is it?"

"Is that old tree house where we used to play still on the property?" Newbury interjected.

Anthony nodded. "In decent shape, too."

"A house in a tree?" Lady Rothwell queried. "How wonderful! Where did you ever get such an idea?"

"'Twas my father's idea," Anthony replied. "We built it together a few years before my trip to Africa."

"And we three played there every time we visited Fairford Park," said Rothwell.

"Lord Sutton allowed you boys to sleep out there on occasion, if I recall correctly. Is that not so, Anthony?"

Anthony bowed to his grandmother's accurate memory.

"Let's go see it," said Rothwell. "Not many remembrances of my childhood remain at Castlelea."

When he stood, Anthony welcomed the excuse to leave the drawing room.

Grace had not spoken to him, nor had she looked at him since Bridewell's departure. Which suited him perfectly. He'd be a fool to become any more entangled here. He would certainly *not* seek her out later, as he'd planned, but leave her to dream of her pretentious suitor.

He joined Newbury and Rothwell, and as they started for the door, Lady Rothwell surprised them by slipping her hand into the crook of her husband's arm and joining them. "Miss Hawthorne," she said, turning back toward those who remained seated, "do join us. This should be fun!"

Anthony decided it *would* be fun, in spite of Grace's continued sour temper. Newbury took her arm, and Anthony resisted the urge to goad her by taking Newbury's place. He picked up a lamp and led the group out the terrace doors and over the cobbled path to the far end of the property. His eyes quickly adjusted to the twilight, but it would be full dark soon.

"Do you remember that time we dug a trench through your grandmother's rose garden?" Rothwell asked with mirth in his voice.

"You didn't!" cried Lady Rothwell.

"Oh yes, we did," Newbury said.

"It was to do battle against the French, as I recall," Anthony said. They'd had wooden swords and pistols, and they'd used them in a fierce battle against their imaginary foe.

"We won, too."

"Not against Lady Sutton, though," Rothwell remarked wryly. "We were all three punished. Remember?"

"As well you should," Lady Rothwell said.

Newbury laughed. "I was terrified of your grandmother after that."

"You were not," Anthony countered.

"I remember it," said Rothwell. "We were sent up to the nursery before supper, but Tony was the one who organized a foray down to the kitchen after dark for sausage pie."

Anthony lost himself in their reminiscing. Their friendship renewed, it was almost as though his twenty-two years in Africa had never occurred. They were chums back at school, joking and laughing together as they'd done as youths.

"Oh my heavens!" cried Lady Rothwell at the sight of the tree fort. "You actually slept way up there?"

"That we did, my dear," her husband replied.

"I would never allow Charles or Peter up there."

"Who are Charles and Peter?" Anthony asked.

"My sons," Rothwell replied. "Got two girls as well, Lilly and Maude. You and Newbury have some catching up to do!" he added with a chuckle.

"Where's the ladder, Sutton?" asked Newbury.

But Anthony hardly heard him. He was dumb-struck at the thought of Rothwell with four children. They were hardly more than lads themselves, weren't they? For the first time, he began to grasp the number of years that had passed in relation to his own age.

"How old are we, Hugh?" he asked before he remembered his old friend was to be called Newbury now.

"You and I are three and thirty this year," Rothwell replied. "But Newbury is younger." He found the ladder and started to climb. "Come on, Newbury."

Rothwell's sons were likely as wayward and roguish as their father had been. And his daughters . . . He glanced at Lady Rothwell, who watched uneasily as her husband climbed to the tree fort, then let his eyes wander to Grace.

She would have children . . . with Bridewell. Her body would grow as it nestled a child beneath her heart. Anthony had no doubt her eyes would glow with the quiet contentment of pregnancy.

Grace glanced at him just then, and he was struck by an image of her holding a tiny babe in her arms . . . of feeding it from her breast . . .

Rothwell laughed, breaking Anthony's concentration. "Come up, Sutton! 'Tis brilliant—just like the old days!"

"I'm not sure it will hold all of us at once," Anthony called up to him. "I'll wait here."

A moment later, Newbury climbed down, carrying the old, wooden box Anthony had left there. "Go on up, Charlotte," he said to Lady Rothwell. "I'll hold the ladder."

When she was up, Newbury held out the box to Anthony. "Remember this?"

He nodded.

"What did we put inside?" Newbury asked as he pulled unsuccessfully at the lid.

"Treasure maps and gold doubloons, if I remember correctly."

They heard Lady Rothwell's light laughter, and then a quiet squeal, and Anthony felt he knew exactly what was taking place up there. He'd done the same with Grace.

"You never married, Newbury?" he asked.

"I am a widower." Newbury's expression changed, his eyes dulling as though he'd drawn a curtain over them.

"*Mbaya*," Anthony muttered, unsure what to say. Such a situation was not something he and Grace had discussed in their lessons. He looked to her for guidance, hoping that her pique would abate sufficiently to respond.

"My sincere condolences, Lord Newbury," she said.

"And mine, Hugh." Since Grace said nothing

further, Anthony decided it must be best to let the matter drop.

Newbury changed the subject and held out the wooden box. "Do you still have the key?"

"I suppose it's still hidden away in the nursery where I left it," Anthony replied. "Shall we see?"

Lady Rothwell let out a shriek just then and started down the rope ladder.

"Wait, Charlotte! You'll fall!" her husband called.

But she pulled her skirts aside and managed to climb all the way down with Rothwell right after her, laughing as she hurried away from her husband.

"Go ahead without us," Rothwell said with a grin as he followed his wife into the darkness.

"Don't mind them too much," said Newbury. "They always seem half sprung when they're away from their brood."

Grace allowed herself to be shaken out of her irritation with Anthony, and observed their amorous camaraderie with wonder. She supposed she should be scandalized, but the Rothwells' wild streak was warmly appealing.

She shivered at the thought of what they might do when they found a private spot, but quickly put such notions from her mind. Her relations with Mr. Bridewell would surely be much more dignified.

"Miss Hawthorne," said Newbury, "has Richmond always been your home?"

"No, I grew up in London," she replied. She felt Anthony's hand at the small of her back as she walked between the two men. She had not taught him that possessive gesture, and wondered if it just came naturally to men, for he'd done the same at the solicitor's office.

Not that Anthony Maddox possessed her. On the contrary, she was looking forward to her drive with Mr. Bridewell. The wildness she'd felt with Anthony was best put aside and forgotten. So was her anger. She would not waste it upon a man who knew no better.

"You have family in London, then?" Newbury asked.

"No, my father died some years ago, and I lost my mother a year ago."

"I'm so sorry," Newbury said. "But you had a connection to Lady Sutton?"

"Yes. She and my grandmother were girlhood friends," Grace replied. "When my mother died, Lady Sutton asked me to come to Fairford Park as her companion. I've been here ever since."

Anthony's hand slid a bit higher on her back. She thought perhaps the movement was meant to comfort. Instead, the warmth of his touch spread through her like a wildfire. Her breath caught, and an unwelcome flush colored her cheeks.

"Your grandmother is a spirited woman, Sutton," said Newbury. "How old do you suppose she is?"

"I hardly know my own age, Newbury," Anthony replied. "How would I know hers?"

"She nearly eighty," said Grace. "She will celebrate her birthday at the St. Andrew's ball."

"Ah, the ball. I plan to attend."

"I'm very glad of it," Grace replied, though she did not intend to do more than make a short appearance, then retire to her own chamber. Anthony had proven himself ready to be introduced to society at large, and Grace had no need to witness it.

When they arrived at the house and entered the drawing room, the gentlemen stood for Grace's benefit, and Newbury set the wooden box on one of the tables.

"What have you there?" asked Lord Carlisle with disdain at the sight of the dirty box with its rusted hinges.

"This, gentlemen," said Newbury, "is an old treasure chest in which Sutton, Rothwell, and I used to hide our most secret, valuable possessions."

Lord Mattingly leaned forward to look at it. "Open it, why don't you?"

" 'Tis locked."

"That is a shame," Lady Carlisle remarked. " 'Twould be interesting to see what three young lads would have put in there twenty years ago."

"Sutton knows where the key is, I'm sure," said Lord Rutherford. "Don't you, my boy?"

"I once knew," said Anthony, furrowing his brow. "But I cannot be sure it hasn't been moved."

"Why don't we find out?" Rutherford asked. "Where do you think it might be?"

Anthony rubbed his forehead and cast a hooded glance toward his grandmother, and it seemed to Grace that he was weighing his options. Show the key to these members of the committee, and he would very likely be hailed as the Earl of Sutton. Decline, and there would still be doubts.

Lady Sutton bit her lip and somehow managed to keep it from trembling. Grace hoped Anthony would consider his grandmother's advanced age and capitulate just this once. Finding the key did not mean that he'd have to stay in England, but it would mean a great deal to his grandmother.

"In the nursery," he finally said, and Grace's heart swelled with affection for him, for he'd chosen not to be unnecessarily callous.

"Then shall we go?" Rutherford asked. " 'Twill take but a moment to see if this lad is the man we maintain he is."

Grace heard a low murmur rumble run through the other men and knew that finding a key in the nursery would not settle anything. But it would add weight to Lady Sutton's claim that the man leading the others up the stairs was truly her grandson.

"Fetch Faraday for me, please, Grace," said Lady Sutton. "He will light the room."

Grace did so, then returned to the drawing room and sat down next to Lady Sutton. "Are you all right?"

"Yes, yes . . . fine," Her Ladyship replied, although she still looked worried. "Go along with them, my dear. Tell me how they react. I want to know what is said."

Grace joined the group at the top of the stairs. Faraday had caught up, and with Anthony right behind him, they entered the nursery first and lit the lamps. The others filed in behind after them.

Grace stood just inside the door and watched as Anthony went to the window that overlooked the terrace. He pushed the curtain back and looked outside, then turned to Lord Rutherford. "I was a good deal shorter when I last put the key up here. I had to pull that bench over here and climb onto it." Without assistance this time, he reached for the top of the window frame and ran his hand along the full length of it.

"Not there, eh?" Lord Nye remarked, clearly unconvinced that the man before him was the true Earl of Sutton.

When Anthony dropped his hand and shrugged, Grace wanted to scream at his nonchalance. Of course he was Anthony Maddox! Lady Sutton had accepted him, and she was no doddering fool. Why could not Anthony say something that would convince these men?

She stood still as the others walked past her, exiting the room. Faraday, who'd been standing aside, spoke up. "My lord . . . What do you seek here?"

" 'Tis naught," Anthony replied.

"If it was a key," Faraday remarked, "I removed it years ago, during a spring cleaning. I put it away, if you'd care to see it."

Anthony had done what his grandmother wanted, but the result had not been unequivocal. Nye and Mattingly still doubted whether he'd truly left a key on the frame of the nursery window, or if the faithful butler had just spoken up in accordance with Lady Sutton's bidding. Barrington and Carlisle were not convinced, either, but they seemed inclined to believe Anthony was the Sutton heir, based on his friends' recognition.

There was nothing more he could do.

He went back to the drawing room, not really interested in whether the men believed him. His grandmother knew who he was, and that was all that mattered.

Rothwell and his wife returned to the house just then, smiling, but keeping what Anthony understood to be a proper distance from one another. Charlotte's pretty face was flushed, and there were a few wrinkles in her gown that Anthony had not noticed before. And Rothwell looked like a contented lion with a full belly, who could not keep his eyes off his mate.

The two sat down upon the settee, and when she laid her hand beside her, just hidden under her skirts, her husband surreptitiously placed his own over it. Charlotte closed her eyes and inhaled deeply, as though savoring the connection she shared with her husband.

An acute sense of isolation came over Anthony. He looked at Grace, who conversed quietly at the other end of the room with Lady Barrington. On the morrow, she was going driving with Bridewell. And, as she'd told him in no uncertain terms, it was none of his concern.

Yet she was not unaffected by *his* touch. Grace had responded passionately to him, up until the moment they were interrupted, or she remembered her damned propriety and drew away from him.

Anthony poured himself a glass of water and turned to Newbury. "Do you know anything more about Thornby?"

"I don't know the man at all, but I've heard a few things over the years."

"What kind of things?"

"That his wife will not live with him at Sutton Court."

Anthony stared blankly. "I don't understand."

"He's become increasingly fond of drink. And when he imbibes too much, he's a beast."

Barrington leaned forward and spoke conspiratorially. "Carlisle was right. Thornby spends all his time in town." He looked round, and saw that none of the ladies were listening. "At the Apollyon Club."

"Ah, yes. Gaming," Newbury remarked.

Barrington nodded. "Seems being in limbo does not agree with him."

"He prefers to go straight to hell," said Newbury.

"I would like to see this place, the Apollyon Club."

"That's probably not a good idea, Sutton," said Newbury.

Anthony looked directly at his old friend. "Nonetheless."

Grace was sure Lady Sutton would sleep now. The cup of warmed milk had settled her nerves, and she was yawning. "Good night, then, my lady." Grace tucked the blanket round the woman's shoulder and blew out the candle. "Sleep well."

She did not bother tightening the belt of her dressing gown as she slipped quietly out of Lady Sutton's bedchamber, for her own room was close by. She closed the door quietly behind her, wishing she had forgone that last glass of wine. She felt quite light-headed as she made her way down the corridor toward her own chamber, and nearly stumbled when she came upon the staircase to the third floor.

Over a pair of bare feet.

She caught her balance and faced the culprit. "What are you doing here?"

Anthony stood, but did not answer. In the faint

light of the hall, she could see that he still wore his evening trews and white shirt, but his cravat and coat were gone, his shirt unfastened. Grace pulled her dressing gown together.

"Lady S-Sutton's chamber is just there," she said uneasily, pointing to the room from which she'd just come. "If you came to see her—"

"I did not." He took a step toward her.

Grace's mouth went dry. She should take her leave, but her feet would not move.

Anthony touched her cheek, cupping her jaw. "Another suitor, Grace? What about your old friend Cooper?"

Grace closed her eyes and swallowed. She could barely think of Preston Cooper when Anthony was touching her. "I only invited him here to advise him of my disinterest," she said softly.

"And now Bridewell."

He came close enough to slide one hand round her waist. Pulling her body to his, he made a low growl when she was flush against him. "So soft."

All at once, he seemed to surround her, his hands skating down her back and pressing her hips intimately against his. He tipped his head down and took her mouth in an all-encompassing kiss. Grace's thoughts scattered, her awareness fully focused upon Anthony's touch, his kiss.

He moved his head again, deepening their kiss, sliding his tongue between her lips. Grace welcomed the intrusion as she moved against him, her body instinctually seeking further pleasure. She wrapped her arms round his neck, sliding her fingers through his unfettered hair.

It seemed she could not get close enough. A melting heat quickened deep inside her, but he suddenly broke their kiss and lifted her into his arms. With seeming ease, he carried her into her bedchamber and set her down inside, sliding her dressing gown from her shoulders as he did so.

She wore only a thin lawn night rail that seemed to glow white in the moonlight. Anthony pressed kisses to her shoulders as he slipped the garment from them, then cupped the naked fullness of her breasts.

It was pure bliss when he grazed her nipples with his thumbs, and Grace sighed when he took one sensitive peak into his mouth. She held his shoulders and let her head drop back, her eyes drifting closed as he pleasured her.

"*Nyinyi hidaya, sana mulia*," he whispered against her.

Grace did not know what the words meant, but they were spoken so tenderly that each one seemed to pierce her core. She felt as though she were falling, and opened her eyes to find that Anthony was holding her securely, in front of her mirror.

She saw herself half naked, a wild wanton skimming her fingers through his hair while he made intimate use of his mouth and tongue. It shocked her.

It horrified her.

With a sharp cry, she pushed him away. "My God." She said the words on a half sob, her voice hoarse with distress. She struggled with her gown and finally managed to tug it up to her shoulders. "I-I cannot—"

"Grace." He sounded as distressed as she.

"You must go. This is too . . . Oh dear God!" She turned away from him and went to the window.

But he did not go. She felt his hand at the back of her neck, his lips upon her shoulder.

"I want you," he said quietly, his breath tickling her ear.

"No!" she cried, though her nipples still tingled, still yearned for his attentions. " 'Tis impossible!"

" 'Tis entirely possible, *uzuri toi*. Now. Tonight."

And then he would go back to Africa as he'd always intended, without a thought or a care for her, or his grandmother. He was a solitary creature, and deep in her heart, Grace knew he would never change. His kisses were as hollow as Preston Cooper's.

She stepped away. "I want you to go," she said, her voice thick with emotions she struggled to control.

"You prefer Bridewell?"

"This is wrong."

He came to her then, and touched her face. She burned with longing, but knew it could never be.

Turning away from his touch, she closed her eyes to hold back her tears. "Anthony, please."

And then he was gone.

Anthony's swim the night before had done little to cool his ardor. He had not been sated by Grace's potent kisses or the touch of her body as he'd hoped. She was beautiful and sweet, as he'd told her in her bedchamber . . .

And he needed something to occupy his mind and body so that he could stop thinking of her. He went out riding with Tom. They took one of the eastern roads, and had been at it for a good hour when Tom said he needed to get back.

"You go ahead," said Anthony. "I want to go a bit farther."

"Ye've got the lay of the land, my lord."

Since they often rode this way, Anthony was familiar with the landmarks. He turned in his saddle and gave a nod toward the north. "That way is the road to Oxfordshire." He looked right. "This is the London road which I've already taken all the way into town, and here is the direction of Richmond Park." He did not mention the path to the river where he'd lost his senses in Grace's arms.

"M'lord, if ye're sure ye don't mind—"

"Not at all. I'll see you in the stable later."

"All right, then." Tom tipped his hat and turned round, leaving Anthony to consider his own road. With the restlessness he felt at the moment, he might have ridden all the way to Oxfordshire and dealt with Thornby. But now he knew Thornby was biding his time in London.

And yet he did not ride directly to the Apollyon Club, where Thornby was sure to be found. His thoughts were much too preoccupied by the woman whose every touch set him to flame. A flash of her eyes aroused him quicker than a butterfly could flick its wings, and the taste of her soft breast had brought him to his knees.

He shifted uncomfortably in his saddle, swearing viciously in English, as well as the Tajuru dialect.

It was well past noon, past the time when Bridewell would have collected Grace and taken her away from Fairford Park. The widower was much too tame for her, even if she did not see it. Anthony had known the same kind of starched and pretentious prig at school, and knew this one would never be able to satisfy her. If Anthony were the one to take her riding, he wouldn't seat her across from him on the soft cushions of a carriage, but pull her onto his horse behind him and gallop until they were both breathless.

He could almost feel the press of her body as she rode behind him, her arms round his waist, her breasts against his back. Their destination would be the riverbank, where he would lay her down in the soft grasses, unfasten her bodice, and push her stiff, prim gown off her shoulders.

Without giving further thought to his direction,

Anthony headed in toward the park at a determined trot.

It should have been a lovely day for a drive. The sun was shining and there was a pleasant breeze rustling the grass and the leaves of the trees. But Grace kept a proper distance between herself and her legitimate suitor, feeling like a sham.

He seemed overdressed somehow, although he wore nothing more than a plain frock coat and trousers. Perhaps it was his hat. She would have liked to see his pale hair gleaming in the sunlight.

Surely it would distract her thoughts from Anthony's thick, black locks and how silky they'd felt as they slid through her fingers.

"Your situation at Fairford Park is quite good, is it not?" Mr. Bridewell asked.

"I would say so, yes," Grace replied.

"Until now, I suppose. What with that African barbarian under your tutelage."

"He is no longer a barbarian, Mr. Bridewell," Grace corrected, and tried not to take offense on her pupil's behalf. "He has amended his ways . . ." She would not think of last night's interlude. ". . . and will soon be a perfectly acceptable gentleman."

"Do you really believe he is Lady Sutton's grandson?"

Grace looked at him quizzically and reminded herself that Mr. Bridewell had not had the opportunity to get to know Anthony, so his skepticism was understandable. "The evidence seems to point to it," she explained tactfully. "Lady Sutton is convinced. So are Lords Rothwell and Newbury, the two men who were his closest childhood friends."

"Hardly reliable witnesses."

"Of course they're reliable," Grace retorted, becoming impatient with his uninformed opinion. "These are men in full possession of their faculties and—"

"No, no . . . That is not what I meant."

She tried unsuccessfully to settle her ruffled feathers. "Perhaps you can explain?"

"It's just that their boyhood memories would have faded in twenty years. They see a dark-haired man of the correct age, who claims to be their old friend, and voilà."

"Or the three of them recall the same incidents from long ago, verifying the identity of the dark-haired man from Africa."

The widower gave her a little smile that felt more condescending than pleasant. "You can hardly credit Lady Sutton's memory."

"Why ever not? She has all her faculties, and would surely remember certain unique traits possessed by her grandson."

Mr. Bridewell drove on in silence for a few moments, then turned to Grace. "Let's don't speak of Lady Sutton's troubles. It is a beautiful Sunday, and we should enjoy it."

Grace took a deep breath and decided to capitulate. Time would demonstrate Mr. Bridewell's error, and there was likely nothing she could say to convince him. Nor should she. Not when Anthony himself did not care to convince anyone.

Grace forced herself to relax. "How is your daughter, Mr. Bridewell? Has her fever abated?"

"Yes, I am happy to say, Sally is much improved today. Though I did not allow her to go out to church."

"Very wise of you, I'm sure."

"Sally has always had a delicate constitution. Takes after her mother."

"And your other daughter?"

"Much more robust, fortunately. As are my sons."

"You are very fortu— Oh my heavens!"

"What is it, Miss Hawthorne? What is amiss?"

Grace swallowed and tipped her head forward. "Lord Sutton."

He was riding his black gelding, and coming directly toward them at a leisurely trot, looking tall and impossibly handsome in the saddle. The occupants of every carriage ahead of them nodded or tipped their hats to him, and he responded in kind, as though he had been raised among them.

Grace's heart sped up and she tried to contain the exhilaration she felt at the sight of him. She pressed her hands firmly into the cushions underneath her.

"Is this a coincidence?" Mr. Bridewell asked.

"I would imagine so," Grace replied, though she doubted it was true. Anthony Maddox might not understand what he was about, yet he was coming close to ruining what appeared to be Grace's one and only chance to secure a husband.

She knew better than to think she could rely upon Lady Sutton's largesse forever. One day the dowager would pass away, and Grace would be alone again, for Anthony would be long gone.

Appalled by such a callous thought, Grace slipped her hand round Mr. Bridewell's arm and braced herself to face Anthony, willing him to be silent about their encounter last night. She was not going to allow him to ruin this outing.

He approached the rig, and Mr. Bridewell brought the two horses to a halt, then doffed his hat and greeted Anthony, although Grace could see he was not happy about it. Anthony was hatless, but he returned the widower's bow and turned quickly to Grace. "You are such a good horsewoman, Miss Hawthorne," he said, "I'm surprised to find you sitting in a carriage."

"Phaeton," Mr. Bridewell corrected, then drew his lips up in a stiff smile. "A rig like this costs a bright penny, I'll tell you."

Grace barely heard Mr. Bridewell's words, not when Anthony looked as wild as a beast atop his horse, with his powerful legs bracketing his mount and his hair in disarray round his face and shoulders. He wore no neck cloth, and his coat was wide open, displaying his shirtfront.

But it was his brilliant green eyes that disturbed her most. They were fierce and savage as they took in the sight of her hand entwined with Mr. Bridewell's arm.

She tightened her grip on Mr. Bridewell, furious that Anthony had seen fit to interfere with her courtship. He had no proper intentions toward her, and yet he wished to ruin her chances here. "Lord Sutton, I believe I spoke to you about proper dress in public." Her tone was polite, but unquestionably censorious.

"I am sure you did, Miss Hawthorne. But I've chosen to ignore convention."

Grace's blood boiled at his hidden meaning. "You did not join us for church this morning as your grandmother requested." Though Grace had been grateful not to have to face him so soon after the near-catastrophe in her bedchamber.

He had the audacity to laugh. "My grandmother's dictates do not bind me, Miss Hawthorne."

"Simple courtesy—"

"—is not the question."

"No, 'tis whether or not you choose to stay in England and become the grandson she longs for. I understand completely."

Grace looked away from Anthony and smiled up at her suitor. "Shall we go on, Mr. Bridewell? I was hoping to see the lake."

Chapter 12

❦

The box from Anthony's tree fort sat open on a low table in his grandmother's parlor, with the key beside it. Lady Sutton drew out a few dirty metal discs and looked up at her grandson, puzzled.

"Toy doubloons," he explained. "I don't know where Father got them, but he let us play with them."

Lady Sutton removed an old, yellowed parchment that had been rolled and tied with a strip of leather. "And this?"

"Open it," Anthony replied. "'Tis a treasure map. I believe Rothwell drew it. He was the artist among us."

Sophia raised her eyebrows as she unrolled the old drawing and smiled wistfully at the young boy's artwork. Anthony recalled the happy times when they'd spent their holidays running like bushbucks—innocent and free—all over the estate.

Anthony reached into the box and pulled out a

roll of twine and a well-worn, miniature painted wooden horse.

"I sent that to you at school," Sophia said.

A pang of nostalgia washed over Anthony, and he felt a burning at the back of his throat. Every time he'd gone back to school, his grandmother had secreted some treasure into his luggage, something he would not discover until he'd unpacked and found himself missing home. He'd played endlessly with that little horse, pretending he was riding it on the adventures he knew his father was taking while Anthony was away.

"This was in my trunk when I started my second year, before Hugh arrived."

"We missed you terribly every time you went away."

He shrugged and told himself it did not matter. Not anymore, regardless of what Grace Hawthorne had said. Sophia had gotten along very well without him. "It was a long time ago."

Sophia sat back in her chair. "Imagine Daniel Bryant—Lord Rothwell—married. And with four children. Where does the time go?"

Anthony started tossing the old toys and keepsakes back into the box. He was an adult with no use for them now.

"Charlotte seems a good match for him, don't you think?" Sophia asked.

"Umm," he said noncommittally. If Lady Rothwell's demeanor when she'd returned from her assignation with her husband was any indication, then she was a good match, indeed.

He'd seen such pleasure in Grace's face, yet she'd ended their tryst to preserve her innocence for Bridewell. Anthony could not believe she preferred his grandmother's neighbor to him, and knew she'd leaned close to the man in his carriage only to goad him.

Which was absolutely fine. By keeping Anthony at arm's length, Grace Hawthorne had ensured that she would be one less memory for him to carry back to the Congo. She could marry her arrogant widower and settle for a man who would never know her worth.

It was exactly as it should be.

He stood and went to the fireplace, and rubbed his damp hands down his thighs, finding it exceedingly difficult to forget about those moments in her bedchamber. He could taste her still.

"I am going to the orphans' home this afternoon," Sophia said. "Would you care to join me?"

His grandmother had felt disappointment on Sunday morning, when he'd declined her invitation to accompany her to church. And though she hid it well, she was not able to completely mask the hope in her eyes. Anthony sighed just as Grace came into the room wearing a plain, dark gray gown.

She did not notice him at first. She'd avoided him since their encounter in the park, and she clearly did not expect to see him now. "Lady Sutton, are you ready to—"

Anthony returned to his grandmother's chair and looked at Grace. When she clenched her teeth together, he knew he could not help himself. "I do believe I will accompany you, my lady."

"I thought you might prefer to practice your riding skills on the way to St. Andrew's, Lord Sutton," said Grace acerbically. It was much too close in the carriage, and the ride to the orphanage just north of London was becoming interminable.

"On the contrary, Miss Hawthorne," he said. "I have done a great deal of riding. My skills are entirely adequate."

Grace knew that was true, for he'd been going out riding with Tom Turner every day. But she could not resist provoking him, especially with the way he strived to irritate her.

She put her feet directly in front of her, but he managed to slip one of his big, booted appendages up against hers. She tried to engage Lady Sutton in a discussion about preparations for the ball, but he stole the conversation with talk of his exploits in the Congo.

He charmed his grandmother with his tales, taking care never to touch upon the anguish he'd felt upon finding himself alone and far from home. Nor did he mention his intention to leave England. In spite of herself, Grace admired his sensitivity to

Lady Sutton's distress over what had happened to him, and how she would feel once he decided to go.

It was all she could do to keep her eyes from alighting upon his broad shoulders and square chin. She wanted to ignore the hum of her body at his proximity and refrain from thinking of the wickedly carnal interludes they'd shared. Grace decided that such passion was unbecoming a civilized woman. Mr. Bridewell was going to prove a perfectly adequate husband and lover, one whose passions would never cause her to lose her own—

"Grace?" Lady Sutton said. "Would you ever want to visit?"

Her mouth was nearly too dry to speak. "Visit?" she croaked.

"Africa. The dark continent."

"The Congo," said Anthony, spearing her with his gaze.

Grace refused to give him the satisfaction of showing any interest at all in the place he considered home. She bit her lip and appeared to consider the question. "I think I would prefer to see Greece," she finally said. "And Spain."

She felt supreme gratification when he shifted in his seat, mistakenly believing his unease was in reaction to her reply.

"Good choices, my dear. I've been to Spain, and of course to Portugal to meet my grandparents," Lady Sutton remarked, oblivious to the undertones of Anthony's and Grace's interchange. "But that was many years ago."

The corner of Anthony's mouth tilted up slightly and he spread out his long legs, taking up most of the floor of the carriage.

Pointedly, Grace turned her head and looked out the window, thinking of the pleasant Sunday afternoon she'd spent with Mr. Bridewell *after* Anthony had left. They'd stopped at the lake, gotten out of the widower's stylish phaeton, and strolled along the woodland paths. The gardens were breathtaking, and her suitor's company had been entirely agreeable. Not once had Grace needed to correct his conduct or help him to improve his conversation.

Never had she been tempted to touch his hair or slip her hand into his.

"Oh look, here we are," Lady Sutton said as the carriage slowed and halted on a gravel drive.

Anthony opened the door and stepped out, then assisted his grandmother down the steps. Grace moved quickly, contradicting her own lessons by starting down the step alone, to avoid gentlemanly assistance.

But Anthony was quick to take her hand, apparently determined to torment her with his touch. She'd made it quite clear that any liaison between them would be wrong. It would be completely improper, and she would not allow it, even though her heart quickened and her step faltered when he touched her.

"I-I will remain with the footmen while they unload," she said. "Please go on ahead, my lady."

Anthony would be compelled to escort his grandmother inside, which would give Grace a few moments out of his company.

It seemed that his every move was calculated to remind her of the sensual encounters they'd shared. The way his gaze lingered upon her lips, then moved down the front of her bodice, could only call to mind her wanton reaction to his touch.

Thankfully, Mr. Bridewell had not made any such improper advances. Grace could trust him to behave as a respectful gentleman who was steady and reliable. One who had no plans to abandon all that was important and go haring off to some uncivilized corner of the world.

Grace watched the footman and gave directions as they unloaded the goods they'd brought. The children always seemed to need clothes and shoes, blankets and other bedding, as well as books for their lessons. The money Lady Sutton raised at her charity ball would go far toward making repairs to the building and buying coal for the coming winter.

The footmen carried the boxes inside and stacked them in the anteroom, which was vacant, as was the matron's office. Grace figured it was likely the woman was taking Anthony and the countess on a tour of the facility.

The arrangement suited Grace. She went to the

room where the smallest infants were cared for, and took an apron from a hook near the door. Greeting the woman and two older girls who looked after these children, Grace went to the cradle of the babe who was crying the loudest, and lifted him into her arms. "There now, young master. What can be done for you?"

"'Tis time for a change of nappies and a feeding," said the caretaker.

Grace was happy to oblige.

Anthony wished he'd had the sense to decline this trek with his grandmother and Grace. He was not generally a foolish man. At a very early age, he'd had to learn what needed to be done under the most difficult possible circumstances, and then carry it out. Yet here in England, things were different. Nothing seemed quite so clear-cut.

The hour spent in the confines of the carriage had been pure torture. That pretty freckle at the corner of Grace's lip had tormented him every time she spoke, and he had not been able to ignore the feminine contours of her body that had melted against him that night in her room.

For one so soft, she'd managed to sit stiff and upright for the entire ride to St. Andrew's, and deliberately kept her gaze from meeting his. She'd been flushed and out of sorts upon their arrival at the orphanage, matching the heated frustration Anthony himself felt.

St. Andrew's Home was a bleak, red brick building, three stories high, with one wide, dingy window in each room. The scuffed, wooden floors creaked as he and Sophia followed the matron down the halls, looking into dormitories and stopping in classrooms.

The children stopped their lessons or their games as Lady Sutton visited each of the rooms, and were clearly glad to see her. Anthony noted the look of sincere delight upon his grandmother's face as the children came to her and greeted her fondly. He came to sense how deeply Sophia must have felt his loss.

He observed her frail form as she went from room to room asking the teachers how the children fared, and calling many by name. It seemed to Anthony that she must have assuaged her grief for him and his father through her work here.

Anthony's efforts to survive had effectively done the same. While hunting for food and trying to keep himself safe from predators, he'd had no energy to waste on his misfortunes. The Tajuru had not allowed him to stay with Dawa and her family, so he'd kept busy building a secure house in his acacia tree—more of a hiding place—far above the dangers on the ground. And when night came . . . he'd been all alone to dwell upon the dangers he faced and the losses he'd suffered.

No doubt his grandmother spent the hours after dark mourning the same.

Lady Sutton finished her tour of the rooms without encountering Grace in any of them. Feeling restless and uneasy with all these abandoned children, Anthony somehow managed to refrain from pacing. He needed to get out of doors, wanted to breathe in the warm summer air and swim hard and long in the Fairford pond. His muscles ached to run and climb, but he held himself fast and gazed through a window at the front of the building.

The Sutton carriage had been pulled off the drive and stood waiting near a stand of trees, unattended. There was no sign of Grace, either.

Finally, his grandmother was ready to leave. Anthony assisted her down the cold, stone staircase to the ground floor, where she went into the matron's office.

"Are you coming?" she asked.

"No." He could not stand another moment in that closed-in space. Could not understand why the children were not outside, running. Playing.

"Well, then, will you see if Grace is in the nursery?" She gave a nod toward a door across the anteroom. " 'Tis where she most likes to visit."

He hesitated, glancing toward the main entrance, intending to escape the bleak place. Instead, he clenched his teeth, walked across to a noisy room on the opposite side of the anteroom, and pulled open the door. There, he saw an older woman with two adolescent girls tending a room full of infants in cradles and cribs. Grace was there as his grandmother had predicted, sitting in a rocker with a very small, but very loud, babe in her arms.

She was rocking and patting the child's back while she sang softly, her lips brushing his downy-haired head. Anthony's arrival in the room drew her attention, but did not distract her from her task of comforting the child. Her posture was more relaxed than Anthony had ever seen it, and as she continued to rock, she stroked the infant, and cooed to him to quiet him.

Her bonnet was gone, and now she wore a plain white apron over her dark gray gown. The infant tangled his fingers in the hair behind her ear, and she gently dislodged them, smiling sweetly as she held his tiny hand in her own. Anthony swallowed hard at the sight she presented, at the languid sensuousness of her actions.

Anthony shuddered with hunger for this alluring woman and cursed himself for a fool.

No doubt she would nestle her own child at her breast in a year's time, given the way her courtship with Bridewell was progressing. She'd sat closer to her suitor in that damned phaeton than Anthony knew was proper, and grasped his arm altogether too familiarly. And the smile she'd given the man . . .

He muttered an unsavory word under his breath and made a hasty exit from the room.

* * *

Grace frowned up at the spot Anthony had just vacated. He had been perturbed, his face ruddy with color, his hands fisted at his sides. She gazed down at the infant who'd just fallen asleep in her arms, then softly kissed his forehead and rose from her chair to put him to bed.

Two years ago, she'd set aside her hopes for a husband and her own children. Her mother's illness had taken all her time and attention, but now Grace could entertain those dreams once again. Mr. Bridewell's affections would surely supplant the impossibly wild cravings Anthony never failed to arouse in her.

She knew better than to trust such passions. A cautious, temperate man was exactly the kind of husband she wanted. *Needed.* One who would never leave her vulnerable, leave her shaken and dazed by a mere touch, or stupefied by a kiss.

Grace took a shaky breath and finished her tasks in the nursery. She removed her apron and went to the anteroom, where she assumed she would find Lady Sutton and the matron. Instead, she found Anthony, pacing the length of the floor.

He stopped when he saw her.

"Is something amiss?" Grace asked. "Wh-where is Lady Sutton?"

He took her by the arm and led her to the door. "Naught is amiss. 'Tis merely time to get out of this dreary place."

"Do not let your grandmother hear your assessment of St. Andrew's."

"She is no fool, Grace," he said tersely as they went outside and walked briskly to the carriage. "She cannot help but know."

Grace pulled her arm away. "What is wrong with you?"

He'd been a pesky annoyance on the ride from Fairford Park, but now he was positively malicious. He braced one large, heavily veined hand against the carriage, and Grace could see him clenching and unclenching his teeth. He did not answer her question.

"Where is your grandmother?" she asked.

He tipped his head in the direction of the orphanage. "Not finished." His words were clipped.

The carriage stood in an isolated spot, yards away from the drive, partially hidden in a grove of trees. The footmen had gone inside for a drink, and so Grace was alone with him. It was the last place she should be.

She tore her gaze from Anthony's strong back and the glossy, dark hair that brushed his shoulders. Grace chided herself for thinking of hot, intimate caresses on a warm spring day. "A proper gentleman would return to the building and escort his grandmother back here to the carriage."

He whirled on her, emotion burning in his eyes. He was visibly struggling to hold himself back, to keep from reaching for her.

"I am *not* a proper gentleman, nor will I ever be, Miss Hawthorne, no matter how many lessons you give!"

To be the cause of such passion was dizzying. Pure, liquid sensation pooled in Grace's nether regions, and her bones started to soften. She took a step closer, but caught herself before she reached him.

"That is quite obvious, Lord Sutton," she said quietly, though at the moment, a proper gentleman was the last thing she could think of. On shaky legs, she returned to the orphanage to collect herself.

Grace entered the building and encountered Her Ladyship coming out of the matron's office. "Where is Anthony?"

She spoke more calmly than she felt. "He is waiting outside at the carriage, but he seems rather out of sorts."

"Oh?"

"Perhaps he did not enjoy our outing," Grace said. "I doubt he is accustomed to small children."

Lady Sutton's brow furrowed. "I do not think that can be it, Grace."

Grace knew that wasn't it, either. But it was clearly not her place to itemize everything that was really bothering Lady Sutton's grandson.

Anthony rode up top with the driver all the way back to Fairford Park, but the brisk ride did little to ease all that ailed him. He felt pent up and caged, like a wild beast taken out of its natural habitat, and forced into a box with too few airholes. They finally arrived at the house, and Anthony stormed through it like the raging wind of a sudden gale.

He stopped abruptly at the sight of half a dozen vases of flowers cluttering the corridor, and saw even more of them filling his grandmother's parlor.

Grace and Sophia came in right behind him. In unison, they exclaimed over the bounty in the room, examining each bouquet, and pulling out the cards that had been inserted among the flowers.

Anthony flew past the maids who were in the process of carrying the flowers from the hall into the parlor, when he heard his grandmother's voice. "All from Mr. Bridewell?" she remarked, sounding altogether too pleased.

Anthony's stomach burned. He needed to get out of there, but Faraday came to him from the back hall. "My lord?"

"Our Mr. Bridewell is in earnest, then," he heard his grandmother say to Grace.

"It seems so," she replied.

Anthony needed fresh air. A climb to the top of his tree. A hard ride. Anything to rid him of the peculiar sensations that had been growing ever since the moment that morning when he'd set foot inside the carriage with Grace and his grandmother.

"My lord," said Faraday, breaking into Anthony's thoughts, "a man awaits you."

"A man? Who is he?"

"Sent from London with a message," Faraday replied. "He's waiting in the kitchen."

Anthony stood rooted to the floor at the sound of his grandmother's voice in the parlor.

"Grace, here's an invitation. He wants you to accompany him to supper this evening."

Anthony snorted and walked back to the kitchen. What did he care if Grace wished to place her hopes in a man who could make a dung beetle appear interesting?

He stalked into the kitchen where the cook and two helpers were busy working on preparations for a meal. A dusty young man stood abruptly when he saw Anthony.

"Lord Sutton?"

Anthony nodded curtly, and the man handed him a folded, sealed note. " 'Tis from Lord Newbury," he said.

Anthony read quickly, then turned to Faraday. "Send someone out to saddle my horse." Then he spoke to the messenger. "I'll meet you at the stable."

He headed toward his cottage to change clothes and began to breathe more easily. As he took steps to make his escape, he felt the late afternoon sun on his face, and it seemed he was lord of all the savannah.

Newbury's man was waiting to accompany him to London.

* * *

The mixture of floral scents was nearly over-powering, and Grace felt choked by it. And after the tension she'd felt all during the ride home from St. Andrew's, she wanted some fresh air. A brisk walk was just what she needed before her supper engagement.

"What does Mr. Bridewell think of Anthony?" Lady Sutton asked Grace.

"My lady?"

"He must have said something during your drive the other day."

"I believe he thinks you should, er . . ."

"He does not believe he is my grandson, does he?"

"Not yet," said Grace. "But he will. He is a cautious man."

"Hmm," said Lady Sutton. "He's always been a bit suspicious, too. No doubt he thinks Anthony a fraud, set up to swindle me."

"I would not go so far, my lady. He merely voiced a few misgivings."

And Grace would not hold that against him. He could not have been more attentive or appealing on Sunday afternoon. And now all these flowers—as cloying as they might be—constituted a grand gesture. His intentions could not be more clear.

"Lady Sutton, if you don't mind, I would like to take a bit of a walk. It will be some time before Mr. Bridewell comes for me."

"Not at all, my dear. I believe I'll have a short lie down myself."

Grace made a quick change of shoes, then headed for the door just as Anthony came round to the front of the property on horseback with a strange man at his side. His expression was one of determination and . . . relief. The two men took to the road at a gallop, and Anthony never looked back.

"Faraday," Grace said to the butler as he came to close the door behind her. "Who was riding with Lord Sutton just now?"

"Lord Newbury's man," Faraday replied. "I believe he came to take Lord Sutton to London for the night."

As Anthony rode alongside Hendrie, he relished the freedom of his ride. He'd had enough of carriages and women . . . and flowers.

He enjoyed riding horseback. It was a pleasure he'd forgotten during his years in the Congo, when he'd traveled only on foot. Here he was able to cover longer distances in far less time, but it was the speed and the sense of flying that enthralled him. It would be difficult to give this up.

The ride to London took nearly an hour, and Anthony remembered the route and landmarks he'd noted on his previous ride.

"We'll take one of the paths through the park, my lord," Hendrie said. "Lord Newbury's house is not far from it."

It was late afternoon and the sky had turned cloudy, but that did not deter the Londoners from walking, riding, and playing in the park. Anthony passed a number of gentlemen on horseback, as well as ladies riding sidesaddle as Grace did. But the London ladies wore much more elaborate clothing than Grace, with hats that were as ornate as the ceremonial headdress worn by Jahi, the Moto chief.

Several of them glanced his way, making eye contact and then smiling in a manner that seemed to invite further interaction. But Anthony did not feel the slightest stirring of interest. These women were much too obvious to intrigue him.

They emerged into a street lined with tall, stately houses. The dwellings were smaller than his grandmother's, but this was an entirely different setting. The houses were much closer together, and there were people walking or riding, and carriage traffic in the street.

"Just down this way, my lord," said Hendrie, turning into yet another busy road.

A few minutes later, they stopped in front of a handsome brick house, where Anthony dismounted, then climbed the steps while Hendrie took charge of his horse.

A servant showed him into a drawing room where Newbury sat reading a newspaper while he sipped a clear, reddish-brown liquid from a crystal glass.

Newbury rose immediately, folding his newspaper and tossing it aside. "Sutton. Glad you were free to join me."

Anthony shook the other man's hand as he looked round the room.

"Do you remember the place?" Newbury asked.

"Not really," Anthony replied. "I suppose I visited here at one time or another?"

"A few times, actually, although I came to Fairford Park more often than you came here. It was always much more exciting out there."

Anthony could see that that would be so, especially from a child's point of view. How would three young boys have amused themselves here?

"I thought you might not mind getting away from Fairford Park, at least for one night."

Anthony felt his teeth clench and put aside the image of Grace standing at the front door of his grandmother's house with her hat in her hand as he rode past. Nor would he think of her at St. Andrew's and her expression of contentment as she'd held the infant in her arms. "You have no idea."

Newbury laughed. "The season is at its peak. You have but to name your diversion and it will be done. I assume you brought evening wear?"

Anthony nodded. "You mentioned it in your note."

Newbury showed him to a guest bedchamber. "I'll send up my valet to help with your bath and get you dressed. When you're ready, we'll start at my club."

Anthony held his tongue at the ridiculous notion of a servant helping him bathe. What was there to it? Water, soap, something to dry with . . .

He dismissed the valet as soon as the tub was full. After bathing quickly, he went into the bed-chamber, where the servant had laid out his freshly pressed clothes. This time, he accepted the man's assistance, for dressing in the English manner was a much more complicated task. When he was ready, he went down to meet Newbury in the library.

His friend handed him a glass of spirits and Anthony took a sip, grimacing at the burning in his throat.

"Sorry. Didn't realize you hadn't had time to develop a taste for whiskey," said Newbury.

"You'll forgive me if I do not finish." Anthony set the glass on a low table. "I prefer water."

Newbury grinned. "I believe you'll be able to get away with it, too."

"What do you mean?"

"Well, look at you. You're obviously a man to be reckoned with. No one would dare call you anything less than a man."

Anthony looked at the awful drink he'd just discarded. "Spirits—this whiskey—it defines a man?"

"Not entirely," Newbury replied, giving a smile that was entirely reminiscent of their childhood.

"There are many factors." Hugh was the youngest and always the mischievous one, playing pranks on most everyone in the household, or hiding when he was meant to return to school, while Daniel was unfailingly good-natured.

"Grace spoke of honor and responsibility," Anthony said. "There was no mention of whiskey."

"Grace? Ah yes, Miss Hawthorne." His voice changed as he spoke her name. "How did that come about? The lovely Miss Hawthorne as your tutor?"

Anthony's eyes narrowed, vaguely displeased by the overcurious tone in Newbury's voice. Having been childhood friends did not qualify him to be privy to Grace's background. "She has some connection with my grandmother."

"It seems strange that she is not already married."

Anthony thought he'd shaken that odd, restless feeling on his ride to London, but it seemed to have returned in full measure, like insects crawling up his legs. "What is your interest in her?"

"She is companion to your grandmother, is she not?"

"Yes."

"I thought perhaps I could interest her in something a bit more exhilarating."

Anthony frowned. "What, exactly?"

Newbury laughed and started down the stairs to the front hall, with Anthony right behind. "It cannot have escaped your notice that Grace Hawthorne is a beautiful woman."

The sensation of red, biting ants increased. Anthony stopped abruptly. "So?"

"And she has a most agreeable air of innocence about her."

"Your point, Newbury?"

"Come now, Sutton, you cannot be as naïve as all that. I would gladly take her as my mistress." Newbury left the house and climbed into the shiny black carriage at the bottom of the steps.

Chapter 13

Anthony refused to ponder the notion of Newbury and Grace, intimate together. She had rejected Anthony's advances, so it was obvious she would reject Newbury's proposition. Surely.

"Miss Hawthorne has a suitor," he informed Newbury, though that situation did not bring Anthony any peace, either.

Newbury dropped the subject and spoke of various functions they might attend that evening. They decided to visit Newbury's club first, and have supper there while they discussed their options.

Anthony found it a good deal more relaxing than he would have anticipated. Warm, wooden paneling covered the walls, and thick, colorful carpets softened the floors. He found the quiet hum of English-speaking voices surprisingly soothing to his ears, and the delectable aroma of simmering meats and other sundries tantalized his palate. There was no such fare to be had in the Congo, and Anthony realized the taste of meat cooked over an open flame had faded from his memory.

Newbury did not mention Grace again, and the two men regained their camaraderie easily. They'd both grown into men with starkly differing experiences, yet their shared memories seemed to provide a deep link between them.

Which was absurd . . . a trick of memory, perhaps, for he had no real bond with Newbury, or anyone else. Anthony knew where he belonged, and it was not in any of these elegant, cosseting drawing rooms.

But there was no reason he could not relax here for the moment, and enjoy the comfortable atmosphere, and the food that had been caught and prepared for him, especially when his other old friend, Rothwell, joined them.

"So, you decided to brave our wild and wicked city, Sutton?" he asked.

"I thought I'd take him round to some of the clubs," Newbury said, and gave Anthony a curious look. "The Apollyon, perhaps."

But Anthony had not decided whether he wanted to confront Thornby just yet. When he'd first awakened at Fairford Park with a bump on his head and a sprained ankle, he'd been ready to take his *kisu* to Oxfordshire, find Thornby, and gut him for what he'd done to him twenty-two years before. Now Anthony knew he wanted more than just a quick, clean kill. He wanted to look the bastard in the eye and show him how badly he'd failed.

Newbury turned to Rothwell. "You seem well-pleased tonight."

"That I am. We'll be heading back to Castlelea on the morrow. Therefore, I must take my leave of you, gentlemen. The children are in a state, anticipating our return to Norfolk, and I do not like to leave my dear Charlotte to deal with the rascals without me."

"That's what nurses are for, Rothwell."

Rothwell turned to Anthony, who saw a glimmer of potent contentment in his old friend's eyes. It was as though he could not bear to be away from his woman for too long. Grace's kisses could do that to a man.

"Good to see you, Sutton. Perhaps you'll come up to Castlelea and we can enjoy more of a visit then."

"You're becoming dull, Rothwell," said Newbury. "Are you sure you wouldn't care to join—"

"Why would I wish to take part in your dissipated evening when my lovely wife will be waiting for me, bouncing our youngest son on her knee?" He grinned good-naturedly, then stood and bowed to all present. "I must beg off."

"*Mbaya*," Anthony muttered as he stood, too, thinking of the warm affection with which Lady Rothwell would greet her man. Which called to mind Grace's sweet scent and the sensation of her fingers sliding through his hair. Would that she would welcome him home, and to her bed.

She'd said their passion was wrong. Impossible.

And yet she'd responded to his touch like a wildfire on the savannah. She was either lying to herself . . . or she was afraid.

Mr. Bridewell took Grace's shawl, folded it neatly, and placed it on the chair next to her. Then he took his seat as Grace looked round the dining room of the Richmond Arms Hotel.

She wondered what Anthony would be doing in London tonight. Surely Lord Newbury had many connections in town, and would have any number of invitations. They could attend a ball, or a fashionable soiree. Or perhaps Newbury would take him to one of those terrible gambling places.

"It looked as though preparations for Lady Sutton's ball were well under way at Fairford Park," Mr. Bridewell said.

"Yes," Grace replied absently, worried that Anthony might get into difficulties at one of those clubs and have to rely on Newbury to rescue him. She had given him absolutely no instruction on how to comport himself in the kind of venues that Newbury would—

"Miss Hawthorne?" He placed his hand atop hers, stilling her fingers. She had not realized she was drumming them lightly on the table.

"I'm sorry . . . I was just . . . admiring the room."

She spoke in a bright tone, even though she did not feel particularly cheerful. " 'Tis very richly appointed, is it not?"

Mr. Bridewell gave it a quick perusal, then returned his attention to Grace. " 'Tis adequate."

He ordered their supper, and Grace forced herself to relax. Anthony's trip to London had been a very good idea. He needed to spend time with his peers in order to understand their ways. *She* certainly could not teach him the nuances of life as an English nobleman.

And she truly wanted to concentrate on Mr. Bridewell.

"Your gown becomes you," he said. "The color matches your eyes."

Grace smiled warmly. "Thank you. And thank you again for the flowers. You shouldn't have sent so many—"

"You must know they represent only a fraction of my admiration."

His affecting words embarrassed her when she should have felt pleased by them. They hinted at an intimacy that made Grace feel vaguely uncomfortable. "I was surprised to receive your invitation to supper."

" 'Tis very soon, I realize," he said. "But our Sunday afternoon together was most enjoyable."

"Yes, it was."

"Next time, we shall bring the children with us," he said. "A Sunday outing does them good.

But weekdays, I do not allow them to become too lax."

Grace peered quizzically at him.

"They have their lessons, and their chores as well, for I have no intention of raising my children to be lazy or careless."

"'Tis . . .'tis very admirable, I'm sure." Grace thought of her own father and his relaxed manner, and fondly remembered their excursions to London attractions. She wondered if Mr. Bridewell ever relaxed his position with his children, and thought perhaps a woman's gentle hand would improve their rearing.

"My late wife did not understand discipline," said Mr. Bridewell.

"I think a mother's instincts might naturally give her a softer attitude, Mr. Bridewell."

"Ah, but you are young, Miss Hawthorne. And inexperienced in such matters." He looked at her with a gaze that felt more condescending than kind, and Grace decided she could not let his remark pass. She was well-read on the subject of children, and many other topics, besides.

"I believe there are several schools of thought on the principles of child rearing," she said.

"No doubt invented by childless spinsters who have little to do with their time."

His harsh dismissal of her statement gave her pause, but their supper arrived and Mr. Bridewell turned the conversation to his fields and his hopes for a good summer crop. He spoke of the improvements he was making to his barn, and the additional plow horses he'd recently purchased.

Grace listened distractedly. Surely that roomful of flowers and his precipitous supper invitation indicated that a proposal of marriage was imminent. And yet the man went on about sheep and plows, and other aspects of life at Bridewell Manor.

He had a deep crease between his brows when he spoke so earnestly, and his broad cheeks grew pink with his enthusiasm. Grace had never known anyone who could speak so extensively on winter feed grain.

"Is your beefsteak not to your liking, Miss Hawthorne?"

Grace looked down at her plate. "Oh, 'tis very good," she said, taking up her knife and fork again. But the next few bites could have been sawdust for all that she tasted them. Her connection with Mr. Bridewell was not progressing as she thought it might. He'd seemed so very anxious to see her tonight, but she could not fathom why. He might have been alone for all the interest he showed her.

She waited until he'd finished his meal and then asked him to return her to Fairford Park.

"Are you all right, Miss Hawthorne?" he asked as he rose from his seat. "You look a bit pale. Did the meal disagree—"

"No, no, I'm quite all right. I just . . ." She

touched her fingers to the bridge of her nose. "I seem to be developing a slight headache."

"Who has your grandmother chosen for you?" Newbury asked Anthony as they rode toward the Apollyon Club. They'd returned the carriage to Newbury's house, and taken their horses.

"Chosen for me?"

Newbury laughed. "A wife, chum. No doubt she'll have invited any number of silly young beauties to her ball whose charms you are meant to peruse."

Anthony's throat went dry. He wanted no wife.

And yet there was Grace, stern but sweet, proper to a fault but vulnerable. She could rouse his ardor with her smallest smile, and make him burn for more. Yet she'd said his kisses were *wrong*.

"Don't worry. No matter who Lady Sutton chooses for you, you can always take a mistress."

Anthony gave his old friend a sidelong glance. "Which is what you had in mind for Miss Hawthorne? That you would pay her to—"

"She could do worse." Newbury said it in an offhand way. As though Grace could be treated as a commodity, like the wheat in Bridewell's fields.

"It would not be the first time a beautiful woman without marital prospects accepted a protector," Newbury added.

"What do you mean—without marital prospects?"

"A woman with no dowry, no family. No father or brother to see to her future. Such women often take lovers—men who support them. Of course these women lose any claim to respectability. Once an unmarried woman lies with a man . . ."

But Grace had prospects. And a room full of flowers to prove it.

Anthony felt his gorge rise at the thought of Bridewell—or any other man—touching Grace. He had no doubt she would decline the kind of arrangement Newbury described, yet he did not care to think about her respectable evening with Bridewell.

If Anthony were with her, he'd drive that damned phaeton to a secluded place and pull her onto his lap and kiss her until neither of them could think.

He drew up short.

"What is it, Sutton?" Newbury asked, already a few paces ahead.

Anthony shook his head just as a wild ape would do when he wanted to rid himself of a pesky fly. " 'Tis naught. How far to Thornby's club?"

"Not very. What will you do when you see him?"

He glanced at Newbury and decided to tell him the truth. "Kill him."

Newbury laughed. " 'Tis pure moonshine, Sutton."

Anthony did not understand his meaning.

"You jest," Newbury explained.

Anthony shrugged. "I am deadly serious."

"For what? For taking Sutton Court?"

"Nothing so inconsequential," Anthony replied. He stretched his shoulders and neck as they rode. Tonight he wanted only to look into the eyes of the man who'd tried to kill him, though he doubted Newbury would understand the nuance of the hunt. Anthony intended to unnerve his prey before he killed him, to show him that his reckoning was upon him.

They soon came to an unassuming building that was much like Newbury's club, though no light penetrated the thick, dark curtains that covered every window. The two men left their horses in the care of the Apollyon grooms and were quickly admitted inside by a servant.

"My lord," said the man with a bow, as they stood in the foyer. The adjoining rooms were closed off by sturdy oaken doors, so Anthony could not see inside. But a large staircase stood directly ahead. "If you would but tell me your preference . . ."

"Vingt-et-un," Newbury replied, and the servant extended his hand toward the down staircase, and the two men descended. " 'Tis Thornby's preferred game," Newbury said once they left the servant behind. "Do you plan to kill him here?"

Anthony shook his head. "Nor do I intend to speak to him."

Newbury frowned in concern. "I'm with you,

old friend, but do you mind telling me what you *do* intend to do?"

"Nothing. Just put him on notice. Draw him out." As he'd have done with his prey in Africa. Thornby would feel compelled to come to him.

A quiet hum of voices reached them when they got to the bottom of the steps. Anthony went ahead and stepped into the first room. He took note of every table and every patron, for it would be useful to know as much as possible when he returned. Some of the men bore expressions of desperation, others looked gleeful.

"Not here," said Newbury. "These are faro tables."

Anthony withdrew and followed his friend into another large room, and then a third, searching for the one where Thornby's game was played.

Finally, they entered a room where a layer of smoke hovered just under the ceiling. Again there were round tables full of men, but these fellows held no cards in their hands. The man in control of the cards sat on one side of the table and served cards to each of the players.

Newbury nodded. "In here."

Anthony perused the tables, but saw no one who looked like the man who'd kicked him into the raging Congolese river. "I don't see him," he said quietly to Newbury.

"Dead center."

Anthony turned his gaze to the table Newbury

pointed out, and looked carefully at each man. Three were too young to be Thornby, and another three were much too old. As he studied the remaining two middle-aged men, one of them looked up and caught Anthony's eye.

It was he. And he had not aged well.

Anthony did not allow his gaze to waver. He met Thornby's bloodshot, annoyed stare and watched him until the man's brow furrowed and recognition dawned. His already florid skin turned a deeper hue, and he picked up the crystal glass at his place and downed the liquid inside it.

When Thornby slammed the glass down on the table, Anthony turned away and headed back up the stairs.

"Is that it?" Newbury asked.

" 'Tis all for tonight."

They left the club and went round to the mews for their horses, rather than waiting for a groom to bring them, for Anthony did not want to chance another encounter with Thornby. They rode out onto Jermyn Street and started back toward Mayfair.

"What is it about Thornby?" Newbury asked. "Is it the title—his challenge?"

Anthony gave a shake of his head. "I'm sure 'tis difficult for you to understand how little I care about the title or my standing in England."

"It could only be one thing, then. You hold him responsible for what happened to you in Africa."

Anthony gave a bitter laugh. "Thornby shoved

me off that boat into the raging river, Hugh. His intent was murder."

Grace had developed a real headache by the time Mr. Bridewell had taken her home the previous evening, so she'd taken a powder and gone right to bed. To her dismay, her sleep had been fraught with images of Anthony Maddox in evening clothes with his hair tied back, displaying his sharp cheekbones and square jaw. In her dreams, she'd seen his hands, and felt them caress her while he'd kissed her mouth and neck.

Her headache persisted for most of the following day.

Grace entered the ballroom, looking for something to help keep her troublesome thoughts at bay.

"Is anything wrong, Miss Hawthorne?" Miss James asked.

Grace bit back a sharp retort and gave Miss James and her companion, Mrs. Drayton, a wan smile. She might be restless and out of sorts, but it was no fault of the ladies who had been working so hard to make the charity ball a success. "No, everything is just fine."

She longed to become Mr. Bridewell's wife. He'd come calling on her at least once a week for the past three months, and she knew he intended to propose. Perhaps he had been nervous last night and unable to take the plunge. After all, he'd been a bachelor since his wife had died more than five years earlier. Such a significant change in status could not be easy after so much time.

And Grace was more than ready. She had always hoped for a home and family of her own, and this was her chance.

"What do you think of these palm trees?" asked Mrs. Drayton, who'd come to help put the finishing touches on the decorations.

"Magnificent," Grace said, though she had a feeling Anthony would not appreciate his grandmother's efforts in recreating his African setting. For all he would know, every English ball was decorated in such a way and this was nothing special.

And yet she could almost hear him asking about the trees and how they'd been made. Grace gazed up at the tall palms and wondered what Lady Sutton's grandson had been doing while she'd gone to supper with Mr. Bridewell. No doubt his activities with Lord Newbury had been much more sophisticated than hers.

And a great deal less disappointing.

"Here are the refreshment tables," Mrs. Drayton said.

"And this is where the orchestra will be situated," Miss James added, and Grace began to feel even more irritable. In two days' time, Anthony would be in this room, dressed in his fine new evening suit, dancing with some of the *ton*'s most beautiful, most marriageable debutantes.

Feeling unfit for company, she left the house and went for a long walk to try and clear her mind. She brushed away tears of frustration and confusion, wishing she had never set eyes on Anthony Maddox, yet feeling pangs of regret that she had not taken him to her bed the night of Lady Sutton's soiree.

Oh, what could she be thinking? There was no honor in such a liaison, no basis for a respectful bond between them. Mr. Bridewell's approach was wholly proper and courteous, and Grace appreciated the sensitivity he showed toward her. He made no unwelcome advances, caused no unhealthy fluttering in Grace's breast.

And soon she would become his wife.

Anthony Maddox was just an inconvenient wrinkle in the cloth of her life. When he returned to Africa, Grace would have her home and her own family here in Richmond, and remain close to Lady Sutton.

She finally returned to the house and was persuaded to join the countess and Reverend Chilton for supper. She should have welcomed a diversion from her bothersome thoughts about Anthony but found no respite at the table as Lady Sutton talked incessantly about him.

The countess was in a fine mood, anticipating the coming ball and Anthony's introduction to society. She turned suddenly to Grace. "Grace, have you taught my grandson to dance?"

Grace felt her face heat with discomfiture when she realized she had completely forgotten that lesson. "N-not yet, my lady."

"Come, come, Miss Hawthorne," said the reverend. "There are only two days until the ball."

"Yes," Grace said, her heart dropping to her stomach. "I . . . I . . ."

"He'll need to know the country dances . . ." the reverend added, "but also the waltz."

"Sutton will learn quickly," said the countess. "He is very agile. Very physical, indeed, wouldn't you agree, Grace?"

Grace swallowed the lump in her throat. "He is."

"My dear," said Lady Sutton, "has your headache returned?"

"A little, my lady."

"Perhaps you should go up to bed?"

"By all means, Miss Hawthorne. Wouldn't want you to come down with something and miss Her Ladyship's ball!" said Reverend Chilton.

"No, of course not," Grace said lamely. She excused herself and went outside for some air.

Before Anthony returned to Fairford Park, he rode down to the dock and dismounted, then started to pace. Leaving was the right thing to do—it was what he'd wanted from the moment he'd left Africa. All he need do was to deal with Thornby, then he would be free to go. He could not allow himself to dwell on the women at Fairford Park. They would go on, almost as before. Grace would marry Bride-well, but would remain close to Fairford Park.

It was the perfect situation.

He jabbed his fingers through his hair and swore, feeling surly and miserable. These crowded London streets and the city's foul air did not agree with him. He wanted to get away from the stink of the river and the suffocating, black coal smoke, and the sooner, the better.

Walking his horse close to the water, Anthony called to the sailors on every ship until he got the answer he sought. A Belgian ship called *L'oiseau de Mer* would be putting out for the east African coast in two days, and the captain was more than willing to take on a paying passenger.

He quickly paid the seaman for his passage, before he could change his mind. Then he mounted his horse and made for the western road.

His stomach burned. Pressure built in his head.

All was progressing as he intended, yet the farther he rode, the worse he felt. He'd taken the first step in his revenge on Thornby, unnerving the man so he would err when Anthony finally confronted him. He tried to focus his thoughts on his next move, but found his mind turning relentlessly to Grace and that pretentious farmer who wanted her.

Mbaya, could she not see how miserable she was going to be, tied to Bridewell? He supposed she would be respectable, but she would know no joy, and certainly no pleasure.

Not like he could give her.

He arrived at Fairford Park feeling even more ill-tempered, more frustrated than when he started out. He left his horse with a groom and made for his cottage in the darkness, peeling off his shirt and dropping it as he moved. Tonight, the smell of the flowers along the garden paths was just as overpowering as the load of nauseating blossoms Bridewell had sent to Grace, and Anthony knew that only a thorough dousing in the cool pond near his cottage was going to clear his head.

Half naked already, he started on the buttons of his trews, but soon collided with a very soft, very feminine object in his path.

"Anthony!"

He gritted his teeth at the sound of Grace's voice, the very last person he'd hoped to see tonight . . . the last person he'd intended to knock down. He quickly shot out both arms to catch her.

Her breathing came fast, and she eased away from him, putting space between her chest and his.

"Are you all right?" he asked, finding it impossible to release her entirely.

She did not protest his gentle grip on her forearms. "Yes. I'm sorry. I didn't see you."

"What are you doing out here in the dark?"

"Walking," she replied. "I was . . . Y-you were not back, so I thought . . ."

"You thought what, Grace?" The burning in his stomach relented.

She smelled of lavender, and Anthony leaned closer and inhaled deeply. It was the only floral scent he could deal with tonight--perhaps ever.

She cleared her throat. "That th-the ball is only two days away," she said quietly.

He did not want to talk about the ball. He wanted her to touch his bare chest. He had nipples, too, and they peaked at the mere thought of her fingers on them. His cock roared to life at the idea of her tongue on them.

"I know."

She hesitated. "I need to teach you to dance."

"Oh aye, Grace, teach me. Right here and now." There was nothing he wanted more than to feel her in his arms.

"But we have no—"

"We have all that we need." He had a vague childhood memory of a dance here at Fairford, and knew that he was to take her into his arms and move in time with musical accompaniment. He drew her close, slipping his arms round her waist.

"No," she said breathlessly. "'Twould be scandalous for you to touch your partner this way."

"'Tis how I want to touch you, *uzuri toi*."

He took her hands and moved them to his chest, sliding them up to his shoulders, shuddering as they grazed his nipples. He tipped his head down and caught her lips with his own, bending his knees slightly to maximize the contact between them.

She took a shuddering breath and angled her

head to accept his kiss. Anthony's heart quaked when she skimmed her fingers through the hair at his nape and pulled him down to her. He slid his tongue into her mouth and tussled with hers as his erection grew and pressed against her.

Anthony feathered his fingers across her breast, then worked the buttons of her bodice, desperate to feel her bare skin against his.

"Grace," he said in a whisper as he broke away. He lifted her into his arms and carried her to his cottage, kicking open the door to get inside. He did not bother lighting a lamp, but took her into the moonlit bedchamber, where he sat down on the bed, keeping her in his lap.

He pressed hot kisses to her throat and worked on the rest of her buttons and laces. In his haste, he did some damage to the stiff device she wore underneath, but her sigh drifted through him, setting his blood on fire as he pulled away the last barrier to his touch.

She let her head fall back, and he kissed the fluttering pulse at her throat. Her naked breast filled his hand, and when he brushed the nipple with his finger, she gasped, but did not pull away. When Anthony leaned down and took it into his mouth, he felt as though his heart would burst.

He laved the taut peak with his tongue, and she made a small sound of arousal, trembling at his sensual touch. Anthony pulled the pins from her hair and let her soft curls cascade down her back, and he slipped his hand through the fragrant mass.

Shifting positions, he laid her on the bed, gazing at her pretty eyes in the moonlight while he teased the tips of her breasts with the ends of his fingers. She shivered and pulled him down to her, taking his mouth in a soul-stealing kiss. She was small beneath him, yet fiery with ardor, her response as intense as it had been the last time he'd kissed her, touched her.

He slipped one leg between hers, but her skirts impeded him. He fumbled with the buttons that trailed below her waist, aware that he'd never wanted anything the way he wanted Grace. But he was getting nowhere.

"Grace, take it off," he said quietly.

Anthony's deep voice vibrated through Grace. His steel-hard body covered her, and the press of his thigh between her legs made her ache for deeper contact. She touched the rough angle of his jaw, and the glittering intensity of his eyes obliterated every coherent thought.

She only knew that she belonged here. With him.

With one hand, she managed to unfasten the buttons of her skirt, and Anthony quickly dispensed with it. The rasp of his tongue against her nipple pulled at the core of her being, quickening her womb with a fierce yearning. Mindlessly, she arched upward, inviting his raw touch.

He slid one hand down her abdomen, and Grace grabbed a handful of his hair, feeling uncertain. But his touch was intoxicating. Addictive. She wanted more, but knew she should not.

"Trust me, *uzuri toi*."

She did. She could risk everything—her heart and her innocence—for this man who was like no other.

He covered her lips with his own as he touched her most private place, a tiny nub she had barely noticed before. The resulting sensation was more intense than anything Grace had ever known. He flicked one finger and she broke their kiss, gasping with pleasure.

"Anthony . . ." she breathed, so unsure.

"There is much more, sweet one." He moved away from her mouth and slid down her body. "You are so beautiful, sweet Grace. I want to touch and taste you."

Grace took a sharp breath when he encircled one hand round her knee and pressed a kiss to the incredibly sensitive skin there. He bent her knee and skimmed his mouth up, pressing searing kisses to each of her tingling legs. His big hand was suddenly under her buttock, and he opened her up, feathering his lips and tongue over the wildly sensitive apex between her legs.

As responsive as a wanton, Grace could not keep from rocking against his mouth, from striving toward a savage need she could not define.

It happened suddenly. Grace cried out and saw stars. Her heart clenched in her chest, and all her muscles squeezed tightly. Anthony growled in response while Grace writhed with pleasure.

Anthony moved again, bracing himself over her. In one quick move, he plunged inside her, then held perfectly still while every one of his breaths came in hard gasps.

It burned, but Grace felt pleasure, too, emanating from that sensitive nub that still reverberated with satisfaction. She made a faint sound at the back of her throat and pressed herself against Anthony, yearning for another climactic explosion. Slowly, he slid out, and back in, then increased his pace to create a rhythm that caused a renewed frenzy of need in Grace. She wrapped her legs round him, and held on tightly.

She peaked once again, her heart beating madly as Anthony shuddered and groaned, then collapsed onto his side, pulling her with him. Grace felt his heart against her breast, and knew he'd felt the same staggering rapture that she had experienced.

Their hearts and lungs slowed, and Anthony gently swept her hair back from her face. He dropped sweet kisses on her forehead, then her mouth.

She felt him inside her, a part of her, as a husband would be. And yet he was not her husband. She'd taken a lover.

At length he withdrew, and Grace winced.

"Are you all right?" he asked.

She swallowed hard and looked at Anthony's handsome face in the faint, silvery light of the moon. Never had she behaved with such utter abandon, rejecting every precept she'd been raised to respect and keep. She'd violated the most basic of society's tenets by sharing Anthony Maddox's bed.

Her heart quaked with the knowledge that she'd ruined everything, betraying not only Mr. Bridewell, but herself as well.

The taste and smell and feel of Grace Hawthorne was imprinted on Anthony's soul, and he wanted nothing more than to take her into his arms and make love to her once again. But slowly this time, drawing out their pleasure all night long.

"Did you enjoy L-London?" Grace asked, her voice soft and tremulous. He felt unsteady, too, as though the earth would not stop trembling beneath them.

"Aye. But not enough to stay. Did Bridewell propose?"

She gave him a startled look. Then, with a strangled cry, scrambled from the bed and started gathering her clothes from the floor. Anthony went to her and took her by the shoulders, loving the soft bounce of her breasts, the feminine crests of her hipbones, the shadowy secrets between her legs. He bent to kiss her, to apologize for his tactless mention of Bridewell, but she moved abruptly and tried to whirl away.

He held on to her waist and turned her to face him. In the moonlight, he saw a sheen of moisture on her cheeks, and he frowned. He cupped her face, running his thumb over her cheek. "Tears, Grace? Did I hurt you?"

She made a low whimper that sounded like despair and pulled away from him, quickly dragging on her clothes.

"Grace, are you . . . Don't go."

"How can I stay when you will not?"

"But I . . ."

Helplessly, Anthony watched as she fumbled and failed to tie her laces correctly. She managed to pull on her gown, and hastily worked on the buttons as she ran from the cottage as though it were on fire.

A hot, painful swell of emotion expanded in Anthony's chest and threatened to choke him. He'd never felt such raw desire before, and he ached with the knowledge that his desperate yearning for Grace had resulted in hurting her.

She was right. He had every intention of being on *L'oiseau de Mer* when it left, two days hence.

Why had he not followed his better judgment and escaped England as soon as his ankle had healed? Had he done so, he would not be pacing here in front of his cottage and wondering how badly his actions had injured Grace.

Mbaya. Marriage prospects. They had naught to do with him. It was well past time he left England and returned to the Congo. The life he knew and loved awaited him there, where he had no duties and no responsibilities, passing his time hunting, fishing, and sleeping.

What could be better?

"*Nothing*," he grumbled. But his stomach roiled, even worse than before. He had to get out of there.

He drew on his trews and took the narrow path to the pond at a run. But a sharp pebble tripped him up, and he stopped to hop on one foot, swearing viciously.

Life was much simpler without women, he decided, although his body still hummed with the pleasure of Grace's touch. He did not want to feel any attachment to her, or to anyone else in this country. He did not want to know whether she wed Bridewell, or see the day she moved from Fairford Park.

He dropped his trousers at the edge of the pond. Diving in, he barely noticed the cool temperature of the water. He swam vigorously to the far end and back so many times that he lost count.

Once he dealt with Thornby, *L'oiseau de Mer* could not depart England's shores fast enough to suit him.

Chapter 14

If misery had a name, it would be Grace Edwina Hawthorne.

Morning dawned and Grace had not managed to sleep at all. She'd torn her bed apart in some kind of mad restlessness, and finally left it to sit at the window and stare outside. Feeling feverish and chilled in turn, she did not know what to do. Perhaps she should just pack her bags and be done with it. She'd done the unthinkable, and now she would surely pay for it.

An ill-omened chill came over her. How could she have abandoned her principles so thoroughly?

Some kind of madness must have taken over in the moonlight last night. Anthony's touch had stirred the impossible longings that lurked deep within her, and an untamed streak she'd never known she possessed. She had responded to him like a wanton, a woman with no morality, no honor.

And now Grace was mortified. In every way.

She took particular care in dressing, as though meticulous attention to her appearance might mitigate what she'd done, might disguise the dark circles under her eyes. She could not bear to think of all that had happened—*all that she had allowed*—in Anthony's bed last night. No true lady would ever have allowed even a kiss . . .

Grace sat down on her bed and covered her face with her hands. She had gone so much further than a mere kiss, and for only one reason.

She'd fallen in love with Lady Sutton's impossible grandson.

Grace's breath came out in a low whimper.

It would never have happened if she'd observed society's rules. Instead, she'd forsaken the proprieties over the past weeks and permitted intimacies that would make a harlot blush. And now she would have to bear the pain of watching Anthony sail away from England's shores.

Or take Lady Aubrey Kinion as his wife.

Grace pressed a hand to her chest and reminded herself that a perfectly suitable gentleman would soon propose to her if he did not learn of her indiscretion.

And how would he hear of it? Grace would not tell him, and she doubted very much that Anthony would say anything. If there was any justice in the world, Grace would marry Mr. Bridewell, and move into his manor house nearby. And she would share his bed.

Grace ignored the gnawing feeling in the pit of her stomach. She had to get herself ready for her day, which was sure to prove a difficult one. She finished dressing, then twisted her hair into a tidy knot and pinned it securely at her nape. It was past time to join Lady Sutton in the breakfast room.

"Perfect!" Sophia said as Anthony entered the breakfast room. "You are just the man I want to see."

"Good. I want to talk to you, too."

"Fill a plate and sit down," Sophia said, casting a glance toward the doorway. "I cannot imagine what's keeping Grace. She is usually ahead of me."

Anthony rubbed one hand across his face and dragged out a chair. But he wanted no food. He wanted to get as far away as possible from Fairford Park and all the entanglements here.

A servant poured tea into his cup, but he ignored it, just as he ignored the ridiculous dream he'd had of Rothwell and his wife, the two of them cavorting happily together. Because it had not been Lord and Lady Rothwell. It had been he and Grace.

Which was pure moonshine, as Newbury would say.

He had to tell his grandmother that he was going to leave. That any plans she'd made for his future were irrelevant. That he intended to bury whatever he felt for Grace and get out of England as fast as he possibly could. What an idiot he'd been to trust that—

"Well. I see you are not hungry."

"No," he said. "Avó, I—"

"What did you say?"

"I haven't said anything yet. But I—"

"You called me Avó. Just as you did as a boy."

He damned his mistake. In all the time since his return to England, he'd managed to keep her at arm's length until he could make his escape. And yet he'd forgotten himself in every possible way. Making love to Grace, calling his grandmother by his pet Portuguese name for her. And now he was about to crush her expectations.

And Grace's.

He felt her before he saw her.

She came to the door and stopped short when she saw him. The sight of her caused an instant arousal, but he was fairly certain she did not feel the same, for she barely looked at him. He damned his hunger for her and managed to disguise it with an expression of indifference.

"Good, you're both here," his grandmother said. "Come in, Grace. Come in and sit down."

Grace wore a white gown with some sort of pale blue pattern in it—a dress that disguised the alluring feminine curves that lay beneath it, curves he longed to touch and caress once again. Her hair was drawn back into a simple knot, and she smelled of the lavender scent she favored.

Anthony fisted his hands at his sides to keep from reaching for her.

"Oh, well . . . my lady," she said in a voice that sounded rough to his ears, "I do not wish to intrude—"

"Are you unwell, Grace? You do not sound good. And your eyes . . . Come here and let me look at you."

Reluctantly, she did as she was told, sliding daintily into a chair next to Sophia. The countess put one finger under her chin and raised her face to study it, and Anthony frowned at the dark circles under her eyes. "Did you have trouble sleeping last night, my dear?"

Gently, Grace took his grandmother's hand and lowered it. "I'm fine, my lady."

"Well. If you say so." Sophia glanced at Anthony. "What I have to say concerns both of you."

Anthony should have felt some satisfaction in knowing Grace's night had been as sleepless as his own, but he did not. He watched her carefully, wondering again if he'd hurt her, knowing why she'd run from him. But she shuttered her eyes, making their expression indecipherable.

Deciding it would be best to make it known to his grandmother that he'd booked his passage to Ouidah, he turned to her and addressed her formally, regaining some distance. "My lady, I . . ."

But Sophia took a small piece of paper from a little leather-bound book that lay beside her plate, and handed it to him. "Here is a list of eligible young ladies that Grace and I have chosen for you. I would like you to dance with each one tomorrow night, and decide on one or two who might suit you."

"To what purpose, my lady?" He kept his voice cool and indifferent.

"To court, of course. You must marry. Soon, my boy!"

He placed one hand over the list, but did not actually look at it. It did not matter whose names were on it. He would wed none of them. He would not even be present to dance with them. "You know my intentions," he said to his grandmother.

Grace stood abruptly. "My lady, if you don't mind," she said, her distress unmistakable. "I believe I'll forgo breakfast this morning."

"You are ill, dear girl. Of course you must—"

The countess did not have a chance to finish her reply before Faraday came into the room with an announcement. "There is a visitor. Mr. Cooper."

"Oh!" Grace said, clearly disturbed by the butler's statement, "I . . . I'm not sure—"

"Be seated for a moment, will you, Grace?" Sophia said, and turned to the butler. "Send him in, Faraday."

Anthony bristled at the thought of Cooper calling on Grace. Had she not refused his suit? He leaned back in his chair and crossed his arms over his chest as the man himself came into the breakfast room.

Holding his hat in his hands, Grace's tall, angular *unsuitable* suitor stopped suddenly when he saw everyone gathered there. He recovered quickly and bowed to Lady Sutton. "I beg your pardon, my lady. I did not mean to interrupt your breakfast."

"'Tis early for a social call, is it not, Mr. Cooper?" The countess spoke with an edge of acerbity in her voice, and Anthony realized his grandmother did not like the man.

Nor did Anthony. Cooper's intrusion put him even more out of sorts when he thought of his treatment of Grace when she would have needed him most.

"*Mbaya*," he muttered when he realized he was making himself miserable for no good reason. He glanced at Grace, and noticed that she seemed to be holding her breath.

Anthony felt immediately better at her unease. She was not pleased to see Cooper, either.

"My lady," Cooper said, fingering the hat he held in both hands. He bowed yet again, and spoke to Sophia. "I've come with news."

Lady Sutton raised an eyebrow.

"The Lords' Committee on Privileges wishes to meet this afternoon. Here at Fairford Park."

Grace realized with chagrin—and relief—that Mr. Cooper's visit had nothing to do with her.

He'd only arrived at Fairford Park to deliver a message from his employer.

Not to see her, thank heavens.

She would not yet have to speak to him while Anthony's touch, his scent, and the influence of his powerful embrace were still fresh in her mind and in her heart.

She felt light-headed and realized she was breathing much too fast. Looking down at her hands in her lap, she inhaled deeply through her nose and worked to compose herself, but all she wanted to do was run from the room.

Anthony had not taken his eyes from her since she'd arrived, and she wondered what he must think of her. She'd run away from his bed like a child who'd misbehaved. And now he looked at her with fire in his eyes.

He was angry.

As if he had the right.

"What time will they arrive?" Lady Sutton asked Mr. Cooper.

"Not until late afternoon, my lady."

Anthony stood and walked to the row of windows opposite the sideboard. His shoulders were impossibly broad, his waist and hips narrow underneath his casual suit of clothes. Grace knew his arms and chest were thick with muscle. She'd felt the wonder of his solid but gentle touch. He smelled like the air outside, fresh and virile, and

Grace closed her eyes with the memory of his lovemaking—so tender, yet as forceful as the man himself.

He did not look back, and Grace felt some relief from the intensity of his gaze. He turned his attention to the gardeners trimming the lawns as though that undertaking was the most important thing in the world, dismissing her. Grace should not have felt abandoned, and yet . . .

"Finally. Well, we are ready," Lady Sutton said, her words causing a deepening of Anthony's color and a tightening of his jaw.

Grace wondered when he intended to leave. Had he booked his passage on a ship while he was visiting Newbury in London? Or did he plan to leave Fairford Park without a plan and take his chances on the wharf?

"Miss Hawthorne." Mr. Cooper faced her and gave a slight bow, oblivious to the way her heart was quaking in her chest at the thought of Anthony's departure. "If you would do me the honor of taking a stroll with me?"

Anthony turned and crossed his arms over his chest, fixing Grace with a look of pure . . . disdain? . . . but it was Lady Sutton who spoke. "Your timing is not ideal, young man. As you know, my charity ball is to be held tomorrow night, and Miss Hawthorne has not yet taught my grandson to dance."

"But my lady, surely Miss Hawthorne—"

"*Now*," Anthony interjected, cutting off Mr. Cooper with an annoyed growl.

The countess looked pleased, but Grace felt confounded. How was she to face Anthony . . . how could she touch him, dance with him?

"Ring for Mrs. Brooks, please, Robert," Lady Sutton said to the footman.

Grace's throat burned. "My lady, I am not a very good dancer. Perhaps Miss James could be enlisted—"

"What do you mean, dear girl? I've seen you dance. And now that your color has improved, I would say that now is a very good time."

Grace saw that there was no escape. Neither Preston Cooper nor Mr. Bridewell could help her to contain all the immoral, impractical, *thrilling* longings Anthony elicited in her. She was trapped.

Mrs. Brooks arrived, and Lady Sutton asked her to make sure the ballroom was ready for a dance lesson. "And of course we wish you to remain and play the pianoforte, so that Miss Hawthorne can teach my grandson to waltz."

The housekeeper left the room happily, always glad to play for Her Ladyship. Grace stood, and almost immediately Anthony came to her side, very correctly pulling her chair back as she stood, but preempting Mr. Cooper, who did not manage to get to her in time.

She turned to her former suitor. "Mr. Cooper,

if you meant to use our stroll as an opportunity to change my mind regarding . . . your suit, you are mistaken. I hope you will respect my wishes and refrain from approaching me again."

She felt hot, angry emotions simmering just below her skin, and when Anthony's hand touched the small of her back, she thought she might ignite.

There was no possible way for her to get through a dance lesson with him.

Anthony managed to avoid grinning at Grace's show of temper, but he found himself gaping at the counterfeit trees standing in every corner of the ballroom and the leafy vines that were strewn from chandelier to chandelier. Servants had strategically placed a number of real potted plants all round, transforming the ballroom into a bizarre semblance of a jungle.

"Do you like it?" his grandmother asked.

"'Tis . . ." He looked round to give himself a moment to think what to say. She'd obviously done it to humble him. To soften his heart. The skin at the corners of her brown eyes crinkled with pleasure, and he could not bring himself to denigrate her efforts. "Very nice. I'm honored."

"Well, good. For 'tis all done for you, my dear boy. To celebrate your return."

That might be so, but he would not be swayed, though at the moment he could not focus his attention on the freedom he would soon enjoy. Not while Grace walked beside his grandmother, wearing her pretty white gown, with her hair curling about her ears. For one so soft and delectable, she had spine. She had been brutal with Cooper, making certain he understood her. His lovely honeyguide was fierce when riled.

"You will have to waltz at the ball, of course," said Sophia, taking a seat near Mrs. Brooks, who sat down at the pianoforte. "While Faraday finds a few servants to help with the country dances, Grace will teach you to waltz."

Grace's discomfort was palpable, and Anthony had no intention of making this lesson any easier for her. She thought they could go back to keeping a proper distance, but he knew differently. He'd kissed her and sucked her nipples . . . he'd been inside her. It could never be the same between them.

She would barely look at him, but she took his hand, extending it and raising it to the level of her shoulder. "Put your other hand here," she said, placing it on her shoulder blade. She put her hand on his shoulder, but did not move close. When he started to draw her in, she looked up sharply at him.

"Try to follow my steps," she said stiffly.

"Try to relax, Grace," he retorted sarcastically.

"When do you plan to break your grandmother's heart by returning to Africa?"

"She is a tough old woman," he replied. He wanted to ask what of *her* heart, but he knew the answer to that question. She would not have run from his bed if he'd denied his intention to leave, for he knew she could not possibly prefer Bridewell's touch . . .

The thought of her suitor put him on edge, made him feel like snarling.

"The dance is not complicated," Grace said. "You take the first step, and two more follow quickly after it. Like this."

While Mrs. Brooks played the music, Grace made the movements slowly. Anthony followed her steps, catching on quickly. She kept her expression a neutral mask, but Anthony felt a tremor with every breath she took. He pulled her in closer, but she was so intent upon the steps that she did not realize it.

Anthony could not help but take pleasure in the brush of her skirts against his legs, and the feel of her slender back in his hand. How easy it would be to toss her over his shoulder and carry her out to the cottage. He was hungry for her, for the slide of her smooth body against his, for the taste of her sweet mouth—

"That's right," Grace said, and for a second, Anthony thought she was agreeing to leave with him. But her expression had not changed. She was forcing herself to be indifferent to him. "Now let's try it in correct tempo with the music."

They moved faster, with Anthony following each of Grace's steps. He felt the music, and loved holding his woman in his arms as they danced, creating a madly sensual prelude to lovemaking.

Mbaya, he wanted her. He wanted to glide naked against her and kiss every inch of her body. He wanted to taste her, to hold her close all day and all night, and make love to her until neither of them could stand.

He took charge of the steps and led her to the far corner of the ballroom. Tipping his head toward Grace's ear, he whispered. "I would taste you now, *uzuri toi*."

She faltered slightly.

"We can leave my grandmother's house and find a secluded bower where I would unclothe you."

"Anthony, don't—"

"I would lick your pretty breasts, Grace."

She made a strangled sound.

"And draw your nipple into my mouth. I want to slide inside you when I do that, Grace. I want to feel your feminine sheath clench with your pleasure."

"Oh, dear heavens," Grace said, coloring deeply. Her blue eyes glittered and darkened with awareness. "You must not say such things."

"Even if they're true? Grace, you enjoyed making love with me. Come back with me."

She released his hand and stepped out of his embrace. "That will do," she said as she started to walk away. "Now you know how to waltz. We're finished."

Halfway across the room, Sophia laughed. "Oh Grace, you do amuse me. There is so much more. Go on."

"There is *much* more, sweet Grace," Anthony said, low under his breath behind her. "But you are a coward."

She returned to him with fire in her eyes, but she said nothing as she took his hand again and placed it on her back, shivering as she felt his heat. Mrs. Brooks began a different piece and they started to dance.

"As y-you will note," she said, fiercely fighting the sensual pull between them, "the steps remain the same, even though the music has changed."

But her lips parted and her breathing quickened. She would already have become moist between her legs, and the tips of her breasts had surely hardened. Would that they were in a private place where he could pleasure her and draw out the same wild response he'd already seen in her.

"You hide behind your etiquette and your narrow propriety," he said, caressing her back as they moved across the polished ballroom floor.

"I am no coward!"

"Come to the cottage with me," he said in her ear.

"Not so close, Anthony!" Sophia called out. "Grace, instruct him!"

"You heard your grandmother," Grace said. "Stand straight and put some space between us . . . B-between you and your partner."

It was frustrating to watch her turn her bland expression on him when he knew there was so much passion in her. He wanted to see sparks lighting up her eyes, fever burning her cheeks. He wanted to feel the same shuddering pleasure she'd squeezed from him last night. "Which of those names would you choose for me, Grace?"

"Names?"

"My grandmother's list. Has she already chosen a bride for me?"

"What difference does it make?" she said in a tone that made him think of the cold, rainy days he remembered from his childhood. "You are leaving."

"What if I don't?" he said, feeling stunned by the very idea. "For argument's sake . . . If I stayed here in England, who should I take for a wife?"

Her answer was clipped and brusque. "I'm quite sure I do not know."

She was stiffer than ever, and he could not resist goading her. "Should we not be more fluid with the music, Grace?"

She bit her lip, and Anthony fought the urge to lean down and suck it into his mouth. If only he could take her behind one of his grandmother's painted trees and press her up against one of the walls while he invaded her mouth with his tongue.

He longed to slide his hands under her long gown and cup her smooth buttocks in his hands.

"Pay attention to this turn," she said, sounding even more breathless than before.

He swallowed hard and executed the move, thinking about all the ways he wanted this woman.

"Well done, Anthony," Sophia said. "Now you must take the lead as you will do at the ball. Take another turn round the ballroom. Mrs. Brooks, a little Mozart, please."

Chapter 15

*G*race was no coward!

And she'd proven it by staying to teach Lady Sutton's inconsiderate, barbarian grandson to dance when she'd have been better off with a walk in the countryside, or a ride to her favorite place by the riverbank. Or even a visit to Bridewell Manor.

She was finally able to breathe when three of the footmen and an equal number of maids joined them to demonstrate the steps of the country dances Anthony would need to perform at the ball. Grace managed to don a pleasant, proper expression and tried not to dwell on all the young ladies who would vie for Anthony's name on their dance cards. She could not bear to think he might actually be considering staying in England.

He'd only said that to . . . to upset her.

And he had succeeded.

Grace knew Anthony still did not care whether the Lords' Committee recognized him as earl. He'd made no concessions to his grandmother, beyond learning to dance. And she knew why he'd done that.

Somehow, she held off her tears until the end, her throat thickening with anguish. She managed to avoid Anthony's touch and quickly bowed to his grandmother, taking her leave before she fell apart. He started to follow her, but Lady Sutton caught his arm. "We have matters to discuss, Anthony."

Grace left the ballroom and started for the staircase, but Faraday stopped her. "Is everything . . . er, Miss Hawthorne?"

She sniffled and took a deep breath. "What is it, Faraday?"

"Mr. Bridewell is waiting for you on the terrace."

"Tell him I will see him presently." Mr. Bridewell could wait until she'd had a chance to wash her face and compose herself.

It took longer than she would have hoped, but the cool, wet cloth she pressed against her eyes prevented them from reddening any further. She found Mr. Bridewell sitting in a wicker chair on the terrace, reading a newspaper. He was well-dressed and genteel, and Grace knew he would never dream of seducing a lady with brazen kisses and the wicked temptations of his body.

Mr. Bridewell put down his newspaper and stood when he saw her, and Grace forced aside every thought of Anthony's touch. She'd made one grave error already, and would not repeat it. She managed a modest smile, for Mr. Bridewell could not have come to Fairford Park just to pass the time of day. She had not heard from him since their supper in Richmond, and she could not help but think that now he was surely ready to propose.

"Miss Hawthorne," Mr. Bridewell said. "Are you free to walk with me?"

"Of course," Grace replied, feeling light-headed at the thought of what lay ahead.

Mr. Bridewell put on his hat and extended his arm to Grace. She took it without going back into the house for her own hat and gloves. Let Anthony try to call her a coward now. She was going after what she wanted.

They went round to the front of the house and down the drive, exiting Lady Sutton's estate. "There is a nice walking path out this way," Mr. Bridewell remarked.

He was so very courteous—a gentleman who knew how to court her. How to treat her. And Grace believed she could be quite content with Mr. Bridewell. More than content. She would enjoy a calm and dignified relationship with him, one that was sanctified by the church and accepted by society. Not some uncontrolled, illicit coupling in the dark corners of a lover's cottage.

"Are you chilled, Miss Hawthorne? Do you need your shawl?"

"No, thank you. I will be fine once we get into the sunshine." And far from the house.

"There are so many servants bustling around Fairford Park," Mr. Bridewell remarked. "Has the countess taken on extra help?"

Only Lady Sutton's most wealthy, titled acquaintances had been invited to the ball, so Mr. Bridewell was not on the guest list. But surely he did not take offense. "Yes—Lady Sutton's charity ball takes place tomorrow evening."

"Ah, right. For the bastards' home."

Grace nearly stumbled at his unkind word, but caught herself from appearing the clumsy oaf. "I beg your pardon?"

"She is raising money for her foundling asylum, am I correct?"

"St. Andrew's Home," Grace said, frowning slightly. " 'Tis a worthy cause. The children are innocent of wrongdoing . . . and they have needs."

He shrugged and moved on before Grace could say anything more, but her mind shuddered at the coldness of his remarks. If only he could see the children at St. Andrew's, he would understand, for he had his own family.

"How are your children?" she asked, picturing each one, and wondering how they would accept her into their household. The eldest was a girl of fourteen, and as much a mistress of her father's house as her mother would have been, had she lived. The boys were quiet, serious young fellows who had been clean and well-dressed on every occasion Grace had seen them. They were lads who would never know a moment's adventure in a tree fort. The youngest Bridewell was a frail child of about six or seven years, who had a propensity for clinging to her father.

"They are very well, thank you," he replied. "Shall we walk up to that rise? I would speak to you on a matter of some importance."

Grace's heart should have swelled with delight, but her emotions floundered. Which was absurd. The greatest moment of her life was about to occur. The hussy who'd shared Anthony's bed last night no longer existed. That interlude had been an aberration, an unexplainable deviation from Grace's normal, refined behavior.

"There is a lovely spot just below that hill," she said, "with a bench in the shade, and a pretty little burn running by. Perhaps we could sit there for a bit."

"It will do." He touched Grace's lower back, and the proprietary touch of his hand gave her pause. Soon there would be many more touches. Kisses. Intimate fondlings.

She swallowed and walked on. She'd had no idea the degree of pleasure that could be found in a man's arms, though she should have guessed it from Anthony's intoxicating kisses. She'd relished the feel of his big hands on her breasts, his mouth on her nipples.

And the rest . . . She pressed her lips together at the thought of his most intimate kiss.

" 'Tis always important for a man and his family to adhere to the most proper behavior," Mr. Bridewell said as he walked beside Grace, jerking her attention from her unseemly musings.

"*Absolutely*," she said with more vehemence than she intended, drawing a sidelong glance from him.

"Which is something I greatly admire about you, Miss Hawthorne. You understand decorum. Propriety. Your behavior can never be faulted."

"Thank you," she said, feeling more than a bit hollow inside.

They walked on through an expanse of flat pastureland, passing through a turnstile where a dozen sheep had gathered to graze. Grace looked down at Mr. Bridewell's fine shoes and tried to imagine seeing his feet bare. Climbing into their bed. Taking her into his arms.

"Ah, here's the bench you mentioned." He waited for Grace to sit on the rough-hewn seat, then took his own place beside her, keeping several inches between them. He removed his hat, putting it on his lap.

"I enjoy reading out here," Grace said, and she could not deny saying it to gauge his reaction. "On days like today, I will often bring out a book and spend hours passing the time."

"My dear Miss Hawthorne, surely there are

many more productive pursuits you might enjoy."

"I am sure that is true, Mr. Bridewell."

"Well, once a woman is married, her responsibilities are too numerous to while away her time."

"No doubt a wife must be judicious with her time."

"'Tis very true. And with sufficient instruction," he added, "there can be no doubt that you will become a satisfactory wife."

Satisfactory? She caught herself gaping at him, but he did not seem to notice.

He moved to take Grace's hand, but she stood and walked to the water's edge. She crouched down and slipped her hand into the cool, running water, remembering their conversation at the Richmond Arms. He had not asked her opinion, even once. He had not asked about her life, her past, her hopes or dreams.

Mr. Bridewell followed her to the water. "I brought you down here for a specific purpose, Miss Hawthorne. 'Tis time I took a wife. Bridewell Manor needs a mistress and my girls need a mother."

Grace chewed her lip. She stood and faced him, and looked into his light gray eyes, feeling somewhat defiant. Anthony had accused her of being a coward. But she was not.

Nor was she the same woman who'd sat quietly eating supper with Mr. Bridewell at Richmond's hotel. And yet once Anthony left, Grace would have nothing. Her life would go on as before, her mornings occupied with Lady Sutton's correspondence, her Wednesday afternoons spent with the countess's dowager friends, and one night a week sharing supper with Reverend Chilton.

She wiped her wet hand upon her skirt, feeling unsure and uneasy. Did she dare risk her one chance for marriage with a confrontation? "Did you know that my late father was a barrister, Mr. Bridewell?" she asked, boring straight ahead.

"No, I did not. But I do not see how it is relevant—"

"And I was nearly engaged two years ago."

He frowned. "I trust that nothing untoward—"

"Of course not."

"Naturally. Nothing occurred," he said. "I apologize. I have never known a more refined young lady. You are exactly the kind of woman I'd hoped would help to mold my daughters."

Grace forced herself to take a deep, calming breath. He was not entirely insensitive. His nerves had likely dictated his conversation on previous occasions.

Besides, she could not allow her feelings for Anthony to cloud her judgment. Mr. Bridewell's proposal was what she'd dreamed of. When Anthony Maddox was long gone, Grace would have her own perfectly satisfactory life at Bridewell Manor.

"I hope, Miss Hawthorne, that you will do me the very great honor of becoming my wife."

Refusing Edward Bridewell would be the mistake of her life. But the words of his proposal did not lift Grace's heart, and a slight throbbing started in her forehead.

She returned to the bench and sat down, while he remained standing with his hands clasped behind his back. Waiting.

Grace moistened her lips. No more Wednesday afternoons with the dowagers? "Thank you for your proposal, Mr. Bridewell. I-I would like . . ."

He came and sat down next to her.

" . . . some time to consider it," she said, surprising even herself.

"What is there to consider, Miss Hawthorne? Grace. We are well-suited to one another, are we not?"

"I th-think we must be. But I . . . 'Tis such a change for me, and a weighty decision to make."

"I understand. With no father or brother to advise you . . . Grace, I hope you will not take too much time. I had hoped the vicar would post the banns on Sunday next."

"I won't."

"Well, then. There is nothing more to say, is there?"

She looked down at her feet, feeling entirely adrift. Perhaps she should just say yes and set the date.

"Let's go back to the house," he said. "The

sooner you begin your deliberations, the sooner I will have my answer."

"Yes." Grace looked up at him, shielding her eyes from the bright sunlight. "But I would rather not say anything of this to the countess. She has much on her mind right now."

Not the least of which would be Anthony's desertion.

She looked at Edward Bridewell's placid expression, at his ruddy cheeks and his stocky hands. As much as she wished otherwise, she knew he would never fill the void that would remain when Anthony left.

There was no reason for Anthony to feel so wretched. He'd been quite clear with Grace and his grandmother from the first. He was going home, and his home was the Congo. Any other hopes or expectations were unwarranted.

But it rankled that Grace had gone walking with Bridewell without even a glance back in his direction.

He'd pushed her during their dance lesson, saying things he knew were beyond the sphere of polite society. He'd goaded her for no good reason, only to punish her for running from him last night. She had not left for lack of satisfaction, for he'd felt her shudders of pleasure.

She'd gone because he'd acted like a savage, and

made her forget herself. She'd discovered that she was not above the same primitive urges that had driven him to take her to his bed.

Urges that had not abated in the hour since he'd waltzed with her in his grandmother's ballroom.

While she was away with Bridewell, the members of the Lords' Committee on Privileges assembled in the drawing room. Mr. Hamilton was present, as well as Cooper—yet another of Grace's suitors.

Anthony gritted his teeth as they all took their seats. He remained standing behind his grandmother with his hands clasped upon the back of her settee. His gaze wavered between Sophia and Newbury, who'd come to lend his support. Somehow, he managed to refrain from watching for Grace's return, with or without Bridewell. He tried to focus his thoughts on the freedom he would attain the moment he boarded *L'oiseau de Mer*, but the solitude of Ganweulu was strangely unappealing at the moment.

The Duke of Epworth, a man of Bridewell's age, started the proceedings. "Our committee has met on numerous occasions since your arrival upon our shores." He squinted his eyes as he looked at Anthony. "But questions remain . . ."

"Well, I am convinced," said Rutherford, quite expectedly, since he was one of Sophia's devoted friends.

"As am I," Lord Carlisle remarked. "Just look at the portrait hanging there. Could this young man bear a greater resemblance to Colin Maddox?"

"Where is Mr. Thornby?" asked the solicitor, Mr. Lamb.

"I expressly asked Thornby to join us. He must have been delayed," Mr. Hamilton said.

"By the contents of a bottle, I daresay," Newbury remarked, and received a number of disapproving scowls in response.

"What of his objections?" asked Lamb. "It is my understanding that he sent agents out to the Congo to determine if the young man's tale of survival is authentic."

Hamilton gave a curt nod. "He did."

Anthony made a derisive sound. If Colin had not been able to find him in six months, Thornby's agents would not find any trace of him, either.

Hamilton ignored Anthony and went on. " 'Tis much too soon to expect news from Thornby's men. Which is why this committee cannot possibly make a ruling today."

"Ah, but we *will* make a ruling, today," said Lord Rutherford. "Several of us are ready to accept Lady Sutton's claim that this man is her grandson."

"Thornby's men in Africa might not return for months," said Carlisle.

"If ever," Rutherford muttered just loud enough for all to hear.

"But the decision must be unanimous, is that not correct?" Hamilton said, though it was clear he already knew the answer.

"My grandson called me Avó today," said Sophia, breaking her silence.

"Which signifies what?" Lord Nye asked.

Sophia's tone was indignant. "Avó was the name Anthony always called me, from his infancy to the day he left on his grand safari."

Anthony could see that Epworth was hardly convinced of the significance of that one word, and he became concerned about his grandmother as she was becoming distraught.

"Faraday," Sophia called to the butler. "Send someone for the box from my grandson's tree house."

"My lady," said Nye, "it does not—"

"You will see that my grandson is familiar with the items inside, the toys and other things I sent to him at school," Sophia said with increasing distress, and Anthony slid his hand down onto her fragile shoulder. She had such tiny bones, he sometimes wondered how she managed to get about as well as she did.

It was clear that Nye was unconvinced by Sophia's insistence on Anthony's identity. As were Barrington, Mattingly, and Viscount Canvey. Anthony had to admit that his nickname for his grandmother had likely been noted by some of the servants years ago. It was not secret knowledge.

But there was something he knew that even his grandmother did not.

"Perhaps Sutton's pet name for his grandmother is irrelevant, but his knowledge of our childhood antics is not," said Newbury.

"Go on, Newbury," said Epworth.

"Sutton, Rothwell, and I were the best of friends at school, Your Grace, and spent several holidays here."

Rutherford spoke up. "And are you prepared to swear that this man"—he gestured toward Anthony—"is that same childhood friend?"

"I am. He remembered the games we played . . . things only the three of us would know."

"'Tis compelling, is it not?" Rutherford asked as Faraday brought the old wooden box into the room and set it on a small table near the countess.

Sophia was wringing her hands fretfully, and Anthony had to fight the urge to sit down beside her and place his hand over hers to quiet her.

"Open it, Faraday," Sophia said, and the butler complied.

Anthony clamped his teeth together. It was frustrating to be drawn into these proceedings, having to worry about his grandmother and the way the discussion was upsetting her.

He moved away from his grandmother's chair and started to pace as the walls of the house closed in around him. He needed some air. There was no room for him in this kind of stilted, overwrought society where a man had to observe ridiculous rules of propriety, where he could not just take his woman and—

Grace came into the drawing room with Bridewell, and Anthony's pacing came to an abrupt halt. Her red-faced swain held a proprietary hand at the lower part of her back, his bearing as pompous as ever. Anthony had to hold back from picking him up by his fancy cravat and tossing him out the window.

'Twas a primitive impulse, but that's what he was. A primitive man. A savage from the wilds of Africa, whose most basic instincts were roused by the sight of soft brown hair, full pink lips, and demure blue eyes.

"Oh! Grace, dear." Sophia extended her hand, and Grace came to her immediately and took a seat beside her. Bridewell did not immediately take his leave, and Anthony glared at him as he resumed his pacing.

Faraday inserted the key into the lock and opened the old box, and Sophia reached in and picked up the metal discs that lay inside.

She looked back at him. "Tell them what these are."

"It will make no difference, my lady," he said. "There is an alternative explanation for every item in that box."

She brought out the little horse. "How did you get this?"

He took it from her and turned it in his hand. "You sent it to school with me, Avó, hidden away in my luggage so I would have something from home, from you, to ease my homesickness."

"There, you see?"

His grandmother's statement was met with silence, but the sounds of a disturbance in the foyer drew everyone's attention. Thornby suddenly staggered into the room, his hair a matted mess, his coat and tie askew.

"Sir!" Faraday called to him indignantly, as two footmen attempted to take him outside.

"Unhand me!" he shouted, his arms flailing wildly, and the footmen backed away slightly. Thornby turned to Anthony and pointed one thick finger at him. "Do not listen to his lies! I never did it!"

Chapter 16

❦❦❦

"**S**it down, Mr. Thornby!" Mr. Hamilton said firmly.

"I will not!" the man replied vehemently. Wavering drunkenly, he staggered into the room, his eyes changing their focus from Anthony to Lady Sutton.

"I won't have you listening to him!" The florid, hateful expression on Thornby's face was enough to alarm Grace, and everyone else in the room.

Anthony moved in front of the settee where she and Lady Sutton sat, ready to defend them if Thornby tried anything untoward.

"Here now, let's be gentlemanly," said Mr. Bridewell, approaching Thornby as any reasonable man would do.

But Thornby threw a sloppy punch and caught Mr. Bridewell on the side of his face. Then he turned unsteadily and lunged toward Anthony.

Grace jumped to her feet with a startled cry.

She barely saw Anthony move. Without a sound,

he surprised his attacker with a quick blow to his stomach. When Thornby grunted and doubled over, Anthony caught his upper body with his shoulder and tossed him over it. Without hesitation, he went out through the door Thornby had entered.

"Faraday!" Anthony said sharply, and the butler regained his composure and followed.

Grace surged in behind Faraday and felt Newbury's hand at her elbow. "Miss Hawthorne, perhaps you should not—"

She shot him a look of determination and he desisted. But he went with her, the two following Faraday while the voices of those who remained in the drawing room erupted into questions and harsh words.

Anthony did not stop moving, even though Thornby struggled to escape him. Faraday opened the front door, and Anthony stepped outside and descended the steps. At the bottom, he dropped Thornby onto the ground beside his carriage.

"Tony," said Newbury. "Don't . . ."

"Don't what?" asked Grace.

"Kill him."

Grace felt wobbly as Anthony drew out his knife, his hatred for the man he'd just thrown to the ground palpable.

"No! You . . . you cannot . . ." she whispered.

Anthony's jaw clenched. He leaned down, putting the edge of the knife to Thornby's throat.

Grace's heart pounded in her ears and her knees startled to buckle, but Newbury supported her so that she would not fall.

Anthony glanced up at her, hesitated, then threw down his knife. "Get him out of here," he said to the driver. "Take him to London and dump him at his club."

"Yes, m'lord," he responded, but before the man could climb down from the carriage, Thornby roused himself and came to his feet. He swayed for a moment, then swung out at Anthony.

With lightning reflexes, Anthony thwarted the man's attack and knocked him to the ground. "You will do me no harm this time, Thornby." He stepped over him as Faraday arrived with footmen and lifted the man up off the ground and put him into his carriage.

The butler picked up the knife, and when they all turned and started for the house, Anthony had already disappeared inside.

"Never seen anything like it," said Faraday, who went inside.

Nor had Grace, who was still trembling. Those powerful hands had touched her so tenderly, had been strong and decisive when his grandmother had been threatened. And yet . . . "He would have killed him," she whispered.

"But for you," Newbury said.

"Why would he?"

"The better question is . . . why didn't he?"

Grace did not know. Surely it could not have been because of her wishes.

She returned to the drawing room, where Mr. Bridewell was half lying upon the settee. A maid was awkwardly trying to keep a thick cut of beefsteak upon the left side of his face. Grace went to him and knelt beside the settee. "Mr. Bridewell, are you all right?"

"Hardly, my dear."

Grace felt duly chastised by his tone, and she pressed one reassuring hand to his shoulder. She should have stayed in the drawing room with him instead of haring off after Anthony.

And yet if he'd truly listened to her plea, then she had saved a man's life. "I'm so sorry. Who would have thought Mr. Thornby would behave in such a manner?"

The meeting of the credentialing committee seemed to have been irrevocably disrupted. Lord Rutherford was making a gallant attempt to get them all to sit down again and resume their discussion, but he was having little success. Epworth had gathered his hat and gloves and his walking stick, and was headed, along with the other gentlemen, toward the same door Anthony had used for Thornby's ejection.

Anthony's voice suddenly rose above all the others. "Come with me."

He did not wait to see who followed, but headed to the rear of the house. Curiosity over-

ruled the lords' determination to leave Fairford
Park, and they all turned to follow him. Grace
burned to know where Anthony was leading
them, but she had left Mr. Bridewell once. She
would not—

"Walk with me, Grace," said Lady Sutton. "Mrs.
Brooks will stay with Mr. Bridewell."

"Go with Her Ladyship," said Bridewell, and
Grace did not hesitate to leave. She and the countess soon found themselves on the path to the old,
run-down lodge. They lagged behind, but were
still able to hear a few dubious remarks made by
the men of the committee.

Anthony pushed open the door. He waited until
his grandmother came to the fore, then took her
arm and, with great care, led her to a chair, where
she sat down. The rest of the party filed inside, but
remained standing, watching in silence until everyone was inside.

"My father always kept a cache of money hidden
here."

"No . . . Where?" Lady Sutton asked, clearly
bewildered by Anthony's announcement. "Why?"

"I do not know, Avó," Anthony replied. He was
in complete command of the room, giving information, even though he did not seem to care whether
these men believed him.

Grace had the feeling he'd brought the committee out to the lodge in spite of himself. That somehow this jaunt had more to do with Thornby than

with Anthony wanting to prove his grandmother's claim that he was truly Colin's son.

She wanted to ask him to explain Thornby's statement, and why he would have murdered the man, but he was speaking to the countess, explaining himself.

" 'Twas some sort of tradition carried on by the men of our family from a time of unrest—I cannot remember the details," he said. "But it was for emergencies."

Lady Sutton appeared dubious. "I've never heard of such a thing."

"Of course not. My father said 'twas only for the men to know," Anthony said.

"Or the women would have spent it, most like," said Lord Rutherford, drawing a chuckle from the men in the gathering.

Grace remained standing near the door as Anthony went to a bookcase in the farthest corner of the room. He dropped down to one knee and reached beneath the lowest shelf, pulling out a drawer. He carried it to the table where his grandmother sat, then tipped it over carefully in front of her.

All the men crowded round the table, and Grace heard Lady Sutton ask for her. "Where is Miss Hawthorne?"

"Here, my lady," Grace replied.

"Come close. I want your hand."

Lord Rutherford took Grace's arm and guided

her to a spot right beside Her Ladyship. She took
Lady Sutton's hand and remained standing as Anthony did something that caused a spring to be
released. Grace heard a popping noise, and the
bottom of the drawer sprang free. Underneath it
was a stack of currency, along with a large number
of gold and silver coins.

The collective reaction was audible. Every man
in the room drew in a sharp breath at the small
fortune that had been stashed under the drawer.

"My father told no one of this reserve. Except
me, just before we left on our expedition." He
pushed the overturned drawer closer to his grandmother, and then left.

They could do what they would with the dem-
onstration Anthony had just given them. All that
mattered was that Thornby would never benefit
from his ignoble actions twenty-two years before.
Had the bastard not kicked him off the *dhombo*
in the storm, Anthony would have returned home
with his father, who might still be alive today. Anthony would not have spent all those years fighting
for his survival in the brutal environment of the
Congo.

Yet he'd learned to love the valley in which he
made his home. His life was his own.

He kicked a stone off the path and kept walking toward his cottage as he thought of the expres-

sion on Grace's face when he'd had his *kisu* against Thornby's neck. She'd been appalled.

And he'd let Thornby go.

He jammed his fingers through his hair. *Mbaya*. He had to get away now before his conflicting emotions paralyzed him. All he needed to do was grab his *gunia* and *kisu*, for he had no other possessions here. Nothing he needed, nothing he wanted. It was only approaching dusk, so he could easily ride to London and arrive before full night. He would board his ship and sail tomorrow on the evening tide.

He slammed into his cottage and pulled off his coat, then his cravat, and tossed them onto a chair. The *gunia* was in the bedchamber, and when he went for it, his gaze was drawn by the rumpled bedclothes. A blanket lay on the floor—the one Grace had held up against her breasts, covering herself from his sight.

He closed his eyes and drew in a deep breath, then whirled at the sound of the cottage door opening.

Grace.

Her expression was tentative, or perhaps even frightened. She did not step away from the door. Her only movement was the slow fluctuation of her throat as she swallowed.

Anthony could almost taste the skin there. He knew how sensitive it was, nearly as much as the tender spot behind her ear. Or farther down.

He might be tempted to stay for his grandmother's ball if only to dance with Grace.

"You stayed because of Thornby."

He gave her a curt nod.

"He was the cause . . ." She furrowed her brow. "You did not fall from that boat. Thornby . . . ?"

"Shoved me and left me for dead. Likely, he persuaded my father to give up on me." He still did not understand why he hadn't slit the bastard's throat and been done with it.

"Thank you for what you did back there—in the lodge—for your grandmother," she said. "It meant a great deal to her."

It was on the tip of his tongue to say it had not been for Sophia, but merely to thwart Thornby. But the expression of admiration on her face halted his words.

She took a step toward him. "The lords made their ruling. The duke said he did not see how you could possibly have known about the hidden drawer unless you were Sutton's son. That if anyone else had known about it, the money would have disappeared."

She seemed different. Subdued, somehow.

"Viscount Canvey agreed," she said. "Then the others—even Mr. Hamilton—concurred. You are now . . ." She caught sight of the *gunia* in his hand.

He clamped his jaws together to keep himself from saying something he would surely regret.

She made a small sound of distress and looked away. When she spoke, her voice was soft and breathless. "Lady Sutton was sure you'd decided to . . . to stay."

"Should you not go back to the house and see to your man, Miss Hawthorne?" he asked harshly. "He took quite a blow from Thornby."

She faced him squarely, then took a step forward. "Even *I* thought you'd changed your mind."

"You are courting disaster, Grace. You know you should not be here. Alone, with me." Because if she took one more step, he was going to scoop her into his arms and take her into the bedchamber, and show her that there was only one man for her, and it was not Bridewell.

"I was alone with you during all our lessons, Anthony," she said, taking yet another step.

"But 'tis different now." *Mbaya*, she was beautiful.

He saw her swallow, and her color deepened.

As he remembered the taste of her kisses and the sound of her pleasure, Anthony's arousal grew. She belonged in his arms, in his bed. He started toward her.

Grace's mouth parted in anticipation of Anthony's kiss. She wanted this more than her next breath. She wanted him to stay.

He slipped one arm round her waist and cupped her face with the other. "Ah, Grace . . ." He'd just begun to lower his head when they both heard the sound of footsteps and voices approaching the cottage.

Grace heard Newbury, speaking urgently. "Rutherford, it can wait. Sutton is probably not even out here." She broke away from Anthony and quickly moved to the far side of the dining table, pressing one hand to the center of her chest, where her heart beat madly.

Lord Rutherford headed a group that came right up to the door and knocked as they looked in through the window. Anthony's face darkened like a storm cloud. He looked at Grace with fire in his eyes, and the promise of future pleasures.

"No, it cannot wait, lad," Rutherford said to Newbury.

Grace's legs trembled, so she took a seat at the table as Anthony growled under his breath and opened the door. Lords Rutherford, Carlisle, and Canvey entered the room, with Newbury right behind them.

"Sorry, old chap," Newbury said quietly to Anthony. "I couldn't manage to divert them."

"Seems Miss Hawthorne has already borne you the good news. Well, no matter. Congratulations, young man," said Rutherford, smiling broadly. He took Anthony's hand and shook it vigorously. "I knew you were authentic from the first."

"The rest will only be formalities, Sutton," said

Carlisle. "For all intents and purposes, we recognize you as earl of all the Sutton possessions."

"And a very formidable one, I would say," said Rutherford. "Dealing with Thornby as you did."

"What was that all about, anyway?" asked Carlisle.

"What was he afraid you'd say to us?" Canvey added.

Grace had wondered, too. Thornby's words had made her suspect some kind of treachery Anthony had never mentioned. Now she knew, but Anthony just shrugged.

"Well, he's off the estate as of now," said Rutherford. "All is yours, Sutton."

Grace's heart sank at the sight of his traveling bag. The kindness and concern Anthony had begun to show—to *feel*—for his grandmother was insignificant compared to his desire to leave England. Grace could not plead ignorance of his intentions.

"If you'll excuse me," she said, rising from her chair. She avoided looking at Anthony as she hastened to the door.

Grace was not sure she could face Her Ladyship just then. Nor could she deal with Mr. Bridewell. She started walking to the big, sweeping tree where Anthony had perched himself that first night at Fairford Park, and soon found herself running, dashing away from the mistakes she'd made, from her hopeless yearning. Anthony had confronted Thornby and chosen not to exact his revenge.

And now he was free.

She took a turn down the path toward Anthony's tree fort. No one would look for her there.

When she reached its base, she gathered her skirts in one hand and made an indecorous climb until she was all the way up. She clambered inside and sat down on the floor with her back against the tree trunk.

Taking a deep breath, she tried to understand where her once-perfect morals had gone, and what she was going to do.

"*Mbaya*," Anthony muttered, looking into his grandmother's happy, sparkling eyes. He should never have allowed his hatred for Thornby to interfere with his better judgment and lead those men to his father's hidden treasure. Now Sophia believed it all mattered to him.

"I am still stunned," she said. "Imagine—your father hiding a small fortune away in that old lodge of his."

"Give it to the orphans' home," he said offhandedly. He had no use for it beyond what he'd already paid for his passage on *L'oiseau de Mer*.

He wondered where Grace could be. She'd slipped away when Rutherford and the others had arrived, and he had not seen her since.

"Why, that's a wonderful idea, dear boy," Sophia said. "Who could doubt you are my grandson with such sentiments as this?"

She looked tired, worn out from the excitement of the day, Anthony guessed. She should already be abed.

"Where is Grace—Miss Hawthorne?" he asked.

Sophia hid a yawn behind one hand. "I have not seen her since you showed us the hidden drawer in the lodge."

"She did not leave the house with Bridewell?"

"Oh no. He went away in his carriage as soon as he could get up. I . . . I do not know where Grace could be."

"Excuse me, Avó," he said. "I must speak to the butler, and you should seek your bed. Where is your maid?"

"What is it, Anthony?"

"Nothing to concern yourself with."

" 'Tis Thornby, is it not?"

Anthony turned slowly to face his grandmother. He returned to her and sat down on a chair opposite her. "Aye. I let Thornby go."

"What happened on that river, Anthony?" she asked.

"Something no young boy should ever have to face," Anthony replied. He decided he might as well tell his grandmother what had happened on that river all those years ago. "Thornby shoved me off that *dhombo* into the raging river."

Sophia gasped and covered her mouth with her hand.

Anthony continued. "He had to know how unlikely it was that anyone would survive such an event."

"Dear heavens. We'll have to notify—"

"I will deal with him if need be, Avó. I only tell you this so that you will understand my actions."

"No! He is an underhanded blackguard, and I will not have you risking your life to—"

Anthony cut her off, his tone dark and deadly. "There will be no risk. Now please, Avó, go to bed."

He rang for a maid to assist Sophia to her room, then spoke briefly to Faraday, advising him to take appropriate precautions against an intruder. He did not think Thornby would come into the house, for he was an underhanded schemer. He would lie in wait and attempt an ambush.

But Anthony was not going to give him any such opportunity.

Leaving his grandmother in the care of her maid, Anthony went to the room he knew belonged to Grace. He tapped on her door, but when there was no answer, pushed it open. Stepping inside, he took note of the locket she'd worn to Sophia's soiree, hanging against the mirror of a dressing table.

Anthony took it into his palm and closed his hand round it. 'Twas a pretty trinket, but she deserved much more—certainly more than a room full of rotting flowers.

He left the room and exited the house, heading for the stable. Perhaps she'd gone riding, even though it was nearly dark. Anthony would like nothing better than to catch up to her at that deserted stretch of riverbank.

But none of the horses had been taken. He knew she had not left with Bridewell, but he did not find her in the main house. Anthony doubted she'd left to go walking, so she must be somewhere on the estate.

He wanted her safe, inside the house where footmen were keeping watch. Once he found her, he could ride to London and do what he'd intended from the first. He should not have allowed Grace's plea . . . and his own conscience . . . to stop him.

He lived by the rule of the jungle and should have finished the bastard when he had the chance. Instead, he'd left Thornby to become a threat once Anthony was gone. It was close to being fully dark when Anthony walked down the path to the lodge, but the moon was full and bright. He circled round his father's old refuge and went to his own, the tree fort. On a hunch, he took hold of the ladder and started to climb. Grace's voice stopped him.

"Don't come up." Her voice sounded strange. Hoarse, even worse than this morning.

Anthony resumed climbing. When he got to the top, he had to walk round to the opposite side of the platform that circled the tree to find her. She stood with her back to him, her hands upon the edge of the half wall, her head bowed.

"Grace."

She took a deep, shuddering breath. "You should not have come up here."

Of that, he was certain. "What are you doing?"

"Avoiding."

"Avoiding what?"

"Everything. You."

He came within inches of her, then stepped even closer, hemming her in with one big hand on either side of her small ones. Closing his eyes, he breathed in her scent and kissed the side of her neck.

"You should not have teased me during our dance lesson," she said.

"That was no tease. I meant everything I said."

She tipped her head to the side, and Anthony felt her shiver. He closed his arms round her, pressing his erection against her. Grace turned slightly, reaching back to close one hand over the nape of his neck, offering her mouth for his kiss.

Desire flared, hot and ravenous, and Anthony took her mouth greedily. He turned Grace in his arms and put everything he had into that kiss—his hands, his tongue, his cock . . .

His emotions.

He broke away suddenly and touched his forehead to Grace's, swallowing thickly and telling himself this had naught to do with any emotion. It was lust. He wanted her, just as he'd had her last night.

It could be nothing more.

* * *

Anthony took Grace's hand in his and placed it over the placket of his trews. "Feel how I want you, Grace." His voice was a harsh whisper in her ear.

The size and iron hardness of his manhood took her breath away. Grace slid her hand up the length of him, and he shuddered in response.

What were stiff propriety and formal pleasantries compared to this? She loved knowing she could elicit such a fierce arousal in him. She opened his buttons and drew him out, feeling inexperienced and awkward, but willing to risk being a fool.

Anthony took hold of her upper arms and pressed a hard, hot kiss to her lips, sliding his tongue into her mouth. Grace felt her bones melt as a searing liquid pooled deep within her. Still holding him, she squeezed slightly.

He broke the kiss, groaning. "Grace."

He unfastened the buttons of her bodice and pushed the sleeves down her arms. Between them, they managed to dispense with her corset, and then she was nearly naked before him.

"I thought of nothing but this while we waltzed," he whispered, tugging at her chemise.

His awkwardness was endearing, and Grace cupped his jaw in her hands, pulling him down for another kiss. He yanked off his own shirt, breaking away to pull it over his head, and shoved away his trews.

"I've dreamed of this, Grace. Of you in my acacia tree, naked, beautiful, so responsive to my touch."

Grace allowed herself to feel no shame, no unease. Her tears of indecision vanished. She wanted this—wanted Anthony—more than she wanted a life in a cold, respectable manor house with a staid and proper husband. Sliding her chemise down her shoulders and off her arms, she stepped out of it and reached for Anthony again.

He gathered her into his arms and lowered her to the floor on top of their discarded clothing. He angled his knee between hers and lavished kisses on her throat and neck. As he touched the fullness of her breasts, Grace arched, urging him to touch their tips.

He rolled, pulling Grace on top so that she straddled him. Cradling his erection between her legs, she reached down and swirled her tongue round one of his nipples while teasing the other with her fingertips. Her breasts brushed the rough hair of his belly, causing exquisite melting sensations deep inside her, hot and powerful.

He groaned when she moved lower, pressing her lips to his belly and below. Grace licked the tip of his manhood, then took it into her mouth, repeating the suction he'd so enjoyed at his nipple. She licked and sucked, and relished the writhing response she elicited.

He made a growling sound, then in one swift move, he lifted her, then lowered her onto his straining manhood. Grace closed her eyes and let her head drop back, her muscles quivering as she accepted his thick length.

He skimmed his hands round her ribs, touching her breasts with his thumbs as he began to move inside her. Grace put her hands on his shoulders and angled her hips to increase the contact of her most sensitive flesh against him. He plunged deeply and withdrew, and she felt the exquisite tightening that preceded her last climax of pure sensation.

An uncontrollable cry escaped her when it happened. The shuddering heat spread from her fluid center and exploded through her veins. Anthony reacted to her pleasure, increasing his rhythm, intensifying the connection between them. Her heart fluttered wildly when he pulled her down for his kiss. Their mouths melded just as he reached his own pinnacle, his body quaking, jerking out of control.

He broke their kiss and whispered her name as he came, and a handful of words Grace could not understand.

When he slid out of her, he drew her into his arms . . . perhaps to keep her from running away as she'd done before. But Grace had no desire to leave. She wanted every moment she could have in his arms.

*   *   *

Anthony held Grace close and felt the beating of her heart against his chest. It began to slow to normal, as did her breathing. He smoothed a wisp of her hair off her forehead, and when he kissed her there, he felt her tremble.

He felt shaky, too.

"This floor cannot be very comfortable for you," he said. "I will not apologize. I wanted you too badly to carry you all the way back to my bed."

And he would want her every other night to come.

Yet his brain reeled at the thought of it. He was a solitary creature with no true liaisons, no obligations, no commitments. It was the only life he could ever want.

The safest.

"I should go," Grace said as she sat up and started pulling on her clothes.

Anthony's mouth went dry at the sight of her soft curves in the moonlight—the full globes of her breasts, the slender strength of her arms. A fierce arousal, more intense than any he'd felt before, swept over him. He took hold of Grace and drew her into his embrace for a searing kiss, then laid her down again and thrust into her quickly, feeling as primitive as a jungle creature marking her with his scent, taking utter possession of her.

She responded with equal ferocity, her hips matching each of his lunges with a fury of her own. She wrapped her legs round his waist and squeezed him while her nails scored his back. Anthony coiled her hair round his hand and held her in place, locking his eyes on hers as they mated with the heat and passion of two wild beasts.

When it was over, they did not speak, but lay together, struggling to catch their breath. Anthony did not want to let go. He lightly nipped her neck with his teeth, feeling like a dominant lion with its mate, primal and wild.

He'd felt her marking him, too, ripping his back with her nails, owning him. Possessing him with all that she was.

"See what you do to me, *uzuri toi*," he whispered. "I have no control with you."

Grace watched him intently for an eternity, her eyes glittering black in the moonlight, her hands grasping his forearms as though she would never let him go.

And he knew she was not the coward he'd accused her of being.

Grace had moved on after Cooper's abandonment, making a life for herself after her mother's death. She had undertaken the nebulous task of educating him, and persisted in spite of his obstinacy and his teasing. She'd given up her respectability— her marriageability—to lie with him.

She released him, slipping out of his embrace, turning her back to pull on her clothes. "I must get back to the house. 'Tis late and I . . . I m-must . . ."

He heard her take a tremulous breath, and a potent impulse urged Anthony to claim her. To tell her she belonged to no one but him. His hands itched to hold her, and the need to take her back to his cottage and lay her down in his bed was nearly overpowering. As was the desire to pull her tight against him and sleep curled round her soft, fragrant body.

But he could not say it. *He* was the coward.

The words that would bind her to him stayed locked in his throat as he watched her pull on all her layers, fumbling with the laces of her corset, and fastening the buttons that marched up between her breasts.

Anthony went down the ladder first, concentrating very hard on his memories of his tropical home, and not the slender ankles and dainty feet that were descending just above him. There was absolutely nothing in the world better than hunting for food in Ganweulu or lying contentedly in the sun to nap.

Staying here was out of the question. He had adapted perfectly to the Congo and loved his solitude. It kept him free from worry, free from betrayal and abandonment.

Yet there were no books, no newspapers. There was no one like Newbury, or his grandmother . . .

No one like Grace.

Chapter 17

It was well-controlled chaos at the house the next morning, though Grace did not feel quite so calm inside. Taking a lover brought many complications with it, not the least of which was embarrassment over surrendering her morals.

It required secrecy and a false façade to hide her lapse, two things at which Grace had had little practice. She was accustomed to being forthright and truthful, which had always served her well.

But there had never been an Anthony Maddox before. A deep whoosh of air left her lungs at the thought of his leaving, and Grace pressed her hands to her eyes to cool them against the hot tears she'd shed instead of sleeping.

He'd said nothing last night while walking her to the house, had given none of the usual pleasantries that indicated she would see him today. She did not know if he had already left Fairford Park, only that he intended to go. She hoped he would not break his grandmother's heart by missing the ball.

Her own was already shattered.

Servants were busy on the terrace, hanging lanterns that would be lit at nightfall. Others were chopping ice, still more were spreading freshly pressed linen tablecloths on the tables outside. The dancing would take place in the ballroom, of course, but it promised to be a warm night, and Lady Sutton wanted to be prepared when her guests sought the fresh, cooler air outdoors.

"My grandson is ready, is he not, Grace?"

"Yes, my lady," Grace replied, though her heart sank at her deception as she answered. "He is prepared."

"He will cut a dashing figure in his evening clothes."

Grace nodded, but could not speak.

"I suppose it was no surprise that he learned to dance so quickly," the countess remarked. "He is very agile, is he not?"

Oh yes, he was agile. He moved with a predatory grace she'd seen in no other man. His touch aroused passions Grace could not imagine sharing with anyone else, and he—

"Grace?"

She swallowed thickly. "I'm sorry, my lady. You were saying?"

"See if he is in his cottage. I wish to speak to him."

Grace's heart leaped at the opportunity to seek him out, but she braced herself for the task. After all their intimacies, he had not shared his plans with her. She knew he'd stayed only because of Thornby . . .

Of course she wished he had changed his mind. He had thought better of killing Thornby, so why would he not choose to remain here with his grandmother . . . and her? Yet he was not at the cottage, and his traveling bag was gone.

Feeling the utter desolation of his desertion, Grace pasted a mask of neutrality on her face and started back to the front of the property. She was anxious to get away from all the festivities at the house, and too much the coward to face the countess now and tell her that her grandson had flown.

But Grace was not to have a moment's peace. Mr. Bridewell met her on horseback at the end of the drive. He alighted; Grace stood paralyzed on the spot. She had not expected to see him before tomorrow at the earliest, when she might have managed to master the art of dissimilation.

"Good day, Miss Hawthorne."

The side of his face—especially his left eye—was scraped and bruised. He stood still and waited, and Grace managed to move her feet, aware that she had no choice but to speak to him. "Mr. Bridewell, I'm surprised to see you."

Her suitor took her hand and touched his lips to the back of it. "I was unable to bid you farewell yesterday, and I wanted . . . well, I have something for you."

He reached for his coat pocket, but Grace did not want anything from him. Not a visit, not a gift, not a marriage. Everything had changed. And even though there was no future with Anthony, Grace could not face one with Mr. Bridewell.

"Please . . . can we delay it a moment?"

She allowed Mr. Bridewell to draw her hand through his crooked elbow and walk away from the house, leading his horse behind him. "Let us walk down to that handy bench."

"I would rather not."

He pursed his lips with displeasure. "I suppose you have much to do?"

Grace ignored the question. "Mr. Bridewell, what are your feelings toward me?"

"Feelings?"

"Yes. You know—the usual: admiration, respect, love, obligation . . ."

"Well, of course I respect you, Miss Hawthorne. And admire you a great deal."

"On what basis?" Grace started walking again, but Mr. Bridewell stood still for a moment, and she could feel his puzzled gaze upon her back. She could not blame him for being perplexed. For her own more conventional attitudes had recently shifted, and she hardly understood them herself.

Mr. Bridewell caught up. "You are well-bred, and appear to be a disciplined young lady. I am partial to children, and I believe you will provide me with a few more. You seem entirely free of fanciful notions—"

"And yet there is something I fancy very much, Mr. Bridewell."

"Eh?"

"When I marry, it must be to a man who has such a passion for me that my contentment, my welfare, *my happiness*, would be of utmost importance to him."

"But marriage is—"

"And he would still care for me if I were not able to provide the progeny he expects."

Bridewell's face reddened. "Well, certainly—"

"And he needs to understand that the appearance of propriety is not *everything*."

"Of course it is everything."

Grace refrained from snorting with disdain. Propriety had sequestered her in the country, had deceived her into believing a satisfactory marriage should only occur between two cold, distant, *proper* people. "I want a husband who would never dream of going away, no matter what the circumstances."

"Miss Hawthorne, I believe you have not completed your deliberations." He frowned and looked at her with deep concentration. "But I can assure you that I am not disposed to leave a wife. What would happen to Bridewell Manor, to the children . . . ?"

Grace could not marry him, or anyone. Not with her feelings for Anthony so intense, so raw.

It would take some time for her to get over them, if indeed she ever could. She could not see herself marrying now, for convenience sake, especially a man like Edward Bridewell. She would die in the mold in which he would shape her.

"Mr. Bridewell," she said. "I regret I must decline your proposal. I fear we will never suit."

"You cannot mean that."

"Truly, I do," she replied, sorry for the puzzlement in his eyes. "I apologize for this. I should have told you right out that I could not accept."

"You are being too hasty, my dear," he said, taking Grace's hand. "After all the commotion in Lady Sutton's house yesterday, I cannot blame you for your confusion. Take another day, by all means. One more day, Miss Hawthorne."

Grace felt the chill of the kind of future he wanted with her, predicated upon mere convenience and cold respectability. Never again would she know the passion or burning desire she'd shared with Anthony. "No, Mr. Bridewell. I've had my day to think it over. I am resolved."

His features darkened further, especially the bruised area round his eye. Grace hoped she had spoken graciously and wished that he would accept her refusal without rancor, for he was a neighbor and she would be compelled to see him every now and then. A muscle in his cheek twitched, but he said nothing, just turned and started back toward the front of the house.

"Mr. Bridewell?"

"I understand, Miss Hawthorne," he called to her as he walked. "And now I will let you return to your duties here. I will trouble you no further."

Anthony sat on his horse and observed *L'oiseau de Mer* floating in its berth, making ready to set sail on the evening tide. It was an unassuming ship, old and weathered, but seaworthy. It suited him. He could board right now. Just forget about Thornby and move on, back to his peaceful life in the Congo.

As he dismounted and started toward the ship, a vise closed round his chest. He thought of his house high in the acacia tree in the Ganweulu Valley, and remembered the hours he'd spent building his solitary dwelling. It was a simple place that suited him perfectly. There were no demands on his time, no compromise to his freedom. He came and went as he pleased.

To nowhere.

His African acquaintances called him Stranger. Even after all these years, neither the Tajuru nor the Moto had altered his name to Green-Eyed One or Tall Friend. It had never bothered Anthony before, because he had not remembered what it was to belong. To truly belong to a family . . . to a woman.

And now he knew he had not understood the first thing about courage, either. During all his years alone, he'd come to believe that independence and self-reliance were his most essential qualities. But he saw that he'd been hiding in Africa, his boyish feelings hurt, his resentment of his father dictating his actions. He knew now that Colin had not just left him to die alone in Africa.

Yet the prospect of betrayal still gave him pause.

One of the seamen gave him a wave. Anthony nodded back and thought about pulling his *gunia* from his saddle, sending the black gelding back to Fairford Park, and getting on the ship. It would be so easy to go back to the Congo, so simple to turn his back on his connections here.

But the thought of Grace working her buttons and laces last night came to him. She'd had trouble performing the simple task after giving herself to him, body and soul, making herself unmarriageable. Their possession of each other had been fierce and passionate, their connection complete.

Mbaya, she was his. He would risk every kind of agony to possess her.

He turned his back on the dock, climbed onto the gelding, and made his way to Jermyn Street, aware that he could not leave the business with Thornby unfinished. They were mortal enemies as much as the lion and the elephant, either of which would kill the other. Anthony had to get to him first.

It did not take long to locate the Apollyon Club, and there was a boy at the front of the building waiting to take charge of Anthony's horse.

He handed him a coin. "Keep it here. I won't be long."

"Yes, sir."

Anthony felt for his *kisu* under his coat, then went to the door and knocked. He used the same words Newbury had said to gain admittance, and the doorman opened to let Anthony in.

"Vingt-et-un," he said before the servant had even asked the question, and started down the stairs.

He went into the room where Thornby's game was being played, even at this early hour. But he did not see the man himself.

A few players sat at the game tables looking a bit desperate, others wore self-satisfied grins. Every one of them, to a man, looked haggard and drawn. But Thornby was not there.

Anthony left the room and made a cursory search of the other gaming rooms, but did not see his adversary. He climbed the stairs, and it took but another minute to locate the servant who'd admitted him. "Is Gerard Thornby somewhere in this building?" he asked.

"My lord, it is not our habit to divulge the—"

Anthony held up a coin. "I ask you again. Where is Thornby?"

The man took the coin from Anthony's hand.

"He has not yet come today. In fact, I have not seen him since noon yesterday."

"Where does he stay?"

"Unfortunately, I do not have that information, my lord," he said, eyeing Anthony's purse. "Truly."

Newbury would know.

Anthony left the club and went north, tracking his friend in a wholly different manner than he would do in the Congo. Here, he had to watch the landmarks rather than the tracks of a herd or a single animal. There were no grasses to be disturbed, and the smells of the city could not guide him, for they were masked by the odors of the river, by horse dung and coal smoke. But he knew that Mayfair lay northwest of the club, and that was where he would find Newbury.

He soon came upon the park near his friend's house. Once he got his bearings, he was able to find the street he wanted, and located Newbury's residence. Dismounting, he tied his horse and made a quick sprint up the steps.

He pounded on the door, and a very surprised-looking butler answered.

"Is Newbury in?" he asked.

"My lord," said the butler. "Lord Newbury is dressing for his evening out."

"Summon him."

"I beg your pardon?" the butler said quietly.

"I need to speak with him. Now!"

"But my lord, as I said—"

" 'Tis very important," Anthony said, remembering the etiquette Grace taught him. Demands were not made. Requests would be considered. "Please."

The butler gave a curt bow. "I shall see what can be done. If you will wait here."

Anthony went into the drawing room and started to pace. Thornby was a real threat, and Anthony wanted to deal with him before he had a chance to do any damage. Newbury could help him. At the very least, he would know Thornby's London address.

It was some minutes before his friend came into the room, dressed in evening clothes, but barefoot. A servant followed, carrying his shoes and stockings and a coat.

He sat down on a chair, and the manservant knelt before him.

Anthony was momentarily distracted from his purpose. "Can you not dress yourself, Newbury?"

Newbury looked up at Anthony with mirth. "No man of fashion would dream of dressing himself, Sutton."

"Then I will never be a man of fashion," he remarked, hardly aware of what he was admitting. "Newbury, I must find Thornby. Where is his house?"

"Not far from here," Newbury replied as the servant used a metal tool like a large spoon to help him slide his feet into the shoes.

Anthony blinked at the sight of it, then dismissed such elaborate doings from his mind. "You'll have to give me Thornby's location, as you are hardly ready to go out."

"No. Wait. It will only take me a minute to finish," Newbury said. "I was just about to start out for Fairford Park, anyway."

"I am out of patience, Newbury," said Anthony, resuming his pacing. "Be quick about it."

Grace took little pleasure in her new ball gown of amber-colored crepe and painted silk. Lady Sutton had given her a pair of topaz ear bobs and a beautiful necklace to match, but Grace had not the heart even to put them on.

She had never realized how much pain she could withstand and still survive. Somehow, she had managed to get through the day. She'd given instructions to the maids and footmen, spoken to the cook on Lady Sutton's behalf, and had finally bathed and dressed . . .

She'd kept her anguish well hidden until she'd had a moment's privacy, far from all the activity at the house, in Anthony's cottage.

And then she'd broken down.

She did not regret the past two days with Anthony and the intimacies they'd shared. Those experiences had shown her how narrow her life had been, relying upon dry, dull correctness and decorum to take her through life. She'd lived without gumption, without . . . *pluck*. She was a coward, just as Anthony had said.

She wished she'd surrendered all her misguided propriety when she'd had the chance, and told him that she loved him; that she would never marry Edward Bridewell. Perhaps if he'd known . . .

Grace wiped her tears and blew her nose. There was no point in deluding herself. She might love him, but she knew he felt no such emotion. He'd wanted her, but not enough to stay.

The muted sound of music came to her from the house, and Grace realized how late it had become. Lady Sutton must be wondering where she and Anthony were, and Grace was going to have to tell her soon that her grandson had gone.

Using the ewer in the bedroom, she washed her face, careful not to splash water on her gown. It was bad enough that her eyes were red and puffy; she did not need to have a ruined gown as well.

Drying her face, she walked into the sitting room just as someone was coming in through the door. Grace's heart leaped to her throat, certain Anthony must have changed his mind and returned.

But it was Gerard Thornby, and he was holding a gun.

"Where is he? Where is the bastard who's ruined everything?"

* * *

"He is not here, my lord," said Thornby's butler. "He said he had a ball to attend, out in the country."

Anthony did not waste a moment waiting for Newbury. With inhuman haste, he mounted his horse and started for the road to Richmond. "I'll have you know," said Newbury, catching up to him, "that only my oldest friend in the world could induce me to forgo my carriage when I'm dressed in evening clothes."

"Duly noted," said Anthony, spurring his horse to an even greater speed.

In silence, they hurried toward the park, but Newbury made a turn. "This way. We'll take the Knightsbridge Road. It'll be faster."

They skirted round Hyde Park's south side, and when they were finally out of town, they gave their horses their heads.

Newbury shouted a question. "What do you think Thornby will do once he reaches Fairford Park?"

Anthony shook his head and leaned forward. "I know what he will *not* do."

"Which is?"

"Harm my family. My woman."

"Ah. Miss Hawthorne. So you've decided to stay."

He gave a curt nod. He did not belong in Africa, far from everything that meant anything to him.

Not without Grace. He'd wanted her last night in every way, and knew that would not change. He wanted her still, and always would.

They rode the rest of the way in silence, and when they arrived at Fairford Park, Anthony dismounted amid a group of carriages that had stopped at the front of the house. He ignored the music coming from the house and went inside, encountering Faraday, who seemed to shine in his formal attire.

"My lord, you are not ready."

"Where is Grace? Miss Hawthorne?" Anthony asked as Newbury came in behind him.

"I do not know, my lord," he said, frowning. "I have not seen her in quite some time."

"What about Thornby? Is he in the house?"

Faraday gave him a disdainful look. "I have not seen him, either."

"*Mbaya*," Anthony muttered. He took the stairs by twos and looked inside Grace's bedchamber. It was empty. Returning quickly to the main floor, he went out the door and down the steps to where Newbury waited.

"Where now?" Newbury asked.

"The stable. Thornby must have put his horse somewhere."

He questioned Tom Turner and the grooms, none of whom had seen Thornby. "What about Miss Hawthorne?" Anthony asked Tom.

"I haven't seen her since she and Mr. Bridewell went walking."

"*What?*" Anthony felt his gorge rise. "Is he still here?"

"No, my lord. She sent him on his way. Tried to let him down gently, like. But I don't think he took it too well."

"She sent him away?"

"Couldn't help but overhear, my lord," Tom said with a wink. "I believe her heart is engaged elsewhere."

"Your cottage, perhaps, Sutton?" Newbury asked.

Anthony nodded. As relieved as he was by Tom's impression of Grace's interchange with Bridewell, his unease regarding Thornby increased with every step he took. Fairford Park was a huge estate and the bastard could be hiding anywhere. And it did not bode well that Grace was not in the house, attending his grandmother as she should be doing.

"He's after *you*, Sutton. Nobody else."

Anthony knew that. "Innocents could get in his way."

There was no reassuring reply that Newbury could make. They both knew that if Thornby had been willing to murder Anthony as a young lad, he would have no compunction against hurting Grace to achieve his purpose.

Which Anthony assumed was to draw him out.

"What do you think he'll do?"

"I cannot imagine. But if he hurts Grace—"

"He won't, Sutton. We've come in time."

Quietly, they approached the cottage, skirting round to look into the windows for any sign of Grace or Thornby.

"She's not here," Newbury said, meeting Anthony at the back of the cottage.

"The lodge, then."

They moved quickly, reaching the old building, and keeping to the trees to avoid being seen through its dingy windows.

"There's a light inside," Anthony said.

"I think you're right," Newbury replied.

"It will make it more difficult for him to see us through those grimy windows. Stay here, Newbury."

Anthony tossed off his jacket, then reached down and pulled off his boots. Drawing his knife from his belt, he was just about to move toward the lodge when Lords Canvey and Nye came down the path, looking concerned.

Newbury hurried to intercept them, stopping them on the path. But Anthony was able to hear Canvey's hushed words. "We understand there might be trouble . . . ?"

"What? How did you—?" Newbury asked.

"The butler," Nye said.

"Aye, well, we're looking for Thornby," said Newbury. "Sutton fears the man might have done some harm to Miss Hawthorne, for she is missing."

The skills Anthony had learned in the wild had never been more crucial. Aware of how ruthless Thornby could be, he knew Grace's life might be at stake, even though harming her could not possibly benefit Thornby.

Anthony approached the lodge soundlessly, going round to the side where he knew a window was partially blocked by the bookcase where the hidden drawer was located. He crouched beneath it and heard Grace's voice, muted, frightened.

"Be still!" Thornby ordered in a harsh whisper.

"I will not," Grace said in a normal tone of voice this time. "He is not coming, Mr. Thornby. He has left for Africa."

Thornby made a derogatory noise. "Is that why you were weeping in his bedchamber like one of Her Ladyship's precious bastard infants?"

Anthony's heart plummeted at the knowledge that she'd been weeping for him.

"You're his whore, aren't you?" Thornby said. "He'll be back for more."

Anthony pressed his lips together tightly at the blackguard's insult to Grace, and raised himself just enough to see through the lower edge of the pane.

Grace was seated at the table with her arms wrapped round herself, clearly frightened by Thornby, who paced back and forth, brandishing a pistol.

Anthony's mouth went dry.

"You might as well let me go," Grace said, and Anthony hoped she would keep him talking, distracted. "Lady Sutton will not appreciate your bringing trouble to Fairford Park."

Thornby snorted and walked toward the window where Anthony listened to their exchange.

"Lady Sutton," he said derisively. "As if I need to reckon with her."

"What do you hope to accomplish here?" Grace asked, her voice shaky and low. She stood, pushing back her chair. "Lord Sutton is g-gone. And I am no one. I cannot help you with . . . with whatever it is you intend to do."

Anthony knew she could not be more wrong.

"Ha! He'll come."

"N-no he won't. He's always intended to go back to Africa." She started to rise from the chair. "He has nothing to hold him h—"

"Where do you think you're going?" Thornby asked. He returned to Grace and put the pistol to her head.

At that moment, Anthony knew true agony. Thornby was going to kill her if he did not act. There was no time for finesse. He crept to the front of the house with only one plan in mind. He had to startle the bastard, then move with lightning speed to get Grace away from him. He just hoped that she would trust him enough to follow his command.

He reached the door and stopped to listen, hoping Thornby would move away from Grace.

"Sit down," Thornby growled at her, "and you might live another few minutes."

When Anthony heard a scuffle, he burst into the room, but Thornby still held Grace in a tight grip, and he raised the barrel of the pistol to her temple. "See? Like a bee to honey."

"Don't hurt her, Thornby. 'Tis me you want. Once I'm gone, the title is yours. The property . . . Everything."

Thornby made a strangled sound. "And there'll be a bloody body this time, damn you."

Anthony swallowed thickly and looked into Grace's eyes. Bright with tears, she looked back at him in despair.

"Let her go."

"Maybe I won't. Maybe I'll just take the both of you."

Lord Nye came to the door and spoke in a level tone. "Don't do it, Thornby. Put down the gun."

"Don't be a fool, man," said Canvey, coming up behind Nye.

Thornby's eyes seemed to grow, taking on a wild expression as they darted from Nye to Canvey to Newbury. A weird, birdlike sound came out of his throat, and the gun wavered in his hand.

Anthony made ready to pounce, but in a sudden movement, Thornby shoved Grace toward him and put the pistol to his own head. He fired.

Grace screamed at the blast and fell against Anthony, who caught her in his arms.

"Dash it," said Lord Nye. "Is he dead?" Nye and the other two gathered round Thornby while Anthony held Grace and led her from the lodge. She was trembling so violently she had difficulty walking.

Anthony caught Grace and lifted her into his arms, though he seemed to be shaking as much as she was. She pressed her face to his chest, clutching him tightly, feeling stunned. She was barely aware that her tears were ruining his shirt, or where he was taking her.

She could not think of what Thornby had just done.

Anthony did not speak until he'd pushed open the door to his cottage and taken her inside. There, he placed her on the settee and knelt before her, taking her hand in his. "Grace, are you all right? Did he harm you?"

"Y-you're here . . . You came back." Her voice, breathless and fragile, did not sound like her own.

"Grace." He started rubbing her hands vigorously, then cupped her cheek and kissed her, ever so gently. "You are so pale. You need . . ." He left her for a moment and returned with a cup of water. "Drink this, *uzuri toi*. It will help."

Numbly, she did as he instructed, keeping her eyes on him as she drank, afraid to believe he had truly returned. "Did you know Thornby was here?" she asked.

He nodded, and her heart sank. He'd come for Thornby.

He took the cup from her hand and placed it on a nearby table. "Grace, did he harm you?"

"No," she said quietly. She was still trembling, still feeling the terror of being at the mercy of that madman. "He fr-frightened me. I thought he would k-kill me."

Anthony gathered both her hands in his and kissed them. Tears filled her eyes.

"He needed me dead," he replied, moving up to sit beside her. He drew her into his arms, and Grace felt his breath at the top of her head, then his lips on her forehead. "I meant to deal with him before I left for Africa."

She'd already understood that he intended to go, but hearing it brought new anguish to her heart.

"I went to the docks this morn," he said, and Grace could not help but make a small sound of despair.

"But as I sat there looking at *L'oiseau de Mer*," he continued, "I realized that Africa . . . It was never home. It was a place for me to lick my wounds, a refuge where I could nurture my resentment against Thornby and my father."

A small sob escaped her. She sat up and looked at him, blinking away the tears in her eyes. "What are you saying?"

He slid his hands to the sides of her face, then brushed away the moisture on her cheeks with his thumbs. "I am done pretending that my isolation in Ganweulu is freedom. I have no wish to leave you, Grace. Wherever you are is where I belong. I love you."

Her chin quivered, and she did not trust her voice to respond.

"Grace . . . You touch me in ways I've never known or understood before. You are my woman, now and always."

"Yes," she whispered. " 'Tis all that I want . . . to be yours."

Grace's heart clenched in her chest when he smiled and pulled her close. How could she have thought him less than perfect while wearing nothing but his breechclout and this smile? Flawed because he did not know which fork to use, or how to assist a lady to her chair?

"Say it, Grace," he said. "Tell me you want me to stay."

She sniffed, hardly able to absorb all that had happened, all that he was saying. She looked up at him with a tremulous smile. "Oh, Anthony, I still cannot fathom it . . . You came back."

"You are part of me, Grace . . . I am part of you."

Grace gave a shaky nod, then allowed him to pull her back into his arms. "I love you, too. Please stay."

"Oh, aye. You are stuck with me. Marry me, Grace."

"Oh yes," she said, and he lowered his head and took her lips in a searing kiss. She slipped her fingers into his hair and drew him down to her as he sucked her lower lip into his mouth. The faint sounds of the music and voices at the house faded away as Anthony kissed her, skimming his hands round her waist, pressing their bodies together.

He broke the kiss and swallowed, breathing hard. "Grace . . . *Ah, mbaya*. I would take you to bed now."

And Grace would have gone.

"But . . . the ball . . . My grandmother expects us at the house." He leaned his forehead against hers, slipping a lock of her hair behind her ear. "I cannot disappoint her any longer."

Grace did not know she could love him any more, but his consideration for his grandmother caused her heart to clench with emotion. "She is so very lucky to have you back, my love."

"Even a wild barbarian like me?"

"Yes, exactly like you," she said, taking note of his bare feet.

While Anthony quickly washed and then dressed in his evening clothes, Grace repaired her hair. But there were smudges on the front of her gown, and she was afraid to look at the back, for fear of what she would see there. She could not wear it into the house.

She reached up to tie Anthony's cravat, and he pressed a quick kiss to her forehead. "Your gown,

Grace. I would love to see you in the ice-blue one you wore when I first kissed you, when I first started to fall in love with you."

His words touched her, and Grace's throat thickened, aware that he did not want to distress her by mentioning the condition of her ball gown. He was as sweet as he could be fierce.

"We can go in through the kitchen," she said, "and take the servants' staircase without meeting anyone."

At the entrance to the ballroom, Anthony spoke quietly to Faraday, whose eyes widened, but he gave a quick nod of agreement. They were beyond late for the occasion, and as he caught his grandmother's eye, she stood still among her guests and waited for him to be announced. Grace was on his arm, smiling shyly, looking beautiful in the simple but elegant blue gown.

He'd not had the heart to tell her that Thornby's blood dotted the back of her special ball gown. Instead he'd helped her to change from the pretty gown she'd intended to wear, keeping the gruesome sight from her eyes.

"Lord Sutton," Faraday announced to the guests in the ballroom. Then he added, "And his fiancée, Miss Grace Hawthorne."

Sophia's eyes widened, and she stood still for a moment, looking from Anthony to Grace. And then she smiled and her eyes twinkled as she started for them, her step lighter than he'd seen it before. She took his hand, and then Grace's, kissing her upon both cheeks.

"My dears, you should have let me know! Here I'd thought that supercilious Mr. Bridewell was going to win our Grace."

"My lady," said Grace, "You're not un—"

"I could not be more pleased, my dear. The granddaughter of my dearest friend is to become my own granddaughter." The countess dabbed her handkerchief against her eye. "I can think of nothing more fitting."

Sophia moved aside, and Anthony took Grace into the ballroom. He bowed ever so properly before her. "My lady, my love, will you honor me with this waltz?"

And when he took her into his arms, he bent slightly and said something completely and unreservedly wild in her ear, garnering the most delightful blush he'd ever seen.

Unforgettable, enthralling love stories,
sparkling with passion and adventure
from Romance's bestselling authors

HOW TO PROPOSE TO A PRINCE   *by Kathryn Caskie*
978-0-06-112487-7

NEVER TRUST A SCOUNDREL   *by Gayle Callen*
978-0-06-123505-4

A NOTORIOUS PROPOSITION   *by Adele Ashworth*
978-0-06-112858-5

UNDER YOUR SPELL   *by Lois Greiman*
978-0-06-119136-7

IN BED WITH THE DEVIL   *by Lorraine Heath*
978-0-06-135557-8

THE MISTRESS DIARIES   *by Julianne MacLean*
978-0-06-145684-8

THE DEVIL WEARS TARTAN   *by Karen Ranney*
978-0-06-125242-6

BOLD DESTINY   *by Jane Feather*
978-0-380-75808-1

LIKE NO OTHER LOVER   *by Julie Anne Long*
978-0-06-134159-5

NEVER DARE A DUKE   *by Gayle Callen*
978-0-06-123506-1

At Avon Books, we know your passion for romance—once you finish one of our novels, you find yourself wanting more.

May we tempt you with . . .

- **Excerpts** from our upcoming releases.

- Entertaining **extras**, including authors' personal photo albums and book lists.

- Behind-the-scenes **scoop** on your favorite characters and series.

- **Sweepstakes** for the chance to win free books, romantic getaways, and other fun prizes.

- Writing **tips** from our authors and editors.

- **Blog** with our authors and find out why they love to write romance.

- **Exclusive content** that's not contained within the pages of our novels.

Join us at
www.avonbooks.com